Data from the Decade of the

DATA *from the* DECADE *of the* SIXTIES

A NOVEL

THANASSIS VALTINOS

translated from the Greek and with an introduction
by Jane Assimakopoulos and Stavros Deligiorgis

Hydra Books
Northwestern University Press
Evanston, Illinois

Hydra Books
Northwestern University Press
Evanston, Illinois 60208-4210

Data from the Decade of the Sixties: A Novel was first published
under the title *Stoicheia yia ti dekaetia tou '60: Mythistorima* by
Stigmi Publications, Athens, 1989. It was reissued in 1992 by
Agra Publications, copyright © Agra Publications and
Thanassis Valtinos. English translation copyright © 2000 by
Northwestern University Press. Published 2000. All rights
reserved.

Funding for the translation of the present edition has been
provided by the Greek Ministry of Culture.

Printed in the United States of America

ISBN 0-8101-1699-5

Library of Congress Cataloging-in-Publication Data
Valtinos, Thanasēs.
    [Stoicheia gia tē dekaetia tou '60. English]
    Data from the decade of the sixties : a novel / Thanassis
Valtinos ; translated from the Greek and with an introduction
by Jane Assimakopoulos and Stavros Deligiorgis.
        p. cm.
    "Hydra books."
    ISBN 0-8101-1699-5 (alk. paper)
    1. Greece—Fiction. 2. Nineteen sixties—Fiction.
I. Assimakopoulos, Jane. II. Deligiorgis, Stavros, 1933–.
III. Title.
PA5633.A4 S7613 2000
889'.334—dc21   00-008692

The paper used in this publication meets the minimum
requirements of the American National Standard for
Information Sciences—Permanence of Paper for Printed
Library Materials, ANSI Z39.48-1984.

To Maria D.
12/16/1976

Behold I will overturn the inhabitants of the land and will distress
them so that their punishment will show. —JEREMIAH

ﬡ

Translators' Introduction

Historians of literature have always known that any person's life could produce an interesting narrative if told with a measure of sensitivity. In *Data from the Decade of the Sixties,* Thanassis Valtinos has created a fictional array of "data" that capture the tenor of an entire decade through the artful juxtaposition of the events of the period as recorded in newspapers and other documents alongside the ephemera of the times as seen through a variety of personal letters and individual applications.

The curtain rises on all the major themes of the book: the distressed letter of a Greek woman to a radio station's Miss Lonelyhearts; an ignorant villager's confused letter to a government emigration bureau; news of a vendetta murder on the island of Crete; and a right-wing exposé of the private life of a left-wing leader (lest we forget we are in the midst of the coldest years of the Cold War). Filing before our eyes are the real-estate ads foreshadowing the building boom and disastrous transformation of the landscape in and around Athens, verbose movie posters announcing the premiere of *Never on Sunday,* and the first hint of the exodus of Greek laborers to Australia, Germany, the United States, and South Africa, with all the social and economic consequences that this exodus will have on this small country for the rest of the period. The heartbeat of the decade resounds convincingly in the daily mix of the tragic and the absurd, the banal and the apocalyptic. The drowning of a baby in a well, the latest results from the racetrack, and olive oil prices are documented alongside reports of men and women losing their citizenship by dictatorial fiat, UFO sightings in Chile, and the death of an incestuous couple by lightning during a thunderstorm.

The events, both in the psychic and the political arenas, are too momentous to be labeled journalistic or regional. By recording the particular concerns and vulnerabilities of men and women in their words and actions, Valtinos's *Data from the Decade of the Sixties* succeeds in the generous art of the novel with its dual strands of realism and imagination. The woof and warp of this tapestry are made up of broad spiritual ironies as well as of the more material trends of the place and age. Radio Moscow broadcasts diatribes on atheism, monks dance to bouzouki music in mixed company, bands of nuns flee their convents, a dead saint's bones are cut up "with a small hand saw" to be farmed out to religious establishments around the country. And then there is the sixties chitchat of the rich and famous—Princess Soraya, Maria Callas, Aristotle Onassis—while the countryside is left untended and engagements between young people separated by continents are broken; Tarzan episodes are interleaved with news of Marilyn Monroe's death; Nigeria is described through the eyes of a Greek immigrant; the JFK funeral (with an Italian voice-over and probably no subtitles) is relayed via the Telstar satellite to a TV set in the town square of Patras; and, finally, a Greek woman has her first bout with depression and is put on tranquilizers in Johannesburg, South Africa. It is the beginning of the end of the century.

Through the variety of characters depicted in Valtinos's *Data from the Decade of the Sixties* and the multiplicity of their "voices," a picture emerges of a society in transition and in doubt, its traditional center no longer holding, its members drifting apart—their disconnectedness to each other and to the major events of the decade skillfully mirrored by the discontinuity between the individual entries. Like the confused and hyperbolic writings of Valtinos's men and women, the novel at its end shows the failing age itself baring its soul and "migrating" toward states that would have been unthinkable at the time, technologically, politically, socially, and even emotionally.

The eye instantly notices the dynamics of Valtinos's page, or rather the double spread: the use of italics to denote printed material in the public domain, as opposed to normal typeface for personal communications, highlighting in this way the similarities between the letters from the lovelorn to "Mrs. Mina" and those from would-be emigrants to the equally impersonal but often personified DEME. The answers to these needy queries are conspicuously absent from the novel and are only occasionally referred to.

Also conspicuous in their absence are many of the actual political events of the period. Ironically, the most important of these, the takeover of Greece by a military junta on April 21, 1967, following years of political instability and tension between and within political parties and the Palace, is not even mentioned in the book. Instead, there is an article on that date describing a belated celebration of National Independence Day (March 25, 1821), consisting of a play written and directed by a second-rate, middle-aged drama teacher, complete with allegorical, flag-draped tableaus and slogans about "National Rebirth"—a term that would soon be used by the Colonels' Junta to describe their own "liberation" of Greece.

Throughout the book historical decisions are similarly downplayed, placing them on the same level as the lives of ordinary people, while the preoccupations, entertainment, obsessions, and tragedies of these same individuals are elevated to a status of great significance.

The seemingly impersonal and unconnected pages of "data" in the book, in other words, are doing some very subtle storytelling of their own. Valtinos's Greece is not simply depicted as a country making a costly transition in order to redefine itself. Through his juxtapositions, omissions, and understatements, Valtinos forcefully conveys the spirit of an era—not simple facts, but their consequences for the ordinary Greek, whose miseries, meanderings, wiles, and foibles are poignantly evident.

The novel's epigraph, a quotation from the prophet Jeremiah (an adaptation of Jer. 10:18–19), implies that this antiromantic vision is only the beginning of woes to come. The last entry of the novel—a report of a cherry bomb exploding in front of the Larisa Courthouse—is almost a preview of the decades that will follow with their routine hijackings and terrorist bombings around the world.

Data from the Decade of the Sixties is a vast canvas of a novel that licenses and authorizes the imagination of the reader even as it "fixes" the frames of human reference in time and place—in the middle of the waning twentieth century and in a corner of south-eastern Europe—during transitions of singular importance both to private and public life.

This is no nostalgia chronicle; it is art out of the fabric of time.

A Note on the Translation

We chose the term "data" in the title *Data from the Decade of the Sixties: A Novel* to render the Greek word "stoicheia"—which can also be translated as "elements," "features," (identification) "particulars," (written) "characters," and "spirit"—because, in addition to encompassing several of the above meanings, it also contrasts more sharply with the subtitle "a novel," thus setting the parameters and polarities of the novel: the fictional nature of the data itself, much of which was in fact invented by the author, and the use of this data as the stuff not only of history but of literary creation.

Data from the Decade of the Sixties, with its wide spectrum of documents and multiple "voices," has required us to use a number of translating strategies.

The novel is made up of three major linguistic strands: (1) the (italicized) printed matter (newspaper articles, etc.), written in the formal, purist language; (2) the letters to Mrs. Mina, plus the odd personal letter, written in "everyday Greek" as spoken by ordinary people; and (3) the letters to the Emigration Department (DEME), in which mainly uneducated individuals accustomed to speaking only in everyday Greek attempt to write in the formal language of bureaucracy.

The difference between purist and everyday Greek in the 1960s is considerably greater than the difference between, say, scholarly or learned English in its written form and spoken English, either four decades ago or today. While it is not possible to reproduce the extent of the difference, we have attempted to reproduce the difference itself by preserving as much as possible of the original "tone" and resonance of individual documents, though some compromises have been made in the interest of readability in English.

We have endeavored to use, when possible, expressions current in the 1960s, such as "postal code" rather than today's "ZIP code," and "adults only" for today's "X-rated," to cite some examples.

As *Data from the Decade of the Sixties* is intended by the author to be read as a novel, not a history textbook, we have avoided the use of explanatory footnotes. We have instead made infrequent interpretive interventions and, following the author's lead, have in general provided only as much information as we felt was necessary for the reader to experience the book as a novel.

For the same reason, we have often preferred a system of equivalencies to more literal translation, especially in regard to government agencies and their initials, such as IKA (Social Security Agency), and OTE (Telephone Company). When initials such as these are actual acronyms in Greek, and especially in cases where they were widely used, they have been transliterated from the Greek, as with the football teams PAO and AEK and the political parties EDA and ERE.

Some clarification is useful in the case of the three acronyms ASPIDA, DEME, and AHEPA. ASPIDA (literally Officers to Preserve the Country's Ideals, Democracy, Meritocracy) is the name for a left-wing conspiracy of army officers in the mid-1960s and is also an acrostic in Greek meaning "SHIELD." DEME (literally Intergovernmental Committee for Emigration from Europe) has been rendered as Department for EMigration from Europe so as to match the transliterated Greek initials, thus preserving the acronym in English. AHEPA is an English-language acronym for a well-known Greek American organization (American Hellenic Educational Progressive Association).

The spelling of proper names in the present translation has also necessitated a combination of approaches in order to reflect the strong relationship between modern and classical Greek assumed on many levels by Thanassis Valtinos's work. In this spirit we have generally favored etymological spellings (i.e., "Glyphada" with *ph*), though again we have made compromises in the interest of pronounceability and sheer visual accessibility (i.e., "Efthymios" with f) and have also taken into account established usage (i.e., "King Constantine"). But, in the main, our transcriptions aim to capture some of the sound and look of Greek words. This explains references to street names in their Greek form and, without translation, in the genitive case (i.e., "Stadiou Street"). In other words, our translation, while striving for idiomatic fluency in English, seeks equally to maintain awareness that we have before us a Greek universe originally conceived in Greek.

We would like to thank Susan Harris, editor-in-chief at Northwestern University Press, for her encouragement and practical help in obtaining relevant English-language documents from the 1960s, and especially Thanassis Valtinos for his availability and patience in going over the text with us.

Data from the Decade of the Sixties

Athens, January 9, 1960

Dear Mina—

Greetings. I am a longtime listener of your program. I have been involved with a 35-year-old man for a year. In the beginning, I didn't know anything about him, and later on I didn't want to find out. He was always, and still is, kind and gentle with me. The only thing is that he never says "I love you" of his own accord. He doesn't deny it but says so only if I press him. I have to tell you that I love him and I show it in every way possible. I am a woman of 35, we are the same age. Not long ago, however, I found out that he is married and has a child and when I told him about it he admitted it. I asked him why he had kept it hidden from me and he said that he was afraid of losing me. He was sure that if I knew how things were, I would have left him. And I would have. But now it's too late, and he knows very well that I can't stop now. I am only able see him once a week. His job keeps him away from me, or rather it keeps him at home, as he lives in a village and sees me only when he comes up to Athens. When I ask him to stay a little longer with me, he says that he can't. I don't know what he really thinks of me and I don't know how he wants things to be between us. In any case, I think it's clear that there is no way he would be willing to spoil his comfortable home life because of me, but then he goes on and on about how unhappy he is with his wife. I very often get the impression that he is just using me to have a little fun. He has never said anything tender to me, as he thinks it might imply commitment. But then he also says that if I ever leave him, he will kill himself. Because he needs me. And naturally I'm half out of my mind with all this. Please tell me how I should act from now on. I will accept your judgment, whatever it may be. God bless you.

Magda Kaliesperi

P.S. Please refer to me simply as Magda on your program.

HERAKLEION, JANUARY II. *From our correspondent. At eight o'clock in the evening, the day before yesterday, in the village of Prosilia, Malevizios, Nikolaos Markomichelakis, 28 years of age, a sheepherder by profession, fatally wounded his fellow villager Emanuel Melissinos, a shopkeeper, age 53, firing nine shots at him from behind, with an automatic German pistol, for reasons relating to a long-standing dispute. Four of the nine bullets missed their target while five of them caused fatal wounds to the victim. The injured man was transported to the Herakleion Clinic, where he succumbed to his injuries at 5 o'clock in the morning. The perpetrator attempted to escape but was later arrested by the police on his way to Herakleion. It should be noted that, in 1958, the perpetrator had asked for the hand of the daughter of the victim in marriage; her parents, however, did not give their consent. This had been the cause of continual friction and the day before yesterday, following a quarrel, the assailant returned to his residence where he picked up his weapon—a Steier—and, subsequently, after meeting his victim on his way back to town, opened fire on him.*

[4]

To: The Officials of the Dept. for Emigration from Europe
(DEME)

Gentlemen—

Good day to you. I received your notice about my departure,
which is set for February 12, where I see you also asked me for
my son Dimitris's birth certificates. Well, listen, things are like
this: First of all, during the time the notice was sent, I was away
working over in the prefecture of Verroia and now realize there
is not enough time left before February 12. This is on account of
my small property and household expense papers still not being
in order. Second, about my son Dimitris's papers, which you
sent back to me for correction. I did submit them to the Office
of the Municipality, they corrected them, put their initials on,
stamped them, and when they were all ready I sent them to you
on January 4, 1960. But I made one small mistake. Thinking on
account of the envelope inside it must belong to the Department
of Emigration, I did not put any stamps on. Not only that but I
didn't put a return address, I mean my name. I sent it to you just
with the address on the envelope enclosed. Then when I saw you
kept asking for those papers, I went to the director of the post
office at Elassona and explained the whole thing to him. He told
me that if it had a return address, it would come back but that by
now it must be at the Central Post Office in Athens, with the un-
claimed mail. So I would like to ask you, if it's not too much
trouble, to please go and claim it yourselves. You can look for the
Elassona postmark and for your printed address. Also, I think you
can tell there are photographs inside. Otherwise, if you do not go,
please send me another set of forms to fill out, blank ones. Because
I don't know if the forms they have at the Municipality are the
right ones or if they're any good, seeing as how they don't say Department of Emigration in Greek and in English. So I am asking
you to please answer my letter as soon as you receive it and write
and tell me if the certificates I sent you for my son have been
found. I will send you the other certificates about criminal record
and debts to the state on January 24. It would be an awful shame

to miss my February 12 departure on account of all this. Anyhow, I would like you to let me know when the next departure is and also, when you send my other notice, could you tell me what other things I should bring, like what articles of clothing, or any other instructions, and also if it would be to my advantage to bring my elementary school certificate with me in person. Finally, could you please write just a little more clearly so we won't have such a hard time reading it and understanding what it means. Thank you for your assistance in getting away from this barren countryside of ours, but we will always be thinking of our beloved "GREECE."

Respectfully yours, Good-bye

Nikolaos Giannou

Tripolis, January 29, 1960

Your Excellencies: The Prime Minister, Ministers
of Industrial Development, Interior, Labor,
Undersecretary Prime Minister, Deputies Arcadia:
Papadimitriou, Kaltetziotes, Bakalopoulos,
Papaíliou, Aposkites, Michas, and Pavlopoulos,
Athens.

Permit issued by Prefecture Arcadia for
establishment DIANA razor blade factory, opening
of which, as result of law concerning protection
regional development, welcomed by entire population
Tripolis and outskirts. Stop. Withdrawal of
permit following order from Ministry Industrial
Development causing great concern. As unaware which
parties continue undermine progress in region
respectfully ask you take matters in hand use
influence to bring about immediate revocation
withdrawal order concerning opening of factory.
Stop. If this not done, rest assured entire
population Arcadia, plagued by economic crisis,
will be irreparably distressed. Stop. Hoping to
have good fortune of favorable reply, remain
respectfully yours.

Association of Shopkeepers and Businessmen
of Tripolis

The President
Spyros Charitopoulos

The Secretary
Giorgios Douros

To Mrs. Mina:

We thank you for being on the air with your wonderful program *The Woman's Hour* and for discussing such exciting and interesting subjects. My particular problem is this: I am 19 years old and very unlucky in love. I was in love with a young man and one day he walked out on me with no explanation. Three months ago I met another young man who is 23. I liked him right away and he felt the same toward me. I didn't fall in love with him, fortunately. Before he met me, this young man had been in love with another woman. While he was serving in the army, she got married. He did not stop loving her and continued to have his hopes. Now I ask you, what could he hope for from a woman who had abandoned him for another man? He told me everything, that their relationship had lasted four years, and only through correspondence. He still has her letters and her photograph. She has been married for two years and has a baby. I want to do everything I can to help the man I care about forget the woman who betrayed him. Now he is working in Thessaloniki. Before he went away he promised me he would try to forget her. He also bought me some presents. A few days ago he came to the village, but unfortunately I didn't see him until the day before he was leaving. The only thing he said to me was that he had come because of me but that I was just stringing him along and playing with him. He also wrote me a nasty letter, well, almost. Feeling unhappy I wrote him back, hoping that he had only written all those things in anger. And he wrote me back another letter that said nothing about me but was all about his betrayed love. He wrote things like: "If you can help me to forget, though it's difficult, my betrayed love, come and find me. If not, forget about me for good." And now I ask you, dear Mina, what should I do? Will I be able to get what I want without being hurt? And then suppose he also leaves me, with no explanation? Please answer and tell me what to do.

Thanking you in advance,

Wounded Gardenia

En route from Melbourne, the transatlantic ocean liner Patris *sailed into Piraeus Harbor yesterday, ending its maiden voyage on the new round-trip route between Greece and Australia. The ocean liner covered 9,500 miles in 23 days on the trip there and in 22 days on the return trip, carrying 1,000 Greek emigrants to Australia and 189 Greek expatriates from Australia to Greece.*

The owner of the vessel, Mr. D. Chandris, announced that in spite of heavy foreign competition the new Greek line is now firmly established and will create substantial tourist travel from Australia to Greece. Serious efforts are also being made to stimulate increased commercial activity between the two countries.

The Patris, *fully booked, will sail with its passengers from Piraeus to Australia on Wednesday, February 28.*

PATRA, FEBRUARY 14. *From our correspondent. By wire from Kalavryta. In the village of Skotani, 9-year-old Konstantina Bei was pitifully dismembered when a hand grenade that she found inside the house exploded as she was examining it. It appears that the hand grenade had been kept in the young girl's house since the days of anticommunist civil war operations.*

[9]

March 2, 1960

Dear Mina—

I listen to your broadcasts every time and all the interested things on them. And please forgive my writing but it's the best I can do. Now I would like your help with something that happened to me. My nickname is Christakis, that's what everyone calls me, but I want you to use my real name, Christos, so that no one in my village will know who it is. My wife, without so much as a single word, left me and went back to her mother's. And seven months later my child was born and it was a boy. People are talking a lot but my son looks like me, just like me. Please tell me what to do. I asked my wife to come back but she won't. And she told me that she had no particular reason for leaving, she just felt like it. So she did. And that's that. Sorry I don't know what I should write in this letter to thank you. All my best.

Christakis

P.S. Mrs. Mina, I forgot to tell you that I am very poor and just barely get by on my low salary. Could that be it?

Members of the First Security Police Squad, following a stakeout on Kolokotroni Street, took into custody Georgios Anthopoulos, a former diver from Volos, as he was breaking into the automobile of lawyer N. Koinis and removing a raincoat from inside the vehicle. Anthopoulos literally preyed upon parked cars, from which he would remove articles of clothing that he would subsequently sell at ridiculously low prices. Anthopoulos confessed to 18 similar burglaries. This arrest is particularly interesting in light of the offender's life story, which could have been taken straight out of a novel. He left his parents' home in Volos at the age of 15 and came to Pireaus, where he joined a gang of small-time robbers and illegal importers of American cigarettes. He was arrested for one of these thefts and was sentenced to be sent to a reform school for one year. He was sent to a prison on Kos, where he subsequently worked as a diver, was afflicted by a serious case of the bends, and suffered paralysis of his lower limbs. Upon returning to Pireaus, where he underwent extensive treatment at the Navy Hospital, he attempted, contrary to his orders, to emigrate illegally to America but was arrested and deported. Since then he has been involved in burglarizing automobiles. It is interesting to note that Anthopoulos comes from a respectable family in Thessaly.

––––––

WANTED. Employee under provision of Bill 751 for position as accountant's aide. Applications, handwritten, to Mr. G. Papagiannopoulos, Notary Public, 14 Charilaou Trikoupi St.

Larisa, March 19, 1960

Dear Mr. Emigration Officer, Sir—

I heard that you are taking people to Australia from another girl who is leaving who is a men's trouser seamstress. Please, if you are still taking people, write and tell me what papers I should get. I am 36 years old, an orphan with no parents. I work as a weaver and as a nurse, a nurse's aide. I worked for fourteen years at the Kalamochera factory, but I quit due to an unsatisfactionary salary, and for four years in a clinic.

I will be expecting an answer from you with all the required papers so that I can be included on your lists and if possible the letter should be sent registered so it does not get lost. Because I am in a big hurry to emigrate.

Respectfully yours,

Miss Maria (daughter of Thomas) Karageorgiou

during that same year, after the fighting at Grammos, when the communist guerrilla headquarters were located at Pyxos, in Prespa, Zachariades abandoned all pretexts and now presented Roula to the world as his legal spouse, and he even went so far as to live with her in a private bunker. Comments were rife among the comrades and quite often the "chief" found it necessary to take strong measures in order to admonish the "gossipmongers." Following the defeat of the guerrillas, Roula, using the name Rhea, common among village women, made her way with Zachariades to Bucharest. The couple took up residence in a luxury apartment in a well-to-do neighborhood at Stalin Park, where mansions housing the foreign embassies were located. There Roula and Nikos brought a son into the world, naming him after the Red dictator. Henceforth the activities of the "chief's woman" became more and more intensified. In October of 1950 she was elected a nonvoting member of the Central Committee of the party, and took part in most of the Communist Party's international conferences, directing a steady barrage of criticism toward Greece from the radio station of which she was in charge. When the crisis broke out inside the Communist Party of Greece, she remained a devoted companion, standing by her "chief" and fighting by his side in order to refute the charges being leveled against him by the supporters of Vaphiades and Partsalides. Her versatility and competence as well as her aptitude for conspiracy during the crisis persuaded the "chief" to entrust her with the "most important mission in her life." The reconstruction of the outlawed Communist Party apparatus was the important mission given to her by Zachariades. So Roula returned to Greece as "Urania Vasileiou" and proceeded to "reconnect" her outlawed party comrades. Her Waterloo, however, was near. After being continually tailed, she was arrested along with Dr. Siganos at the residence of an Athenian family where she was in hiding, when she could not explain away some "suspicious papers" in a cellophane case that she kept hidden close to her breast.

The same fate was shared, one month later, in September of 1955, by communism's other first lady, Avra Vlassi, the wife of ever-powerful Mitsos Partsalides. Avra also became active when still a schoolgirl in Athens, distributing leaflets. For an English teacher, however, the distribution of propaganda leaflets was not a serious assignment. So Avra, increasingly cited for her consistently Red sentiments, gradually worked her way up the hierarchical ladder of the Communist Party. First she became the liaison officer for the Politburo and for the Local Branch Office in Pireaus, but she was arrested in 1938 and initially sent away to the island of Gavdos and subsequently to Kimolos. In 1941 she escaped from there along with some of her comrades and took up residence in Athens, where she took over the post of secretary of the seventh "branch." During the anticommunist civil war operations she was elected a member of the Central Committee of the women's organization, but was again arrested and exiled to Ikaria. She managed, however, to escape and rejoined the outlawed Communist Party apparatus in the region of Attica. The dragnet of persecution by the authorities was drawing nearer and in January 1949 Avra, using falsified identification papers, escaped with the help of her comrade Ventires to Thessaloniki, and from there she continued on behind the Iron Curtain. At the plenary session of the Communist Party of Greece she was rewarded for her activity by being elected a permanent member of the Central Committee. Henceforth Avra took part, with her rival Roula Zachariades, in many international conferences and continued to level propaganda at her country. Like her implacable enemy, she was sent, in 1954, to Greece attached to Erythriades and his group and began acting as a spy. She enjoyed her illegal freedom for another year before Security Police bloodhounds discovered her whereabouts and placed her under arrest. Avra admitted to her activities and exhibited more courage than Roula during her defense. Would she do the same when, on Wednesday April 28, High Prosecutor Polychronopoulos offered proof that she and Roula were Greece's two Mata Haris?

May 13, 1960

Gentlemen—

Please inform me if I may emigrate to Australia. My birthday is 1943 and I am able to speak a little English. I have been working for three years at the Xenia Hotel in Nauplion. I have completed my primary school education. I have two sisters in Sydney, Australia. They both went there on DEME Lines. They are twins and they attended the Kifisia School, 40 Levidou St., where they learned a couple of words in some foreign languages and whatever else they teach there. They're residing over in Sydney 5 months ago now. I work at the Xenia as a waiter's helper, and I am real good at my job in the restaurant. I don't know if you've ever been there but I'm sure you must know all about really high-class service. I have parents, they will sign whatever I need to leave. I'll be waiting for your answer.

Micky

LONDON, MAY 15. *By special correspondent. Aristotle Onassis, who arrived here the day before yesterday, announced that "a reconciliation with my wife Tina would make our close friend Mr. Churchill extremely happy." These words, coming, in fact, from a person who is "not given to speaking much," lend even greater credence to the opinion most commonly held here that Sir Winston is doing everything in his power to reconcile the couple. As we know, Mr. and Mrs. Churchill returned here with the Greek shipping magnate following a cruise to the Caribbean on the yacht of Mr. Onassis, who subsequently concluded his statement with the following words: "Unfortunately, I am not able at this time to say anything concerning the future of my marriage. I do not know if we will be reconciled or even if I will see my wife again." Mr. Onassis's happy smile and pleased look indicated that something was in the wind and that things have reached a very crucial point.*

LADY, with widow's pension, educated, good-looking, in good health, serious, with superior moral qualities and without family obligations, 50 years old, with luxury rent-freeze 4-room apartment on Skoufa Street (Kolonaki), seeking to meet gentleman 55–60 years old, serious, good-looking, in good health, of high social standing and similar education, may even be on pension, with monthly income of 3,500–4,500 dr., with view toward marriage only. Only serious proposals will be favored with reply. Reply to Ta Nea, Mrs. M.P.P.

well-to-do *cross out*

Dear Mina—

I am twenty-four years old. Three years ago, for personal reasons, I had to interrupt my studies. Lately I have been extremely preoccupied with the subject of marriage. I believe that I am at the right age to make a good family. For years I have been looking for someone to love—a pure, honest love with a view toward marriage, of course. Lots of proposals, but unfortunately things never turn out the way I would like them to. I will explain exactly what happens to me, and ask you please to be perfectly honest in the advice you give me. From the time I was twenty I could never keep up a relationship with a young man for more than a month, at most. After that, the young man would come straight out and make suggestions concerning matters of sex. He would have demands that I, of course, would reject. And so, inevitably, we would break up before ever really getting started. I did not want, nor do I now want, to have sexual relations before marriage. I know we are not living in the year 1900 but in 1960, and many things have changed. I believe, however, that every person has the right to have his own principles, even if other people don't like them. Or am I perhaps in the wrong? Am I asking too much? Is there no point in a girl having had no sexual contact before the day of her wedding? Several days ago, after he had been pressuring me continuously, I agreed to go steady with a young man who lives in the same neighborhood as I do. Not wanting to waste my time, I thought it best to talk to him. I explained my views to him clearly. He, by some miracle, accepted the idea of getting to know me spiritually first and, in fact, also said that he considered it only right to be patient when the other person really deserves it. Of course, he immediately added the following: Naturally, after some time has passed, six months or a year, there most certainly has to be physical contact as well between two young people, so as to get to know each other better. I said it was out of the question, but he continued: I am sure that deep down you too want to have sexual relations with me, which is why you should not rule out anything at all. You don't even have to think about it. You can be sure that it will just happen by itself. As I am by nature the type who worries about every little thing, I have been driving myself crazy for days now thinking about what I should do. Should I stop while there is still time whatever it is I am beginning to feel inside me, or should I compromise with him and the things he has been telling me? Neither of these things suits me. And this is the dilemma I'm in. The truth is that I like this young man a lot. He is smart, he has personality, but my age and my circumstances are such that I can't just take my chances with him. I am from a poor—or to put things more crudely, an impoverished—family, however honest and respectable. I don't have a father, only a mother and brothers. They all respect and love me. I wouldn't want, in the event things fail to work out, to tarnish my name and that of my family. Nor would I like to cause them grief. Nor of course to make my present position even more difficult. Oh, Mrs. Mina, I am so unhappy. My heart and my mind are in constant conflict. Again yesterday when we met, he told me that he believes in me 99.9% and that it's only about 0.1% that he has his doubts. And that sexual contact will reveal everything. That it is only after this act that a person's character is clearly revealed. He told me: Don't be a coward, I'm sure things will turn out well. And at some point you have to play the game; to succeed in life you have to make some sacrifices.

To be honest, Mrs. Mina, I can't find a way out or a solution. I mean, do I really have to accept trying things out, no matter what? I have faith in myself, but I don't have faith in other people completely. And then how can I keep ignoring such possibilities as our relationship progresses? In the unlikely event that my young man meets another young lady—someone with a lot of money, who can guarantee, since there will be nothing legal between us, that he will not be tempted by self-interest? So all I do is think about this problem and worry about it. And of course the temptation remains quite strong. I see my young man once or twice a week. And every time we go out, he keeps stressing the fact that he would like to belong to me completely but, because I refuse to give in, he is obliged, for purely physical reasons, to go with "women of ill repute."

I ask your forgiveness, Mrs. Mina. But I am beginning to feel so tired from all of this. So very, very tired, and I need the support of someone experienced.

Best Regards,

A.T.

JULY 9. *Yesterday afternoon in the seaside region of Varkiza, at a distance of one-half mile from the coastline, two sharks were caught, each about two meters long. The sharks became entangled in the nets of fishing boats from the Taxiarchos fleet. At first there were three of them, but the third got away as they were being dragged off the boat. Later, when the beasts were opened up, inside the belly of one of them, the left heel of a bronze statue was found. The find was turned over to the 17th Department of Classical Antiquities (Lavrion branch).*

PROPERTY FOR SALE

Seaside, at Selinia. On the island of Salamina, short distance from Pireaus. Near sea, sandy beach, mountains, pine trees. Lots will be drawn for 10 free housing lots. Ask for your entry ticket, free. Separate trip for every customer.

SUBURBS: AVLONITIS AREA
42 Veranzerou St., 8th floor, tel. 522-753
21 Agiou Konstantinou St., 1st floor, tel. 522-293

SUMMARY OF COURT DECISION

Drosoula Gatzis, widow of Philippos, née Pan. Christou, housewife, resident of former Euxeikoupolis, presently called Volos, 22B Botsari St., has, on the 17th of March 1960, duly petitioned the Court of the First Instance of Volos that her son, Christos Philippos Gatzis, laborer, born in 1947 in Kouphovouno, Nea Ionia, Volos, at 54 35th St., be declared missing and that the Court of the First Instance of Volos, under decision 1112/1960, call upon the missing person Christos Philippos Gatzis or any other party having information concerning the life or death of said missing person to step forward within a time period of fifteen (15) months from publication of the present.

In Volos, the 12th of August, 1960

Duly Authorized Legal Representative
Anastasios Margarones

Xiniada, October 19, 1960

To: The Department of Emigration from Europe

DEME—

This is to remind you about my application for Australia. Christos George Louridas. Also about Vasilis Daïs's and we have not had any answer. Well, only Mr. Daïs got word that you sent his application to the Office of the Prefecture on 9/20/1960. Did you send mine there too or not? Because the State Welfare Officer came to the village but only asked about Daïs. That was on Saturday, 10/15/1960. Did my application get lost or what? I have no more to write you.

So long,

Christos Louridas

KAVALA, NOVEMBER 22. *From our correspondent. A brutal crime was committed yesterday in the region of the village of Megisti (formerly Tsal-Dag), near the easternmost part of Mt. Aereton. The offender is 59-year-old Demosthenes Kiopeoglou, a farmer, father of two married daughters from his first marriage and the victim, his wife Kastalia, née Arphani and four years his senior. The murder took place at 12:00 noon. The previous day Kiopeoglou had located his wife in Thessaloniki, following an absence of one month, and brought her back home with him but she, upon their return, told him: "I'll just leave again." A struggle ensued, during which the murderer repeatedly and brutally attacked Kastalia with a kitchen knife and when he finally realized that she was dead, he removed her undergarments so as to "leave her as naked as the day he found her," according to his statement, and gave himself up to the police. The couple had wed four years ago in an arranged marriage (the second for both of them); it soon became clear, however, that their union was not destined to last. Several weeks after the wedding, the "bride" began leaving her husband for days at a time in order to see various former lovers.*

Announcing, on Monday, November 28, 1960
the opening of the new movie theater

TRIANON

21 Kodriktonos St. (corner of Patision St.)
the theater Athens has been waiting for

Offering the very latest in modern technology.
Open year-round, summer and winter. With a new system,
never before used in Greece, for electronically opening and
closing roof in a matter of seconds.
Deluxe theater, beautifully furnished, with inclined
seating for easy viewing.

Premiering with the movie the whole world
is talking about

NEVER ON SUNDAY

("The Children of Pireaus")

starring Melina Merkouri

also starring world-renowned director
Jules Dassin

and with music loved the world over by
Manos Hadzidakis

Today, November 26, first showing in Greece of
the movie *Never on Sunday,* under the auspicious
patronage of H.M. the Queen of Greece.

Proceeds will go to the International
Social Service organization.

Tickets on sale at the King George Hotel.

Dear Mina—

Hello there. I am seventeen years old. Last Easter I got engaged to a young man. It was an arranged marriage. We planned to tie the knot in August. By that time, the house that he was building was supposed to be finished. I'm the type of girl who expects to get married, and I know that I want a man to be part of my life. Finally, under pressure from him while we were engaged, I gave myself to him. He is withdrawn and stingy, and whenever he's not at sea everything gets on his nerves. From that time on, we have done nothing but yell and scream at each other. My parents are unhappy and upset at this situation. As I have many sisters, I'm not getting a dowry worth speaking of, and he keeps telling me every day "this is no dowry they're giving you. Here I am building a whole house and you don't own even half as much." He said this not at the beginning but only after a long time had gone by. He is now asking for even more money in order to marry me. The construction of his house ran into difficulties and has now stopped. We keep telling him to go ahead with the wedding, but he hates having to pay rent anywhere. That's what he says. And he changes his mind all the time. He says one thing in the morning, a different thing at night. We can't trust him anymore. He's away now. He's a seaman, near Piraeus, and my family doesn't allow me to go see him.

What am I to do, Mrs. Mina? They tell me I should break up with him, but I don't want to. I know that I will have an unhappy life with him, but if I break up, what will happen to me then? I have no dowry to take care of all this, and here in my village people so often make mountains out of molehills, as the saying goes.

Mrs. Mina, I would appreciate some advice. He's completely insensitive. I look forward impatiently to hearing from you. (Do not read my letter on the air.)

Young and Disillusioned

NEW YORK, FEBRUARY 19. *By special correspondent. The entire U.S. press is giving extensive coverage to the second case of a "weeping" icon of the Virgin belonging to the family of Mr. Petros Koulis, residing at Oceanside, Long Island, near New York, and not far from the house where, a few weeks ago, the same phenomenon was noticed on still another icon of the Virgin, part of the collection belonging to the family of Mr. Katsounes, also a member of the Greek immigrant community. A team of American journalists was on hand to observe the phenomenon of the weeping icon. Not only did they carefully examine the icon, they also took samples of the tears, which were sent to a New York chemical laboratory. The scientific analysis, according to a statement issued by the laboratory, demonstrated that the tears could in no way be considered similar to human ones. They further reported that the liquid contained "oily substances, and minute traces of calcium chloride in marked contrast to human tears, in which this substance abounds." The statement also stresses that the liquid under investigation was totally lacking in nitrous chemical compounds, which form the basis of human tears. The teardrops of the icon flow every fifteen minutes from the right eye, and a little more slowly from the left. The icon is a copy of a lithograph of the Portaritissa Virgin. Following the second occurrence of this phenomenon, Archbishop Iakovos, accompanied by members of the Greek Consulate, visited the Koulis household in order to witness these events firsthand.*

Rodoula Photiadou, 30, a permanent resident of Thessaloniki, arrived in Athens to file suit at Central Security Police headquarters against G. Dalkos, M.D., 33, who had promised to marry her, defrauded her of 30,000 drachmas, then left her in order to marry a colleague of his. Subsequently, Officer Giannimaras called the physician, who did not deny he had a relationship with the young woman, but did deny having promised marriage to her and swindling her out of the 30,000 drs. Following this, they were summoned to testify in each other's presence, whereupon Miss Photiadou, enraged by her friend's attitude, opened her purse, took out a small dark blue glass bottle containing vitriol, and proceeded to throw it at him. Realizing her intentions, however, both he and the policeman managed to push her away in the nick of time.

———

We mend clothes. Tears, burns, moth holes, worn flies,
weave-repaired by specialist trained abroad.
We turn suits, overcoats, and raincoats.
The New Save-Wear Shop, Lolou Bros., Tailors.
5C Dorou St., 1st floor, tel. 55-314.

Dear Madam—

I am in need of your advice. I am without a father and I live with my mother and sisters. They love me, naturally, but there is something I do that they think is sheer stupidity. Do you think, dear Madam, that it is at all possible for someone to be born with a great, powerful imagination, all her own? This is exactly the case with me. Ever since I was 12 years old I knew what direction I wanted to go in. I liked writing stories. Even now, though I'm quite grown-up, I am still writing. Yet during all these years, my tears have not stopped: I write something, and my mother and sisters tear it up. They always laughed at me and they still do. They tell me I never finished high school and make lots of spelling mistakes. They tell me I should stop writing and then they won't make me cry.

For some time I have had my own room. I write and I keep it locked at all times. All those years when they burned what I wrote, it hurt me a lot. It felt as if they were burning my very life. They refuse to understand that I enjoy what I am doing and that they are making me unhappy. They believe it is stupid of me to waste my time like this. In my opinion, the stories I write are beautiful, and good enough to be made into movies. This is exactly what several more knowledgeable ladies have told me, and this is the reason why I am writing you. Please write and tell me if I should go on writing. And let me know where I could apply to. Is there an address where they could tell me if my stories are suitable for the movies? How many should I send?

No matter how many words I might use, believe me, they would not be enough to thank you. So let me not burden you further with my letter. Write to me at this address: Miss Andromache Karanikoli, 12 Navarinou St., Perama, Piraeus.

With many thanks,

Andromache Karanikoli

past the halfway point of the race Galaxy easily dominated his rivals, Andros Captain, Beethoven, and Smog, who finished 3rd, 4th, and 5th, respectively. Their differences at the finish: 1¾ length, 1¼ length, and less than a head.

In the third race, Pluto started out in the lead, then Spercheios after the 1,000-meter point but only up to the turn where the order was reversed again until Spercheios was outrun by Typhon. Attalos came in second. The differences: 1¼ length, 1¼ length, and 4 lengths.

Rita took an early lead in the fourth race, and despite pressure from Hellas, won with a 1¾-length lead over Crete who, in the last four meters, passed Hellas. Nena finished fourth. Kirdan won the fifth race after a battle against Argoan, whom he beat by a difference of less than a head. Third (by half a length) came Ibn Sobe, and Shabet a distant fourth. Finally, in the sixth race Andros Seaman took the lead away from Proteus in the final few lengths. Golpho, far behind, came in third, and Nostos was fourth.

APRIL 4. *It is anticipated that more than 50,000 Greek workers will be employed by German industries by the end of this year. The first treaty between Greece and Germany was recently signed in Bonn concerning the qualifications of those wishing to travel and work in West Germany, as well as the conditions and criteria for their qualification. The above treaty, signed for the Greek side by diplomatic envoy Mr. Tetenes, Ministry of Labor representative Mr. Malatestas, and one official from the Emigration Office of the Ministry of Internal Affairs, establishes, among other things, that travel expenses will be covered by the German government and the German employers. It also defines the nature of the collective agreement governing employer/employee relations, which has yet to be signed, and the issue of expenses for the return trip.*

---

74 ACHARNON STREET

We will exchange your old icebox with an electric one.
No down payment. Come visit us.
Corner of Pheron and Acharnon Streets.

Dear Mrs. Mina,

I listen to your show daily. I am married to a man I did not know and did not love. Today, after seventeen whole years of marriage, I am extremely unhappy. My husband has proved to be cold and insensitive. He does not understand me and does not even try to. He wants nothing to do with my family, I think out of pure envy. We have no children, and this is one reason for our unhappiness. Now, after so many years, he wants us to adopt a relative of his, a fourteen-year-old boy, to help him at work. I agree, provided he is a source of joy for both of us. But will he be? Our life, so far, has been empty. My husband doesn't care about me or even about himself. All he cares about is his work. He is not generous and keeps count of everything. What do you think? Can this child change our life? Can he bring us closer together? And will the child be happy? And how should I behave in this situation? I have often thought of leaving my husband, but I can't bring myself to do it. I do think about him and I do not want to hurt him. He seems even sadder and more bitter than I am. My dear Mrs. Mina, your advice would be most helpful. I live in a village and I am often away on errands. If it's not too much trouble, could you answer me by letter? Many thanks to you and your show. May God grant you happiness.

Pen name: In Search of Light

It has been officially announced that at a forthcoming meeting the State Health Council will, following statements made by American scientists, examine the matter of lipstick and the tendency of certain brands to cause that most accursed of illnesses. It was also announced that samplings of cosmetics, hair coloring products, etc., are taken and tests conducted regularly on the quality of the ingredients, under the supervision of the General State Chemical Laboratory. Items deemed harmful are confiscated, and their manufacturers or importers prosecuted accordingly.

VOLOS, JULY 23. *From our correspondent. Yesterday's first parachute jumps by England's 16th division in the region of the village Stephanidakion were most spectacular and extremely successful. Having boarded four airplanes at midnight in Malta, the parachutists arrived at 6:45 A.M. at a clear stretch of land on the southwest side of the village, from where they began to jump from a height of 500 meters. After landing, they gathered at a designated location for a roll call, after which they were driven in motor vehicles to the temporary camp of their division near Volos. The head of the unit, Lieutenant-Colonel Anthony Faron Hawkley, responded to questions by reporters as follows: "We made a perfect jump. Although we had traveled for seven consecutive hours, the parachutists arrived in good spirits and excellent shape. Today's exercise was unusually successful." Lieutenant-Colonel Hawkley is well known for his activities during the Korean War, when he was captured and held prisoner, undergoing extensive torture for 18 months but, as he reveals in his memoirs, he was saved by his faith in God.*

Athens, August 25, 1961

Dear Mrs. Mina—

How do you do? Well, I am 23 years old, an elementary school graduate only, and I work at home as a seamstress. Six months ago I met, through a friend, a 30-year-old man, who is a foreman and a painter by profession. I got involved with him without feeling anything special, I simply liked him but that was all I felt. As for him, he showed a lot of understanding and love. We spent a month and a half without his pressuring me or asking me for anything. We went out, enjoyed ourselves, talked about different things, as friends. As time went by, I was touched by his behavior, because it was plain to see that he wasn't just trying to pass the time of day with me. He was waiting for me to show him something more than friendship, and not only that, he wasn't like some young men who only think about themselves. I decided to bring up the subject that was on his mind by asking him what he wanted from me. His

"I love you and I want you." I explained my point of old him that I love him, because in fact I wasn't head over heels in love, of feeling of security around him. That's fter my own confession, his love grew w, he didn't simply love me. I returned est I could. In every way. What I felt for ent. He was really the perfect man, dy- sonality.

love for five months filled with dreams, gs lovers do. He came to my house, met about us, and set us a one-year time limit o my father. We accepted because we were ame to the house once a month and we n ith my mother's permission. My mother to y and loved him like her own son.

bothering me about the deadline he had ten appear thoughtful or sad, as if he had other thing nd. Whenever I asked him what was the matter, he avoided giving me an answer, and I couldn't figure out, not even with my woman's intuition, what the problem was. I kept asking him, without making a pest of myself, of course: Theodore, why don't you come and speak to my father now? What's holding you back? Not that I was in a hurry, mind you, Mrs. Mina. It wasn't that. But I knew he had no obligations and between two people in love there should be no secrets. But he always answered that I shouldn't be concerned and that I should stop asking all those questions. All I needed was to have faith in him. The truth is that for a short time I didn't bother him again about it and that made him cheerful and pleasant again.

But a few days later the bomb dropped. A girlfriend who saw us together recognized him as the workman who had painted her house. With great difficulty she broke the news to me, as gently as she could so as not to hurt me. And what was the true story? He was married with two children, ages 8 and 6. At first I didn't believe her. I just couldn't believe her. I asked around, though, and the answer was yes, it's true. I asked some friends to check and see and they came up with the same results. How horrible, how awful. How unbearable! All that time he had been deceiving me and laughing at me behind my back. I told my heart to be still and when he tried to see me again I told him I knew everything. I told him I felt sorry for him. I left complaining bitterly to him, without saying good-bye and without waiting for him to give me any explanation. Explanations no longer meant anything to me, since he hadn't had the courage to tell me the truth on his own for so long. To think that it was only after he took advantage of me that I found out about it, and then from someone else.

Days and days went by without any word from me. He kept on telephoning and standing underneath my house for hours on end. But I had made myself scarce. I didn't answer, nor did I acknowledge his desperate gestures for me to come downstairs so he could talk to me. That went on for three weeks. One afternoon as I was leaving the dentist's office I ran into him. I couldn't avoid him and I have to say my knees went weak. Really, Mrs. Mina, from all that emotion, and all the time we had been apart, love and hate were battling it out inside me, with neither side winning. I accepted his offer to buy me a coffee so that he could have a chance to explain himself, since he wanted to so badly. I also wanted to see what other lies he would tell me. He began by asking me not to interrupt him until he was finished. After that I could leave if I wanted to, and never look back.

He admitted that he was indeed married, that he had two children, and that his life was hell. When he was in the service he had gone on leave to Stylida to visit an aunt on his mother's side who was married and living there. That's where he met his wife. They went out a few times and then he went back to his unit. Three months later they brought her to him and she was pregnant. They insisted that he marry her, since it was his child. He resisted as much as he could. But when you're a soldier you can't do whatever you feel like. In the end he married her. In fact, he was only married on paper since he no longer wanted her after all her scheming. He began living his own life and asking her over and over for a divorce. But she refused, as would most any woman, and I have to admit, Mrs. Mina, that I understand her. She insisted they carry on, in the hope that he would gradually learn to love her. But it was a lost cause. Their tortured life together dragged on and on. Soon a new child entered the picture, making things even more difficult. He didn't want it, but she believed that it would bring him closer to her. But the child had been born without his wanting it. From then on, you can imagine how things went. Every day there were quarrels, screaming, nagging, and all that in front of the children.

Nine years went by. While he waited for her to agree to sign divorce papers. But obviously with no result. Then he met me and without my wanting to, I became the main reason why his plight became even more terrible. That's what he told me, Mrs. Mina, and then he let me think for a while. He assured me that he would go as far as he had to in order to force her to give him a divorce. Of course, there was no way I could agree to that. I love you, I told him, but I don't want to be a cause of unhappiness to your poor, innocent children. Get a divorce, do whatever you think is right, but forget about me. It will hurt, there will be tears, but I'll get over it. We agreed to separate as friends. I made him promise not to cross my path again, but he just won't give up. He keeps on phoning me. To find out how I am. Or about anything at all. And he says I want you to be strong, you're the only one I love, the only one I want, our trials will soon be over. Of course I pay no attention to what he says because I don't want to have any false hopes that one day he might belong to me. But yesterday he called me up all enthusiastic and shouting, he was so excited he could hardly speak. He told me that she went with him to the Magistrate's Office and signed the divorce papers. In two months' time he will be free and if I still want him, he will come to get me.

Now tell me, Mrs. Mina, what I should do. Should I be glad or not? My mother doesn't want to hear a word about him. After all his deceitfulness. She has threatened that if I marry him I can forget about having a mother. She's threatening to tell my father everything. And he's so hard to talk to, so insensitive, all he does is make money. How can I make such a fool out of him by taking up with a married man, and what will his friends say and all that? I don't know what to do, which side to choose. My parents, who had dreams of a different kind of marriage for me, or the man I love? There's one question, however, I have to ask myself: Sia, are you sure that you will have a happy life with him? Or will you end up like his first wife? I ask him the same question. And he assures me that with me he will be different. Because he never loved her. She was just someone he met when he was young and it didn't work out. Now I am hoping for some advice from you, Mrs. Mina. I hope I haven't made you tired, dear Mrs. Mina, with all this but I needed to talk to someone. Because no matter whose opinion I asked for, they all said: What are you, crippled or blind or some old maid, why should you marry a divorced man? That's why I'm asking you now. Please answer me without hesitation. I will anxiously await your reply. Better still, answer me in writing, if you can. I include my address, in case you write. Sia Marou / 12B Bizani St. / Lophos Axiomatikon / Peristeri, Athens.

In the event you broadcast this on the radio, do not mention my last name. I'll be waiting.

Gratefully yours,

Sia Marou

LAMIA, AUGUST 29. *From our correspondent. As of the present moment, the hiding place is still unknown of five nuns who allegedly disappeared along with the monk Glykerios Vam-| vakites on the night of July 22 this past month. As of late last Sunday, the Phthiotis Village Police Precinct has taken charge of the case and is making efforts to discover the nuns' hiding place. In the meantime it was learned that Vamvakitis was sighted four days ago in Athens, where he paid a visit to an ailing relative of one of the nuns. According to the same source, Vamvakitis also visited the office of an Athens newspaper. Meanwhile, in light of his frequent visits to Athens, it is believed that he has been sheltering the nuns somewhere in the metropolitan area, which does not preclude the possibility of their having gone to a different monastery. In any event, Vamvakites is hoping to win his current court case against the diocese of Phthiotis over the ownership of the Metenekteou monastery.*

Razi, September 3, 1961

Dearest DEME,

Hi there, pal. I want to ask you to please do me a big favor. What I want is if I can get on one of those boarding passes for Australia. To go and work there. I want you to send me whatever papers I should fill out. I want you to know I am unmarried and have fulfilled my military obligations. That's all I have to write you and I will be expecting an answer with the best information.

Obediently,

Veretziotes, Konstantinos

had to try as hard as she could not to burst into tears. Because at that moment she felt that it was all over between her and the man she thought had loved her. The next day Orsini took his leave of her and said a formal good-bye as though there had never been any kind of intimacy between them. And when he returned to Rome he was quick to announce to reporters: "I do not intend to marry Soraya. There was never the slightest chance of that. In the first place I don't believe I am mature enough yet for marriage and, in any case, my position prohibits me from marrying a divorced Moslem woman."

Some heartless friends were quick to pass on Orsini's statement, with all the juicy details accordingly exaggerated, to Soraya, whose pride was deeply wounded by this. Because her well-meaning informants also let her know that Orsini had made it perfectly clear that it would be impossible for him to marry anyone who was not a virgin. She realized that her beloved Raimondo had, until now, simply been going out with her to amuse himself and that all his attention and supposed declarations of love during the past two months were nothing more than a means of enjoying her feminine charms by pretending to be in love. He was, moreover, flattered by the fact that his girlfriend was a former empress and he did not hesitate to toy with her, without troubling himself about the fact that Soraya, in addition to her title as "former empress" (an unbearable thing to her), was also a woman. All of this overwhelmed her with unspeakable indignation. After Orsini's departure, she stayed for a while in St. Tropez before returning to Vienna. And when she arrived there she was nothing but a woman in love, heartbroken and in pain. She could no longer sleep and was afraid of living. Her mother thought it wise to remind her every so often of all the declarations of love that had been made to her up to that time, in addition to the marriage proposals she received daily. At the same time she advised her to seek another meeting with Harald Krupp. The

German-born Mrs. Eva Kalil Esfandari, Soraya's mother,
was swept away to the depths of her being by the magic
`  `*that the name Krupp conjured up to anyone German. And*
Harald had always been, in her eyes, the ideal marriage

———

SEXUAL THERAPIST Dr. Georgios Zourares, graduate of
the Institute of Sexual Research of Berlin and a student and
collaborator of the distinguished Magnus Hirschfeld,
founder of Sexual Research in Greece and author of twelve
books on sexuality, receives patients suffering exclusively
from sexual disorders. 37 Akadimias St., 9–12 A.M. *and*
5–7:30 P.M.

17

3
2
4

689

E 302.H22 2017

- 2 volumes

Athens, Sep

Dearest Mina—

I am twenty-five years old and an airline stewardes
married at the end of the month. The man I'm mar
an American airline company with a salary of 8,00c
month. My salary is 10,000 drachmas. I am think
doing any flying after our wedding. In that case, I
ferred to the offices of Olympic Airlines with a lowe
a month. Now, for at least the first few months of ou
the 10,000 drachmas will come in quite handy. So I
ing. The problem I must deal with now is this: As I v
more money than my husband, can this give him
inferiority complex? This is something I would not w
and I am willing to make any sacrifice for our happir
you advise me to do?

Rania 1 + 1

[43]

FIFTH THIRD BANK

On Sunday, September 22, nuptials were held uniting the distinguished Roumeliote from Panormon Doridos, Aristotle Nikolas Virmanes, a businessman living in California, U.S.A., and the charming and stunningly beautiful Sue Palaiothodoros, daughter of Dimitrios Palaiothodoros, a native of Palaioxarion Doridos and a businessman residing permanently in California.

The wedding was held at the chapel of Agias Zonis in Kypseli, imposingly decked out with flowers. The archimandrite of the chapel officiated, along with five priests.

The bride wore an extravagant bridal gown made in the U.S.A. by the fashion designer Jack Davis of Hollywood, who also fashioned the wedding gown for the daughter of former Vice-President Nixon. The groom wore a pale blue velvet jacket. The couple made a handsome pair, well matched and perfectly charming, as they accepted the admiration, love, and heartfelt congratulations of all present.

The best man at the ceremony was a close friend of the couple, the businessman Anastasios Sknipas, whose family is from Attiki and who is also a long-term resident of America.

At the wedding ceremony 500 people were present, among them the Greek businessmen, now well established in America, Ioannis Migakis, Louis Touloumis, Vasileios Kappatsos, Panagiotis Pagouris, Konstantinos Karavasilis, and Christos Thomaïdes as well as the actress Miss Liz Taylor. The uncle of the groom, Mr. Neoklis Virmanes, the American tycoon originally from Panormon, was unable to attend the ceremony with his wife as he had hoped to do, and sent a telegram warmly congratulating the newlyweds. Also in attendance were the parents of the groom, Nikolas and Aspasia Virmanes, as well as the parents of the bride, Dimitrios and Marigo Palaiothodoros.

In the evening a reception was held with a sumptuous meal at the well-known nightclub Babis, in Kifisia, attended by some 400 guests and followed by Roumeliote dancing until all hours of the morning, accompanied by the nightclub's own

[44]

musicians but also by another group of popular singers performing pure Roumeliote music.

Good spirits prevailed, centered around the newlyweds, who danced to the loud applause of their guests while continuously receiving congratulations and best wishes from everyone present.

To this perfectly matched couple we extend our very best wishes as they embark on a new life. May their path be cloudless and strewn with flowers and happiness.

D. I. Thomaïdes

―――――

YOUNG MAN FROM VILLAGE, *15–16 years old, honest and in good health, needed for work at gas station. Offer includes room and board, clothing, salary, and other incidentals. 146 Vasileos Paulou St., Voula, Attiki, tel. 04412.*

TRIPOLIS, OCTOBER 31. *From our correspondent. Yesterday at noon, in the village of Agios Nikolaos, Kynouria, law enforcement agents arrested Dimitrios Papanikolaou, alias Skaphidas, a farmer, for illegal possession and use of firearms. The perpetrator, who has declared himself to be an advocate of the conservative National Radical Union (ERE), fired, in a state of inebriation, four shots "in the air" from his hunting rifle to celebrate, or so he claimed, his party's victory in the elections. It should be noted that the rifle, either stolen or borrowed, belonged to the arrested party's first cousin, Michaïl Papanikolaou, presently in the U.S.A. An additional bit of news: in the region of Alonistainis, the goatherd Paraskevas Sountris bit off the ear of Antonios Pepas, a logger from Chrysovitsion, when the latter refused to pay off a bet he had lost concerning the election results, claiming that the outcome was the result of fraud and violence. The perpetrator was arrested.*

Lixourio, December 10, 1961

To: The office of DEME

Good day to you. First, I would like you to tell me if I can emigrate by air, with my family. Not by ship, because I'm scared and it's a long trip by sea. If there is a way to go by plane, that will be fine. Also, I have two young children, under seven. Please let me know how much money I will need for all the expenses, by land and by air. I also have a brother in Australia, he is there for five years now. He went there through DEME and writes very nice things. Nothing further and I am in patient for your reply.

Panagis Pylarinos Konstantelatos, son of Gerasimos

I am very sorry but I forgot to mention that I am a shoemaker.

MOSCOW, DECEMBER 28. *United Press. Radio Moscow broadcast a scathing attack against the "bourgeois" celebration of Christmas, denouncing it as an "imperialist weapon." The station went on to question the existence of God as man, characterizing the entire doctrine of Christian love as "harmful to the workers." During a lengthy program, the radio station claimed that the icon of the Savior and "supposed founder of the Christian religion" is clearly a product of human fancy and that the existence of this "myth serves the interests of the ruling class." "The existence of Jesus is contrary to history and has been proven by science to be inexact, as writers contemporary to Jesus make no reference to him." The above-mentioned program referred with sarcasm to the Christmas messages of Western leaders, attributing their use to the need to keep their people in subjection. "Kings, presidents, prime ministers, archbishops, and capitalist officials," said the station, "once again invoke these holiday wishes, deceiving the masses with preaching about love, without making clear to us whether—if at all—the worker can truly love the factory owner or the field-worker the landowner."*

Dear Mrs. Mina—

I am 26 years old and have been married for 4 years now to a man
15 years older than me. Everything was going just fine during our
engagement, except for a few times when my older sister-in-law
stuck her nose in things. You see, I have two sisters-in-law and a
brother-in-law who are always saying things to my mother-in-law
and my fiancé. But no one paid them any mind, especially not my
mother-in-law, who I should point out was, in my eyes, quite a
remarkable woman. And with whom I got on wonderfully. I say
"was" because when we got married, before two months had
passed, my mother-in-law died at the age of 56. And so there I was
in that house for a whole year, with my brother-in-law, my father-
in-law, and my husband. After my mother-in-law passed away, my
husband and his brothers and sisters began quarreling about in-
heritance matters. So then my father-in-law and the other three
tried to get me and my parents involved and, believe me, neither
me nor my parents ever wanted to get mixed up in anything. Until
then, Mrs. Mina, my husband had never said a word about me or
my family. Not until after the first year. A month before our first
child was born, we moved into a rented apartment because the
house we had been living in was being torn down. My husband
and his brother agreed to build a big bakery shop there. So then
they also moved into a rented apartment, although I kept telling
them to move in with us. At least until my brother-in-law got married. To continue: when we moved into this house is when all the
trouble started, a month before our son was born. He started saying all sorts of things about my mother, saying that my parents are
no better than his, that they try to boss him around and silly nonsense like that. You see, the house we rented is near my parents
who, I don't mean to brag, are people beyond reproach. Particularly my mother, who is a very smart and sensible woman. When
I came home from the hospital, he kept saying the same old things,
picking the same fights, until the baby was 5–6 months old. Then
one night he came home from work in a rage and began breaking
plates, glasses, slamming doors, and shouting: Didn't I tell you that

your mother shouldn't come here again? I'll go and tell them myself, I'll get rid of them. And he took himself over there, at one
o'clock in the morning. You can understand how awful it all was
for me. So naturally I started being nasty back to him and things
went from bad to worse. I don't know what caused such a change.
I assume it was because of ideas his sisters and his father put in his
head. Because he certainly did get an earful from them, like how I
had dragged him to live near my mother and how we could make
him do whatever we wanted. After a few months things calmed
down. And so we assumed then that he had done what he had done
so they would see him in a better light. But there was one difference, my parents would never come back to our house or go anywhere near the bakery. After all that, Mrs. Mina, you can understand how put off I was by everyone and everything. I reached the
point of saying I didn't want to have a second child. A month later
my brother-in-law got engaged and then married, but he and his
wife turned out to a worthless pair. They threw my father-in-law
out of their house and so we were obliged to take him back in with
us. In the meantime I had, quite unplanned, a second child. My
husband and his brother also opened a second shop, but that's another story, because they are constantly disagreeing and quarreling.
I don't need to tell you how upsetting this is for me. And whenever
my husband has a misunderstanding, he starts sulking, doesn't eat,
won't talk to me for days, sleeps in another bed. When he feels
better, he comes back to me, acting like he always does, and then
he says he has no hard feelings. The only thing I can make of all
this, Mrs. Mina, is that he is a very unstable character who carries
on and enjoys insulting people, always wants to have his own way,
and acts like a know-it-all. Mrs. Mina, I implore you, please give
me some advice as to how I should behave toward him, what to do
about him. Because I can't stand it anymore. Whenever I get upset
I get headaches, they're killing me. Let me also tell you this: The
one good thing about him is that he is a good provider and a decent
man. I await your helpful advice. I wish you a happy New Year.

A very good friend and listener of your program

PATRAS, JANUARY 28. *From our correspondent. Athanasios D. Athanasopoulos, a 54-year-old businessman, was arrested by agents of the local Aitolikos police force and sent to Central Security Police headquarters in Athens, where he has been on the wanted list for many years. He had been sentenced to a 26-month prison term for failure to pay alimony, perjury, credit fraud, and other criminal acts. Athanasopoulos appeared in Aitolikos on January 3 in the guise of the Reverend Father from the Sion Monastery in Jerusalem. He had a beard, wore a white robe, and his head was uncovered in accordance with the regulations of the above-mentioned sect; he stayed for three days in a modest rented room, subsisting on tea and crackers. On Epiphany Day, he attended the ceremony of the hallowing of the waters at the side of Archbishop Egnatius of Arta, the officiating vicar of the vacated seat in the archdiocese of Aitoloakarnania. Due to all this, the "Reverend Father" soon became the subject of much discussion. Many said that he had come to remove from the historic church of the Dormition of the Virgin the tombstone that was kept there, a work dating from the seventh century and of considerable archaeological value. Others said that he was an important ascetic and confessor. In the meantime, because some of the impostor—Reverend Father's activity was deemed suspicious by police officer Michaïl Konidas, the latter had him arrested on the 14th of the month; from that time until the day before yesterday, intensive interrogations were carried out, revealing not only Athanasopoulos's true identity but his entire story. It was learned that he was born in the year 1908 in the village of Oreini, Ilias, and that he was a silk merchant operating in Athens. He had left Greece about eight or ten years ago, at which time he owned factories in Anavryta and in Nea Ionia. He returned to Greece with a forged passport bearing the name Petros Athanasopoulos and his date of birth as 1918. During his time abroad, according to his testimony, he became a monk in the well-known Greek monastery of Agios Savvas, built in the fifth century, 12 kilometers from*

Jerusalem, in the Kedron Valley, and renovated under Emperor Justinian. Feeling homesick for Greece, he returned via Constantinople, and before coming to Aitolikos traveled throughout the country for reasons unknown.

March 7, 1962

To DEME and Co.—

I have worked for twenty years as a tailor. I am good at my job and a good cutter. I am married with three children, two girls and a boy. My wife is 38, I am 39. Our children are: one girl, 17, one boy, 15, and another girl, 6, our youngest. Can you please answer me if our papers have been sent to your office, because I gave them to the village clerk and he said that he filled them out and sent them. But I have not had an answer from you so maybe the clerk still has them. Or maybe they got lost. Please, if our papers are not in your office, let me know where, what, and how, so I can get things ready for our departure by myself.

Respectfully yours,

Paraskevas Kapernaros

The first witness to testify was Marianna, 18 years old today, who stated, among other things, the following:

WITNESS: *I was born in 1944 in a village outside of Pyrgos. My father was killed by communist rebels and my mother remarried. My stepfather, however, was not at all fond of me. I decided to come and work here in Athens, as a maid in a private home. It was for a family with three children. They paid me 300 drachmas per month. After I left there, I met someone named Christos. We lived together for a while in a hotel, but he didn't give me money. He only paid the rent. And then he tried to persuade me to engage in another line of work, but I didn't want to. I started looking for another job and I went to a factory that made baby carriages. When the factory owner realized that I didn't know how to use a sewing machine, he introduced me to Mrs. Jenny, who was looking for a maid. While I was living there, however, aside from the housework I did other things.*

JUDGE: *Did she introduce you to any "gentlemen"?*

WITNESS: *One day someone telephoned and after she hung up she told me that a gentleman would be coming and that I should keep him company.*

Giannitsa, April 28, 1962

Dear Mrs. Mina—

I listen to all the *Woman's Hour* programs and I must tell you that I admire you tremendously for the good, solid advice you give to your listeners. I would like, if it is all right with you, to join your lovely group and to tell you my problem, which is romantic in nature. I am 18 years old. Until now, the young men I have met are all liars and cheats. Fifteen days ago I met a young man who I can honestly say is a "tower of strength" when it comes to love. I believe that he really loves me and that his intentions are good. What bothers me is that he has a child and is separated, that is, he was married and separated five years ago. I accept him because I love him, but I don't know if my parents will accept him. What will they say when they find out that their daughter is in love with a married man, and with a child to boot? That is my problem, Mrs. Mina, and I hope to hear a response soon on the radio.

Love Plus a Child

From Giannitsa

MAY 9. *A rehearsal was held in the Catholic Chapel of Agios Dimitrios of the hymns and psalms to be performed by two mixed-voice choirs during the wedding of Sophia and Juan. The rehearsal was attended by the King and the Queen, the Archbishop Benediktos Printezi of Athens, the Crown Prince, Princess Sophia and Princess Irene, Don Juan Carlos's sister, Infanta Maria de Pilar, and the Lord Chamberlain Dimitrios Levides. During the rehearsal the mixed-voice palace choir, consisting of 110 persons, conducted by Michaïl Vourtsis, performed Handel's* Hallelujah *and* Amen, *and the 80-member mixed-voice choir of Agios Dimitrios, led by the conductor of the Catholic church Michaïl Kornelos, performed Mozart's* Coronation Mass *and Perozzi's* Magnificat. *Mozart's* Coronation Mass *will be performed at the wedding by request of the Queen and consists of three parts: "Kyrie," "Sanctus," and "Benedictus." The soloists taking part in the performance by the Catholic church choir are from the National Opera Company: Mireille Fleury (soprano), Sakellariou (contralto), Axiotis (tenor), and Michaïl Zarbis (baritone).*

May 25, 1962

To: The Chief of Emigration from Greece

We respectfully request you to send us enrollment forms for emigration to Canada, or anyplace.

Konstantinos Kotrones family, 4 persons
Evangelos Tingas family, 8 persons
Dimitrios Damaskinos family, 2 persons, no children
Leokratis Damaskinos family, 7 persons
Dionysios Bartsos family, 6 persons
Village of Keramidi, Trikala

We thank you

VOLOS, JUNE 29. *From our correspondent. Panic struck Volos this morning as a result of the appearance of a large sea monster in the middle of the harbor. The creature, belonging to the whale family and resembling a capsized boat about 10 meters in length, appeared suddenly just off the Theophilos coast, gliding slowly along with its black hump protruding just above the water. A crowd of people immediately gathered on the wharf and looked on with curiosity at this most unusual event in their own harbor. In the meantime a harbor patrol boat was ordered by harbormaster Laïnis to pursue the creature. They fired repeatedly at it with automatic weapons, but the creature, unperturbed by these minor wounds, continued nonchalantly on its course, occasionally diving below the surface and then reappearing. It continued to dive and resurface, under fire all the while, until it finally left the harbor and moved on to Pagasitikos Bay. As we know, the above-mentioned creature has been "patrolling" Pagasitikos Bay for ten days, although it is reported by offshore fishermen to be harmless, as it has yet to exhibit aggressive behavior. Even yesterday, when it was under fire, it did not act at all disturbed nor did it attack its pursuers. To avoid any mishaps, however, the harbormaster has forbidden the circulation of small crafts as well as swimming in the sea around Pagasitikos Bay. At the same time the authorities are attempting to find a practical way to exterminate the creature. Suggestions have included firing at it with bazookas or dropping a depth charge on it from a helicopter.*

ENGAGEMENT

Mr. Alekos H. Pantopoulos, owner of the ASPA stocking factory, and Miss Gianna D. Iliopoulou, granddaughter of Lieutenant-General Charalambos Markouzos, have announced their engagement.

My dear friend Mrs. Mina—

Before I broach the subject that is on my mind, allow me to express the warm sentiments and admiration I feel for you. It is after much hesitation that I decided to write to you, less so that you can help me than so that you might offer me a little sympathy and kindness. I am 21 and the problem that has been bothering me for the last five years is quite serious. I tried to get over it but it was impossible. Fate has ironically played one of its worst tricks on me, causing me to fall in love with an artist, a movie-screen star. When I first saw him, I was 16 years old and I felt something that I never ever felt before. Until quite recently I didn't even know his name, and yet from that moment on, my life changed completely. I thought about him often and at night when I went to sleep I cried bitter tears on my pillow. At first I thought it was just a passing fancy, a crush that would pass in time. I realized that it was foolish to live with a dream, but however hard I tried, it was impossible to forget him. I tried to forget about him by looking at other men but his image was right there in front of me. His manly voice would ring so loudly in my ears that my heart would ache desperately. My sister, seeing how despondent and absentminded I had become, tried to find out what was wrong with me. I realized I needed to talk to someone. So I told her everything. I just had to share my great secret with someone, but she is incapable of understanding how much pain I am in. There are moments when I wish I were dead, only then can I be really free of love and not suffer any more.

I began, Mrs. Mina, to avoid going to his movies, hoping that if I didn't see him I would forget about him, but that only made my predicament worse because I needed the warmth of his presence. Whenever I saw him, however hard I tried to restrain myself, my eyes clouded over with warm tears and my heart ached through and through. Little by little my secret was uncovered, the few girlfriends I had found out and then my mother did. But I didn't care what they said. What's more, I had begun to feel like I was living among strangers. At last I could be alone with him, with his beloved name.

If you could only understand, my dear friend, how bitter one-sided love is. It has been five whole years and it is still painful to remember him and I continue to think of him. Perhaps one day I will marry and have a family, but I will not be happy. And I feel sorry that I will not be able to make whoever I marry happy either. Because he will always be there between us, his shadow I so adore. My dear friend Mrs. Mina, thank you for reading my letter and I ask you please to help me if you can. I will be eternally grateful to you. Please convey my affection for you to whoever is in charge of your program.

Very sincerely yours,

Disappointed in Love

HOLLYWOOD, AUGUST 7. *United Press. On a cold marble slab in the cemetery here lies the lifeless body of Marilyn Monroe,—the sweetest woman in Hollywood. In the opinion of the investigating committee of psychiatrists and coroners who arrived here at her villa on Sunday at dawn to carry out tests to determine the true cause of the violent death of the blond bombshell, it was due to an overdose of Nembutal sleeping tablets. The original diagnosis of suicide was later disputed by spokesmen for the major film corporations, most probably because in Hollywood, as in Monte Carlo, it is customary to cover up suicides by attributing them to accidents. At any rate, the international symbol of femininity, with her graceful, provocative walk, the perfect sex symbol who was copied and emulated by millions of women throughout the world, the idol whose peach-colored flesh was desired by millions of men, put an end—due to mental illness or to fear of her first wrinkles—to her anguish-ridden, unhappy life, through an act of desperation, which she tried to undo at the last minute, as she was found with her hand on the telephone, in a hopeless, mute call for help, which never arrived. And Marilyn Monroe, following the first autopsy, set out for the cemetery in an ordinary hospital ambulance, covered by an ordinary sheet, unaccompanied by relatives or friends, completely alone, which appears to have been how she lived, at least in spirit. Regarding her funeral, it has been announced that her half-sister (on her mother's side) released her body either to her lawyer, Mr. Rowden, or to her second husband, the baseball star Joe DiMaggio. It was also announced by the Coroner's Office that several days will be needed for the cause of death to be determined, that is, whether it was due to an accident, to misuse of pills, or to the actress's own*

LADY, single, age 41, with strict moral principles, Christian and family woman, medium height and full-bodied, excellent housewife, with dowry, fully furnished four-room house, worth at least 700 pounds sterling, also with liquid assets totaling 100 pounds sterling, seeks husband in good health, upstanding with honorable past, up to 47 years old, with steady job, bus driver or technician, any type of work. Send details as to job, age, etc. to Ta Nea, c/o Mr. Nikos *(brother).*

Makronas, August 16, 1962

To: The Department for Emigration from Europe
1 Sophokleous Street, 2nd floor, Athens

Dear Mr. Employment Agent—

Sir, could you please answer my questions? My son Antonis Daskalakis left for Australia two months a go. I have three more sons.
The youngest is sixteen and wants anyway he can to go where his
brother is. You settled my Antonis in the Australian state called
Melbourne. If it would be possible for my youngest son also to go
to the same state, then write me.

    I have two more children for emigration, but first they want
to be insured that they are giving out plots of land. They are tractor
drivers and want their own land, because we hear they're giving
away lots of acres out there to cultivate and plant trees on. This is
what my sons have in mind. But the fields should be close to a
highway or to a railroad line, because if they are giving them out
in the wilds of Australia, then they will be no use.

    Please, clear up the truth for me. Nothing further, that's all.

Greetings,

Georgios Daskalakis
My address is: Village of Makrona, Kissamos, Chania, Crete.

AUGUST 18. *The Minister of Public Works, Mr. Solon Ghikas, during an inspection of Lakes Yliki and Paralimni, which, as we know, feed into the lake at Marathon, discovered that the water level of Lake Yliki has dropped by 9 meters and that of Lake Paralimni by 16 meters. As a result of this drop in the water level, attributed to the presence of large fissures, especially at Paralimni, concern was expressed over continued leakage of water into the sea. The minister subsequently pointed out that, because of the ongoing record dry spell, his ministry is obliged to begin taking all the necessary precautionary measures. It was therefore decided to send for two foreign experts, from France and from Switzerland, to look into the matter of water-proofing Paralimni so that the leakage of water can be contained. The minister also stated that companies specializing in such matters have already undertaken studies concerning various projects to reinforce those already in existence for collecting water and increasing the supply. Meanwhile work on the construction of a second pipeline is nearing completion and during the first fifteen days of this coming November, double the quantity of water will be pumped from Lake Yliki to Marathon. Finally, the minister stressed that by next summer, even if this unprecedented dry spell persists, there is no cause for concern about the possible implementation of restrictions on water consumption.*

HOLLYWOOD, AUGUST 21. *By special correspondent. The coroner's report was submitted today to the prosecutor, Mr. Curfen, in which it states that for every 100 cubic centimeters of blood taken from the dead body of Marilyn Monroe, there were 4.5 milligrams of barbiturates. According to experts, a dosage of 2.5 milligrams is enough to induce death. The report states clearly that death did not result from natural causes.*

Athens, August 29, 1962

Dear Mrs. Mina—

I came to Athens when I was 10 years old. I worked and went to school until I finished elementary school. I lived with an aunt of my father's who used to hit me, I didn't like it there. Then I worked as an apprentice to a seamstress. I also had other jobs. Now I work at a doctor's office and I live in at night and do the housework too. My salary is a little better, except that nothing here is mine. The doctor is a bachelor. He is going out with a lady his age. He is very polite and kindhearted, whereas he could have taken advantage of my situation. Mrs. Mina, six months ago I met a young man thirty years old, I'm twenty-seven. An honest man with a good job, a plumber. At any rate, he is a person like everyone else. He wants to get married but I am not an innocent young girl. You understand what I mean. And I can see that he believes that I am. Because he has never tried to touch me, Mrs. Mina. A girlfriend of mine says I should go and get myself sewn up. That I'm lucky to be working for a doctor and that I should ask for his help. I am ashamed, Mrs. Mina. And not only that, but I love this young man too. How can I do that to him? And how can I love him afterward? What do you advise me to do?

Patra M.
Rigilis St.

MILAN, AUGUST 30. *Special correspondent.* *"I am and always will be ready to take back Maria at any time. If not out of love, at least out of pity." This statement was made by the Italian industrialist Gian Battista Meneghini, the husband of Maria Callas, to a reporter from the influential magazine Epoca. Mr. Meneghini, with his usual loquaciousness, related a good many details from what he described as the "happy years" he spent with his diva wife. "She was always good to me," he said. "It was only with other people that she was difficult and high-strung." He subsequently filled in the following details on the subject: "Maria was a wonderful, sensitive woman, an enthusiastic housekeeper and an obedient wife. Our life together was always a perfect example of sympathy and understanding. In those days Maria loved family life more than the theater. She is less interested in opera than one would think. I had to fight to convince her that she should sing in Paris, in London, in Germany. Although I was never able to make her accept the invitation from the Shah, who wanted her in Tehran." Next Mr. Meneghini stressed that the problems he had as Callas's husband were due to outside influences, to their relationships with other people. He concluded with the following statement: "What happened can only be a kind of madness that possessed my wife. There is no other way to explain this change from one day to the next. And for whose benefit? For Onassis, about whom she said several weeks ago: 'He is an unhappy man.'"*

———

GENERAL ELECTRIC appliances at 42 Acharnon St., Radio-Stringli. PROGRESS mixers-juicers. Technology in your home. IZOLA appliances. 42 Acharnon St. Radio-Stringli. Thousands of electric washers, stoves, refrigerators. Amazingly low monthly installments.

September 12, 1962

From: Dagiakas, Sophocles; son of Ioannis; village of Eustylon, Thesprotia, Epirus

I kindly request the honorable Department of Emigration to please reply regarding the question of my sentence, which is of concern to me because I am interested in emigrating to Canada, with my whole family. I have been condemned to 5 months for a petty infraction; 4½ months for perjury; 2½ months for illegal possession of firearms; 20 days for using them negligently; 42 days for causing bodily harm; and 1 month for insulting authorities. Answer me immediately if it is possible to leave having these sentences. I am sending you a copy of my criminal record that lists all my convictions. Please answer me specifically about which convictions an emigrant cannot emigrate with. In other words, does everything count, or just felonies, pimping, robbery, etc.? Such things are not the case with me.

That is all and I am waiting for your answer.

CHALKIS, SEPTEMBER 17. *From our correspondent. The case of the vicious murder in the village of Kaminari, Evoia, which had local police authorities baffled and was being followed by the public with fervent and sustained interest, has been solved and closed as of yesterday morning. After the initial discovery that 20-year-old Dimitra Lagoudes was murdered by her father Anastasios, the investigating authorities, through exhaustive efforts, also learned of the undisclosed pregnancy of the unfortunate young woman. The responsible party was Dimitra's younger brother, Michaïl, age 13. (This is the age officially mentioned but his real age is 18, according to detailed information below.) The investigating committee was originally of the opinion that Dimitra had become pregnant through an incestuous relationship with someone in her immediate family. That is, with one of her brothers or with her father. In fact, suspicion had been centered primarily around the child-killer himself, because his alleged act did not seem sufficiently justified by his avowed explanation that he murdered his daughter because she would not reveal who her lover was. The investigating authorities persisted in their efforts and, early yesterday morning, Anastasios Lagoudes amended his confession, stating that he became irate with his daughter when she revealed to him, last Sunday afternoon, that she had been having relations with her brother Michaïl, who had made her pregnant. Following this terrible revelation, the father, Lagoudes, in a state of frenzy, murdered his daughter by covering her mouth and nostrils with his hand, causing her to suffocate to death. Following the father's confession, the brother, Michaïl, was questioned yesterday morning and the whole truth was revealed. According to him, it was out in the fields last September or October that he and Dimitra began having sexual relations. He confessed that he often slept in the same bed with her, which gave them ample opportunity to develop a sexual relationship, one which continued in the ensuing months. That is how Dimitra found herself pregnant. Fond of her brother and his warm embraces, she told no one about him, in spite of the fact that, for all practical purposes, she was living with him. Recently, the father, Anastasios Lagoudes, had become suspicious about their relations and had, for several months, been expressing to his wife his fear that Dimitra might be pregnant. To that same end and in order to verify things, last Saturday Dimitra was taken by her mother to a doctor. Following the above revelations and ensuing confessions by the child-killer and the incestuous brother, the veracity of which was fully ascertained, the remaining members of the Lagoudes family were released from custody, except, of course, for the perpetrator who, after being charged with premeditated murder, was taken yesterday afternoon to Chalkis so that he could be brought before the prosecutor this morning. The incestuous brother of the victim, Michaïl, was also released after being charged with incest. He was not held in custody because he had not been present at the scene of the crime. In the meantime the victim's mother, Panagiota, her older sister Ismini, and her brothers Vasileios and Apostolis are in a state of shock, both mental and physical, after the incredible ordeal and trying times they have been through. It was learned, finally, that the incestuous brother Michaïl, although his official birth certificate states that he was born in 1949, is in reality 18 years old, his birth date having been entered both erroneously and illegally. This finding was considered a substantial reason for not disputing his confession that it was he who was responsible for his sister's pregnancy.*

Dear Mrs. Mina—

I once sent you a letter, as you may remember, under the pen name "Love plus a child." Although it is late, considering the answer you gave me, I cannot help but tell you how very thankful I am for your advice. Since then, Mrs. Mina, almost five months have gone by. I have thought things over and I see that really, in some way, what I told you was very superficial. You asked me how the child was behaving. The child's behavior was normal; that is, in the beginning, when I first met him, he acted shy. No, Mrs. Mina, the child was not to blame for anything, I mean not for our splitting up. The cause of our breakup is, and was, my boyfriend's personality. In the beginning, he acted with me like everything was just peachy. Then, when I found out what kind of person he was, I told him to get out. I told him again and again, I love someone else, that I am going to get engaged to him. But he keeps insisting. You may be wondering: And you, since he loves you, why don't you just accept him? I would gladly accept him if he were not the person he is, that is, a liar and a blackmailer. Yes, Mrs. Mina, a blackmailer. Telling me he won't leave me alone and, more important, that even if I'm married he'll steal me back. You'll say, of course, that it's only words, but he is capable of anything. What I would like, Mrs. Mina, is for you to help me with this most difficult problem, at least in my opinion. I can't stand it when he stops me in the street because it may make people talk. Please tell me, Mrs. Mina, some way to make this person go away from me forever. In answer to the question you raised after my last letter, his child is almost illegitimate. He had been engaged to someone, but they broke up before it was time to get married. And he took the child. But all that didn't matter to me, people make mistakes. And I don't want you to mention that on the air. For me, not only as far as he is concerned but for everyone, what matters is their character. I have now found the person I was looking for, Mrs. Mina. We are both very happy and intend to get married. I am talking about another young man, Mrs. Mina, who loved me long before he did. You see, Mrs. Mina true love is like a diamond, no matter where you put it or throw it, it remains *true love*. True and pure.

[71]

I have written too much, Mrs. Mina, and you have other letters awaiting your wise counsel. I close my letter with much gratitude for your support in dealing with my problem.

Best regards from your faithful radio fan,

Begging for True Love

Good-bye

HERAKLEION, NOVEMBER 26. *From our correspondent. Early yesterday morning local police agents in the region of Phoenikas, just outside Herakleion, arrested the robber and Communist Konstantinos Patramanes, 50 years old, from Anogeia, Mylopotamos, who was hiding out in a farm hut. He was a member of the Podias communist guerrilla group operating in Crete during 1947. Since that time he has been in hiding for 15 years and his whereabouts were not discovered until today. There was a 200,000 dr. reward out for Patramanes, who made no attempt at all to resist arrest. He is one of 11 communist guerrillas still at large and in hiding in various places in Crete.*

MAGNETIC HEALTH BRACELETS FROM JAPAN
AIMANTE

For rheumatism, arthritis, headaches, high blood pressure, fatigue, insomnia, bronchial asthma, sexual impotence.

Genuine AIMANTE products bear the patent number 6393 – 4715 – 199777.

Exclusive representative for all of Greece, 22 Triti Septemvriou St., tel. 525 – 171

Gerani, December 8, 1962

I received your reply and I thank you for informing me immediately, and sorry for being a little late writing back, but I am down near Chania harvesting olives, because this year there was no crop in our village, and I may not be finished in December. And so I can't send the certificates now because it's not easy for me to get from Chania to Rethymno, not till we're done harvesting. Anyway, do not neglect to keep me informed. In January will I be eligible for those emigration shipments? Because I'm down here with the rest of the girls and we all want to leave together.

We send you greetings and I am waiting for your reply,

Ariadne Em. Krassaki

DECEMBER 21. *The bones of Saint Nektarios are being cut up and spirited out of Aegina. Where are they taken to? No one knows. It is believed that small and large pieces have already been sent to Athens, to Crete, to Chios, and elsewhere. It is also rumored that a portion of the saint's sternum was donated to the metropolitan church of the Holy Trinity in Piraeus. The cutting up of St. Nektarios has naturally caused a great commotion among the residents of Aegina, who consider St. Nektarios to be theirs, and also among the nuns of the Church of the Holy Trinity, where the saint is known to have lived and in whose courtyard he was buried in accordance with his wishes. In addition, widespread reaction to and discussion of the events were in evidence both among segments of the general population and of the church establishment.*

The elevation to sainthood of the metropolitan of Pentapolis, Nektarios Kephalas, was proclaimed last September in Encyclical 1161 of the Ecumenical Patriarchate of Constantinople. Nektarios Kephalas was born in Asia Minor in 1848 and died on September 20, 1920, in the Aretaion Hospital in Athens. It is noteworthy that St. Nektarios is the sole saint in the history of our church whom the population has become acquainted with through a photograph rather than a religious icon.

We asked members of the church whether the parceling out of bones conforms with the canons of our church. Theology professor Amilkas Alivizatos told us that there is no church regulation either forbidding or permitting the parceling out of saints' relics. Theology professor Gerasimos Konidaris told us that, beginning in the fourth century, there was a custom whereby, at church inaugurations, saints' relics were placed on the church altar during the inauguration ceremony. In particular, concerning the parceling out of saints' relics, Mr. Konidares stated that he had not encountered a similar case in the history of the church. The president of United Lay Theologians, Mr. Andreas Keramidas, stated that the transporting of saints' relics is a matter for the juris-

diction of the local metropolitan. There is neither a legal nor canonical prohibition in this particular instance concerning the parceling out of St. Nektarios's bones, which he characterized as macabre. Theology professor Andreas Phytrakes informed us that there is a long-standing controversy surrounding the Monastery of the Holy Trinity in Aegina and refused, for that reason, to answer questions, so that his comments would not be construed as supporting one side or the other.

In the meantime, the parceling out of St. Nektarios's bones, carried out by the use of a small handsaw, by mutual agreement between Msgr. Prokopios, who is in charge of spiritual matters in the church, and the Mother Superior, has caused quite an uproar among the nuns. One of them claims that at night she dreams about St. Nektarios with blood dripping from his chest (at the spot where the portion of his chest was removed and sent to the Church of the Holy Trinity in Piraeus), and that he has been complaining to her about the parceling out of his bones. St Nektarios's bones, excepting his skull, are kept in an iron strongbox for which there are two keys: one is kept by Bishop Prokopios of Hydra, Spetses, and Aegina and the other by the Mother Superior. His skull is kept in a gold-studded reliquary.

April 22, 1963

Dearest Mina—

Greetings. My problem is different from most. I live in a village and I am 16 years old. Three years ago I was carefree and happy. One day my father took me by force. Now I have become nervous, stubborn, and have no respect for anyone. I have often thought about putting an end to my life, but that's not really a solution either. I want to get back at them by leaving home or becoming a streetwalker. I don't know what else to think. My mother is a very hard woman. She treats me horribly. Maybe she does that because I have no respect for her. When my girlfriends come to the house, she flies off the handle at the slightest provocation. She hits me in front of my friends. She often tells me that I'll be the death of her. I don't know how I manage to control myself and not blurt out the truth to her at that moment. That she's to blame for my ending up like this. Not to mention that sometimes I think she knows about it and that she's jealous. I can't take any more, Mrs. Mina. I'll go crazy. I can't stay in the same house with a person I hate. I've asked him to let me go and work in town, but there is no way they will let me. They are conventional people. And of course he wants to keep me within his reach. No one else knows my secret. Please answer me very soon. What can I do? Should I leave? What sort of work could I do? My pen name is: "Maybe Death."

Thank you and good-bye,

Dimitra Katsaropoulos
St. An., Larisa

Do not repeat my story. Only my pen name: "Maybe Death."

Dimitra

LONDON, MAY 7. *From our correspondent. Great Britain intends to take no position vis-à-vis the possible postponement of a trip already planned by the Greek king and queen to London. This was made clear yesterday in a statement by a spokesman for the Foreign Office to journalists to the effect that "To the best of my knowledge, there was no discussion between the British Embassy in Athens and Greek authorities concerning the probable cancellation of the official visit to London by King Paul and Queen Frederika of Greece, scheduled for this coming July 9–12." Certain British newspapers, as well as the BBC, cited information yesterday and the day before indicating a trend in Greek public opinion, even in pro-government circles, in favor of the postponement of the royal visit because of the political unrest caused by the demonstrations against Queen Frederika. In the meantime, British police refused to comment yesterday on newspaper reports according to which H.M. Queen Frederika of Greece was assaulted by demonstrators on April 21 during her recent visit to London to attend the wedding of Princess Alexandra. A spokesman for Scotland Yard, asked about the accuracy of newspaper statements printed in* The Daily Mirror *(Labor),* The Daily Worker *(Communist), and* The Sunday Telegraph *(Conservative), refused to make any comments on the subject.* The Sunday Telegraph *writes that, according to the report submitted by Scotland Yard to the British government, the allegation that the Queen of Greece was molested has not been substantiated. The wife of the imprisoned communist, Betty Abatielou, who is English by birth, claimed that she attempted to give the Queen a written request but denied that she slapped her. Finally, the British Home Office announced that there is no evidence indicating that the demonstrators laid a hand on Queen Frederika. According to* The Sunday Telegraph, *the plainclothes officer assigned to the Queen was thrown to the ground by six Greek-Cypriot protesters in an attempt to free Abatielou from his grip, but they dispersed when the said police officer revealed his identity. According* to another version, the group of young Cypriot communists attacked the security officer, who fell to the ground before the group attacked the limousine driver, who sped to the rescue of the officer. Due to these circumstances, H.M. the Queen was obliged to request shelter at the door of the first house she encountered. It was, in fact, the house of Miss Marty Stevens, a professional singer, whose permission to enter was sought by Queen Frederika in order to escape from the threat of raving communists led by Abatielou. The Sunday Telegraph goes on to claim that the Queen of Greece was to blame for creating the situation in the first place because, although she had been informed about the presence of demonstrators, she insisted on entering the hotel through a side door without alerting the authorities.

———

WANTED, specially trained threaders and weavers for synthetic thread. Daily salary 75–100 drs., tel. 683-625, 6–8 P.M.

Areopolis, May 7, 1963

Honorable Sirs—

As I was preparing for departure for Australia, on the 8th day of the present month, along with my spouse, Popsie, she gave birth to a female child, and now her 40-day confinement period has almost elapsed. Please inform me when we may come to the city of Athens to undergo the proper medical examinations. Likewise concerning the matter of the birth certificate for our infant. It is not registered in the Town records of female births and consequently I am not able to procure the papers that I was told by you to submit. Would you be so kind as to write me what type of certificate I should ask for or, in the case that such a form exists, please send it to me so that I can fill it out. I await your reply.

Yours truly,

Ilias Plagiannakos

OPEN INVITATION TO PLASTERERS

The ecclesiastical council of the Agios Pandeleimon Church on Acharnon Street invites plasterers, on Friday, May 10, between 6 and 7 o'clock, to submit to the church's office sealed bids for the construction of imitation marble pillars in the church interior, as well as for the decoration of interior railings and external circular railings in the bell tower. The above works will be carried out in accordance with plans drawn up by the architect Mr. Georgios Stavros Nomikos and approved by the Ministry of Education, using imitation marble resembling that from Tinos and Eretria made by the use of a special plaster cement in West Germany. Applications accepted from plasterers with previous experience in this medium. A guarantee of 12,000 drachmas has been set, to be paid by promissory note, letter of credit, or cash. The bid will be made by filling out an invoice issued by the church. For further information, interested parties may contact the church or the architect, Mr. Georgios Stavros Nomikos, telephone 664-974, between 6 and 7 P.M.

In Athens, April 30, 1963
The Ecclesiastical Council

PATRAS, MAY 28. *From our correspondent. By telegraph from Aigion. On its way to be slaughtered, a bull escaped and began running on a wild rampage through the central streets of the city, with its owner in hot pursuit, spreading panic everywhere. After a dramatic chase, the bull made its way, at 1 P.M., into a branch office of the Commercial Bank. The employees, terrified by the sight of the animal, abandoned their posts and took refuge under some tables, while clients ran helter-skelter toward the exits. At one point the bull smashed in one of the teller's glass partitions with its horns, overturned a desk, and subsequently entered the bank's Files and Records Room. There, after causing untold damage by trampling on the books, the bull threw itself with great force at a barred window in an attempt to get out onto the street. As a result, its head was caught in the window bars and it was finally taken into custody by the police, who had been alerted in the meantime and hastened to the scene to pacify the residents of Aigion.*

———

Our brother Grigorios Lambrakis, athletic champion, university professor, and M.P., Piraeus, will be buried today, Tuesday, May 28, 1963, at 4 P.M. in Athens Cathedral. He is survived by his wife, children, sisters, brothers, and relatives.

[82]

Elizabethsville, June 1, 1963

Dear Grigoris—

About a month ago I sent you a letter asking you to please get my
package from the clinic, so that it doesn't get misplaced, and to
take it to your house or to any other safe place. I have not heard
from you since then. Not even a letter since February 25, and I am
worried. In case my package has actually been held somewhere, call
my cousin, Mr. Theodoros Michaïlides, 29 Sithonias St. (look him
up in the telephone book), to come and get it.

Grigoris, you should know that the Katanga stamps, as well as
its paper money, have been withdrawn from circulation. I had anticipated this and have a certain quantity in my possession; and I
would be most grateful if you could let me know if you know anyone or if you can possibly put me in touch with collectors who
might be interested in buying them. We are talking about complete series. Let me know as soon as you can, if possible before the
end of next month, because otherwise I will have to return them to
the bank at that time.

With my best wishes for a happy Easter,

Pericles K.
P.B. 48
Elizabethsville
Katanga—Congo

P.S. I may be moving to Nigeria, due to better working conditions,
salary-wise, that is. I will let you know beforehand.

JUNE 12. *Following an extremely long and stormy meeting, the Central Committee for Athletics decided yesterday to impose a two-month suspension on the Panathenaïkos Athletic Club (PAO) player Takis Loukanides. However, because committee members were threatened and vociferously heckled by numerous Panathenaïkos fans, the president of the CCA, Mr. Stasinopoulos, did not announce the penalty. He merely said that a decision had been made but that it would be announced on Thursday (tomorrow), after its ratification by the Board of Directors of the NFL. During the dramatic CCA meeting, the PAO representative, Mr. Vgenopoulos, stated categorically that in the event that Loukanides is punished, Panathenaïkos will withdraw from the league. This statement was reiterated after the announcement of the penalty by Mr. Vgenopoulos, who added angrily as he was leaving that after Panathenaïkos played with Loukanides on Sunday against AEK, it would withdraw from the league.*

ROYAL COURT, JUNE 11, 1963. *His R.M. the King received this afternoon His Excellency the Prime Minister, Mr. Constantine Karamanlis, who submitted the resignation of his government. The resignation was accepted. From the Office of the King's Chamberlain.*

[84]

Adelaide, June 16, 1963

Dear Mrs. Galanou—

Greetings. My name is Georgios Maglares. I hope you remember the dark, short young man you helped so much and I thank you for that. I think a lot about you all, because you were the only ones who showed me kindness and gave me courage when it was needed. You are such a good person, Mrs. Galanou, that you will understand me. I would like very much for you to help me in something concerning my fiancée. I did not get the invitation done in time because I had no affidavit with it. I have recently received permission to use the invitation. I want so much, and I am not ashamed to say so since you are not here next to me, for you to help the girls at least to come over. I will go crazy, Mrs. Galanou, waiting here. We have been waiting for so many years, she and I both, to get engaged. Her parents didn't want us to and the circumstances were not right either. And now that they are we are separated by 12,000 miles. Help us, Mrs. Galanou, to get together soon. At least let her come with my sister. Everything is fine here and I have a good job, but it is very lonely and my mind has stopped working. I keep thinking about her and it's like a thorn in my flesh, Mrs. Galanou. And now my sister has written that they will come separately. Please do something so that they can leave together. If necessary, let my sister wait. I know it is difficult, but I know that you will help the girls to come over, both together and soon. I am counting on your sympathy and your kindheartedness, Mrs. Galanou.

Regards to Mrs. Sokou and the other lady in your office as well as to Mr. Antonopoulos and the girls in room 407. Be well. I remember you always.

Respectfully yours,

Georgios Maglares

JUNE 17. *Following protracted operations conducted by the vice squad of the Pireaus Security Police, a clandestine brothel was discovered yesterday in Neo Phalero in a house on Ka-nellopoulos Street. It was being run by the Tezedaki sisters: Kymatini, age 31, and Pelagia, age 19, who were selling themselves to respectable members of Pireaus society. The names of the brothel's clients were found through listings in notes and visiting cards found on the premises and also in the telephone book. There was also a small notebook with the telephone numbers of clients of the clandestine brothel where, according to information revealed during the interrogation by police, other young women were also engaged in prostitution. The two aforementioned sisters were arrested and the investigation continues in the utmost secrecy in order to ascertain the identities of the remaining persons involved in the case.*

The lake at Marathon contained 32,250,000 cubic meters of water yesterday as compared with 32,271,000 the day before yesterday and 24,586,000 on the same date last year.

June 28, 1963

Dear Mrs. Mina—

We live in a village in Chania and I am obliged to help my husband with the work in the fields. Although I don't like it in the country, I do it because I have to and I want to help him but he is never satisfied. But that's as much work as I can do. He doesn't believe me but, Mrs. Mina, I'm not lying, I just can't. As soon as I bend over, I feel a sharp pain, I swear to God I do. I learned to love my husband over time, even though I was fond of him from the beginning. My fondness plus some pushing from my parents made me stop high school after the tenth grade to marry him, even though I was still young. And it's terrible, now that I love him, he's very aloof with me. We quarrel often and things keep getting worse. I try at least as far as the housework is concerned to do everything perfectly so that he won't have too many excuses to start complaining at night when he gets back. I have tried to make light of his complaints but he just won't stop. And I can't hide from you the fact that our mutual respect is gone. In the beginning I didn't talk back to him but now I behave the same way. I regret it afterward, but not at that moment. Then sometimes when I'm feeling desperate I think of taking my child and going away. He's four years old, a boy. Just going away and not telling anyone where I am, except my brothers, who live in Athens. So that I could work, so that he'd stop throwing it up at me that I don't earn a single drachma for him. Bear in mind, Mrs. Mina, that we are poor and poverty brings nagging into the home. If I were a little bolder I could convince him to leave the village and come to Athens, where three of my seven brothers and sisters are living. Like so many of our fellow villagers who move away to improve their own and their children's lives. But I'm scared. Perhaps such a move will change our routines and our customs. What do you think? Won't it be better in Athens? Please give me your advice. I thank you.

An unhappy friend from a village in Chania

And the young girl disappeared, returning a short while later with a chunk of natural ice.

—Wow, what's that?, he said, startled.

—Ice, mister, ice from the mountain.

—Alice wasn't far wrong when she said that we had arrived in a wonderland castle, remarked Baker.

For fifteen minutes he paced around the veranda, while Athina served him the cocktail Smith had made.

—How nice it is here, said Mrs. Berkeley.

—It's fabulous, agreed the journalist.

—I wonder what other surprises are still in store for us, added Alice.

—Do you think they know down there that there's a villa like this up here? said Baker, changing the subject.

—Who knows, maybe they don't, said Mrs. Berkeley.

— Only Tsakitzis himself can tell us that, Smith chimed in. They spent a half hour drinking and talking. The bright light from the petrol lamp cast marble streaks on the water in the lake, which shone like Bohemian crystal. Mrs. Berkeley, full of enthusiasm, could not stop expressing her admiration. Inside, the women prepared the meal and the men on the veranda sat smoking; some smoked pipes and others cigars.

—Where's Tsakitzis? Alice asked Stavros at one point, as he held out an ashtray to Smith.

— Tsakitzis will be here in half an hour, Stavros answered in English.

— Oh, everyone here speaks English, remarked Alice.

— That's right, miss, answered Stavros. There are quite a few of us in Smyrna who speak your language.

— That's nice to know, remarked Alice.

— Tomorrow I'll set up my easel right over here, said Mrs. Berkeley.

—You're not going to paint Tsakitzis, are you? her husband cut in.

—Why not? If he poses for me.

(To be continued)

FLY TO AUSTRALIA
ON THE WINGS OF
PAN-AM

Easy payments by installment
Down payment, 2,000 drs., balance in two years
From PAN-AM for Greek emigrants
6 Eleftheriou Venizelou St., tel. 612-695, 611-047

Sunday, June 30.

Theater: ALSOS, *Pagrati,* From the Polka to the Twist; ATTIKON THEATER *(Patision, Angelopoulou bus stop),* Four Queens; *GEORGIOS PAPPAS THEATER (4 Sina St.),* The Three Angels *(comedy), Albert Isson;* KATERINA'S *(former* NEW THEATER, *91 Patision St.),* Mommy Wants Daddy; METROPOLITAN, A Silly Girl; OLYMPIA, *Pireos St.,* Dewdrops; POREIA *(69 Triti Septemvriou St.),* Dreams of Our Own; BUDAPEST CIRCUS *(Vasilisis Sophias Ave., behind American Embassy), two performances daily;* FIRST, Nouveau Riche *(starring Avlonitis, Vasileiadou, Rizos);* HERODOU ATTIKOU THEATER, *Thymelikos Theater Company, and Nikos Karzis,* Bacchae.

Dear Mrs. Mina—

I am 25 years old and married for four years. I have two boys three and two years old. I married my husband for love. I met him as soon as I graduated from junior high school. I had a sheltered life as a girl; I was an only daughter with a very strict father. I grew up without girlfriends. There was also an ongoing family drama, with quarreling between my mother and his sister, who lived in the apartment below us. Every day we had the police around and lots of crying. That was my childhood. I grew up with a desire to marry early to get away from my father's tyrannical rule. And so I found myself in love—or so I thought—with a man who was 14 years older than I was and had serious health problems. I met him three years before we were married. He was always bad-tempered and insensitive. But then the inevitable happened, and my mother had told me that girls who are no longer virgins can't get married easily. And that was the reason I decided to marry him. The quarreling started from the first month. I'm the sensitive, romantic type. I want tender love and care. He is curt, rude, and bad-tempered. He is also insensitive during sex, he hurts me. Instead of pleasure he fills me with disgust. In addition to that, it is very difficult for him to finish. He sweats and tries and tries and often he doesn't even get there. I think he must be on the verge of impotence. He has never kissed me. Or caressed me. All that is unnecessary, he says. I had given up on the idea of getting any pleasure out of this life. I believed, moreover, that this was the way it was meant to be, a chore. He tells me I'm frigid. But it's not true. He has just made me grow old, he has made me feel numb, and my nerves are shot, because he's always making fun of me. He's so mean. We have often come to the point of separating, but in the end I come back because I think of my children. But is it worth living such an unhappy life? When I am so unsatisfied and want so much to enjoy everything I missed out on. I just met a 32-year-old young man. Four months ago. I think it is true love. He is everything I've been missing. He's tender. And he loves me. I adore him. He is honest and hardworking. He says we should keep living like this, so as not

!?

to deprive my children of a stable home life. Stable? When their father and I are constantly fighting? With him I discovered love and found out that I'm not frigid. Tell me what to do. I love him so much. It's driving me crazy. They say that the children of divorced parents become unhappy. Is it true? I have a house and parents and he doesn't. Will I get my children, by law, if we separate? I forgot to tell you that my husband has had tuberculosis for a year now. So does my youngest boy. Please help me. Answer me soon. Don't reveal any details or my name. Just the pen name: "Chloe."

Very respectfully yours,

Angeliki Voskopoulou

MOSCOW, SEPTEMBER 20. *Associated Press. The president of the Soviet Red Cross disclosed yesterday that Lenin's body is periodically immersed in a special fluid, thereby facilitating preservation of the embalmed corpse and duly impressing visitors to Moscow, where the body of the founder of the Soviet Republic is on display. The above disclosure was made by the president of the Soviet Red Cross, Mr. Gyorgy Mitroiff, in response to a question by American actor Danny Kaye, who was in Moscow for an international film festival. Mitroiff stated that Lenin's body is removed from the bier on which it lies and is immersed in a special fluid for between six and twelve hours every two or three months.*

———

By decision of the Mayor of Vyron, as published in the Official Government Gazette, *no. 241, Mr. Ioannis Sapounakis, son of Michaïl, administrator in the borough of Vyron, has been promoted, by election and with the full agreement of the official committee of the Ministry of the Interior, from the position of City Manager 2 to City Manager 1.*

My dear Grigoris—

My first impressions of Lagos: The city has a population of 500,000 to 20,000 Europeans. It is the capital of Nigeria—the Federal Republic of Nigeria—which has 40,000,000 inhabitants. The country is extremely fertile, eleven times larger than Greece, and covers an area comprising the lower bed and delta of the river Niger—from whence its name. The river should be familiar to you from the novel *The Dark Mistress,* which takes place on the upper bed of the river, a former French colony and present Republic of Niger—République du Niger—whose capital is Bamako. Note that in bookshop windows in the Congo I often saw the same novel in French—*La maîtresse noire.*

Some people call Stockholm the Venice of the North, because it is built on several small islands. Perhaps they should call Lagos the Venice of Africa—for short. It is built on five or six small islands, linked by bridges, landfills, and even by small boats. Instead of the palaces along the banks of the bride of the Adria, we have shacks here with tin or grass roofs, and instead of elegant canals with blue water we have small, dull, cloudy lakes full of algae that reflect the cloudy sky. In the center of the city rise about fifteen skyscrapers 20–35 stories high. The harbor, which does a lot of exporting, has about 40 ships these days. Pleasant and sanitary housing is available in a suburb 7–8 kilometers from the center, where my government-allocated house is located. It looks like a villa in Philothei, with a garage, a large garden, three bedrooms—it was meant for a family—etc. I have only one servant at my disposal and I refused to hire a gardener, an action which earned me disparaging comments from the snobs in our colony here. You see, my dear friend, I came here to make money and I have no desire to waste it on foolish things, such as motorboats, for example, or deluxe automobiles, bulky radios, or any of the things that interest my vain compatriots.

The center of the city has most unusual avenues. Traffic is directed, for the most part, by tall, slim-bodied black women sporting tight blue skirts, short-sleeved white blouses, black ties, and police caps. They are said to be quite merciless when it comes to fines. Would you like me to send some photographs of them I took a few days ago?

My job combines urban medicine and sanitation, that is, I inspect food stores, restaurant kitchens, road hygiene, employees—mainly chefs—women of loose morals, etc. One good thing is that the hours are fixed and they never wake you in the middle of the night. His Excellency the President of the Republic had his birthday the day before yesterday. So the newspapers were plastered with his picture. Wearing glasses and a uniform, in his general's hat. I found out that he once served in Nigeria's colonial army, in which, as we know, black men could attain the high rank of Warrant Officer. Do you hear that, my friend, you who have remained in the lowly position of a second lieutenant in the reserves?

In addition to what I mentioned before regarding servants, you should know that all of our simple-minded countrymen—as well as the rest of the Europeans—have at least three: a chef, a butler, and a gardener. There are no women servants, unless you want a girlfriend, in which case you must feed her, clothe her, and give her a large allowance, only to have her go out almost every night with her native friends, as it is practically impossible to keep her at home for yourself only. By the way, let me also inform you that the legends about the anatomical endowments of black men are without any basis. I have already examined hundreds of them and I assure you that I rarely encounter any which exceed European measurements. The only peculiarity I have to report—one which concerns women, however—is the frequency of hypertrophic inner—or small—vaginal labia.

Be well and do not forget me,

Pericles K.

THESSALONIKI, SEPTEMBER 23. *From our correspondent. At 11 A.M. yesterday Xenofon Giosmas, president of the now defunct Association of Northern Epirote Veterans and Victims of the Resistance, accompanied by his lawyer, Mr. G. Goulas, went before the interrogating officer of the Third Precinct to defend himself against charges leveled against him for moral complicity in the murder of M.P. Gr. Lambrakis and the injury of M.P. K. Tsarouchas from Kavala. Xenofon Giosmas asked to be given access to the court documents and evidence on which the accusations against him were based. The interrogating officer, exercising his legal right, refused to make the requested documents available to X. Giosmas. Following this, it was learned that the latter refused to make a deposition, stating that he knew nothing.*

———

It has been announced by the Society for the Protection of Animals that current rumors concerning the purchase of cats by the Budapest Circus, now stationed here, are completely unfounded, as was ascertained by the S.P.A. official in charge of the matter.

Ano Ilioupolis, September 25, 1963

Dear Mrs. Mina—

Good day to you. I am 19 years old, a wife and mother of two adorable children, a boy and a girl, four-month-old twins. I have a wonderful husband, 25 years old, with a steady job. Our happiness is completed by our two little angels. But my problem is my mother-in-law and my sister-in-law, who is separated because she couldn't have children. I try, Mrs. Mina, to be very nice to her because she is jealous and mean. She's always trying to hurt my feelings by telling me that I'm only holding onto my husband because of the children. She's jealous of my house, because I have a very luxurious house, that my parents gave me as a dowry. I am an only child and my family has taken good care of me. Believe me, Mrs. Mina, I married my husband because I cared for him and he, too, adores me, me and our children. He never goes out alone, he always takes us with him, because we have our own car and don't have any problems with the children. My mother-in-law is worse than my sister-in-law, she says that she made me her daughter-in-law because I had a dowry. I say nothing to my husband so as not to upset him, but what should I do, should I tell him, Mrs. Mina, or not?

I am anxiously awaiting your reply.

Vicky

NAUPLION, SEPTEMBER 28. *From our correspondent. Yesterday at 5 P.M., the illustrious Princess Margaret and her husband, Lord Snowdon, accompanied by the Duchess of Blandford and former Mrs. Onassis, arrived incognito aboard a "flying dolphin" hovercraft as guests of Mr. Niarchos. The royal couple, after visiting the archaeological site at Mycenae, returned to Nauplion and then continued on to Bourtzi. Princess Margaret was asked by the manager of the small island's local hotel to kindly sign the guest book, but she refused, excusing herself on the grounds that she was traveling there incognito.*

ROYAL COURT, SEPTEMBER 27, 1963. *H.R.M. the King received His Excellency the Prime Minister, Mr. P. Pipinelis, who submitted his resignation, as he wishes to run for election. H.R.M. the King has reserved judgment. From the Office of the King's Chamberlain.*

October 2, 1963

I am interested in emigrating to Australia. I am married and have a child three months old. I am working as an electrician, have very little schooling, and do some other technical work with no license yet. Please send me instructions what I should do. I am interested in a quick answer. I don't know any foreign languages.

Nikolaos Asimis
Kyparissia

OCTOBER 17. *The district attorney of Pireaus, Mr. G. Poly-chronopoulos, dispatched to Hydra by order of the government to carry out an on-site investigation of rumors concerning flag-draping of the local courthouse there during the recent visit of former minister of finance, Mr. D. Alibrandis, ascertained that the rumors were unfounded and due, in all probability, to the hoisting of a single flag in front of the Justice of the Peace office, located on the ground floor immediately below the Court of First Instance.*

————

Kifisia police arrested I. D. Mitsakis, nightclub owner, E. K. Karanases, a waiter at the same establishment, and G. D. Veloudakis, a restaurant owner from the same neighborhood, for facilitating licentious behavior (in private booths). They were brought before the magistrate at the Misdemeanors Court and sentenced to prison, the first for five months, the second for four months for the same offense, and the third for three months.

Koryphasion, October 21, 1963

Dear Mr. Stranger—

From me to you who will be reading this letter, please don't get me wrong.

I want you to tell me if I can emigrate through DEME. Where to, when, and if. I mean, to which country, like for instance, Germany, Africa, Australia, Canada. I want to get away from life on the farm. Anywhere at all.

I am waiting anxiously for an answer from you. Write me whatever I need, everything. I am 19 years old.

Paraskevi Kanellou

OCTOBER 24. *The Prime Minister, Mr. Stylianos Mavromi-chalis, announced that no decision was made concerning the setting of a price for olive gathering. A decision about this matter will be made after the elections by the new government. The Prime Minister made it clear that the above view-point was accepted by the olive producers concerned. We are also informed that the committee in charge of Corinthian raisins, convening at a special meeting, decided upon an in-crease of 25 lepta per kilo on the price of raisins from the present crop delivered by producers to the Independent Raisin Growers. The committee reached this decision after ascertain-ing that there was a great demand for Greek raisins in mar-kets abroad and after establishing satisfactory prices. If the above committee's decision is ratified by the I.R.G., the prices of Corinthian raisins will be readjusted according to area as follows: from Aigion, 7.85 drachmas per kilo; from Corinth, 7.50 drs.; from Patras and the Ionian Islands, 7.35; from Amaliada and Triphylia, 7.25; Ileia, Pylos, and environs, 7.15; Messinia and environs, 7.00.*

Dear Mrs. Mina—

Today I heard your answer and I thank you. I am your listener who
signed with the pen name "Chloe." Now I have to explain something I found out on the same exact day I mailed you my letter.
The young man in question is married, with two children, but he
is separated. It's been almost three years that he's lived apart from
his wife. He married her when he was twenty, after a lot of pressure
and scheming. He never loved her and because of that there was
always rancor between them. He is not ready to ask for a divorce
because he loves his children and he is afraid that if it goes to court,
his wife will keep the children. I am still seeing him. I love him. I
am ashamed to say so because I have certainly broken all the rules.
And I feel guilty. But what else can I do? He is kind and gentle
with me, he's not just flattering me, and he really talks to me.
About his troubles and about his problems at work. He has also
lacked the affection of a family. He grew up with no mother and
had a rather uncaring stepmother, and he has been working since
he was a child of eight. You told me to talk it over with my husband. How could I possibly since we cannot communicate? Let me
remind you just what my situation is: I married my husband for
love. He is 14 years older than I am. He is in poor health. He treats
me badly, makes fun of me and looks down on me. When someone
from his family or a friend does something to hurt me, he never
takes my side but makes me suffer even more. His brothers and
sisters have a lot of influence over him and they say things against
me to him. In fact, his sister is constantly advising him to be careful
and not to let us push him around. We live with my parents, and
they help us a lot, especially financially. Could this be why he behaves that way with me? In our intimate relations he is very abrupt.
I go with him out of a sense of duty. He says I am cold by nature
and that I should see a doctor. But why should I, now that I've
met someone else, how come I feel differently? I had even begun
to believe it myself about being frigid. Could it be that's just the
way marriage is? That after two or three years it becomes just another routine? But I see so many happy couples around me and

I'm jealous. I don't want to separate because I'm worried about hurting my children. Even though I have the means to support them. Should I perhaps just accept my fate and resign myself to it? But then again how can I live that way? I'm still young, 25 years old. And he insists that I have aged. Once he hit me in public. I didn't say anything. I've been patient, how long can I keep this up? I miss having love, I need to be cared for, and my husband can't give me all that. I think that if I lose the young man that I am involved with now, I will go crazy. His presence is very soothing to me. And I have someone to talk to. What should I do? Should I continue seeing him? He says there is nothing worse than being a stepchild like he was. He is careful and sensible. Please help me. Should I perhaps visit a social worker or a psychiatrist? Answer me once again under the same pen name: "Chloe."

My heartfelt thanks,

Angeliki Voskopoulou

PARIS, NOVEMBER 13. *From the Athens Press Agency. The newspaper* France Soir *has published a long, three-column interview with Crown Prince Constantine entitled: "I will marry Anna-Maria of Denmark when she becomes 18 years old." It goes on to cite an announcement made by the Greek Royal Court in Athens on the subject and has printed the following statements made by the prince: "The date of my wedding to Princess Anna-Maria of Denmark has been set. For the moment it must remain secret. It will be announced in the very near future, at the latest within two months. There has been quite a bit of false information printed here and there on this subject without consulting the interested parties. Our wedding will take place after the princess reaches the age of eighteen. In Denmark young women are not allowed to marry under that age. This is a state law which a princess can hardly violate. Our wedding will take place in Athens. I am here in Paris for work. I was invited to take part in the NATO Council, where I will be examining Western Alliance defense issues. It is very likely that I will be visiting my fiancée in Montreux, Switzerland."*

NOVEMBER 17, 1963. *The Minister of Justice signed several decrees ordering the release from prison, in accordance with the Pacification Law, of the following 15 "political prisoners," formerly convicted for violations of various laws:*

1. *Styl. Spiliotopoulos, in violation of Law 509.*
2. *Ger. Podaras, Law 509.*
3. *Eustath. Kalphas, in violation of Resolution No. 3.*
4. *Ioannis Karatsikos, Resolution No. 3.*
5. *Stephanos Doukatsas, Law 509.*
6. *Christos Manoukas, Resolution No. 3.*
7. *Athanasios Papagiannis, Resolution No. 3*
8. *G. Giannakopoulos, Law 509.*
9. *Christos Koteles, Resolution No. 3.*
10. *B. Raïkoudes, Resolution No. 3.*
11. *A. Platanias, homicide during German occupation.*
12. *Ioannis Balianes, homicide during German occupation.*
13. *G. Vozias, Resolution No. 3.*
14. *N. Karasavvides, Resolution No. 3.*
15. *Ioannis Konstantinou, Resolution No. 3.*

November 19, 1963

Gentlemen—

I wish to emigrate to Australia with my family for a ten-year period. For this reason would you please be good enough to invite me for an examination. My name is Kallistratos Charalambos Karageorgiou, resident of Larisa, 49 Avenue of Thessaloniki Street. Marital status: married. My wife's full name is Panagiota (wife of Kallistratos) Karageorgiou, daughter of Konst. Datsios. One unbaptized female child. Please inform me promptly as to what type of work I could perform there and what my possible salary might be.

Yours obediently,

The interested party Kallistratos Karageorgiou

PATRAS, NOVEMBER 26. *From our correspondent. Hundreds of residents were able to watch the funeral of President Kennedy on television at 7 P.M. yesterday, the hour at which it actually took place. This was made possible at a downtown shop in Patras (belonging to Mr. D. Michalopoulos), where a television set was tuned in to an Italian television network. According to the Italian television announcer, moreover, the program was broadcast in Italy via the Telstar satellite. The crowd of people watching the funeral was so large that at one point traffic stopped and some lights were broken when some youngsters climbed up on a traffic pole.*

CHIOS, DECEMBER 25. *From our correspondent. The much-publicized news that the State Chemical Laboratory has, by recent decision, permitted the manufacture and distribution throughout the country of the American soft drinks Coca-Cola and Pepsi-Cola has outraged citrus-fruit producers on the island, already blighted by insufficient consumption of their products. This will lead to the incapacitation of the newly opened soft-drink factory, which this year alone has processed 20,000 tons of oranges. A telegram was sent by Chios M.P. Leonidas Bournias to the Prime Minister and to the Ministers of Coordination, Industry, and Agriculture protesting the licensing of the manufacture and distribution in Greece of the above foreign soft drinks. Mr. Bournias stresses in his telegram that the withdrawal of this measure is imperative in order to protect the citrus-fruit producers, who will otherwise incur great damage, as has already happened in neighboring countries.*

ROYAL COURT, DECEMBER 24, 1963. *H.R.M. the King received his Excellency the Vice-President of the Government and Foreign Minister, Mr. S. Venizelos. H.R.M. the King received his Excellency the Prime Minister, Mr. George Papandreou, who submitted the resignation of his government. H.R.M. the King accepted the resignation. From the Office of the King's Chamberlain.*

Dear Mrs. Mina—

I am 27 years of age and so is my husband. We have two little boys, three and five years old. Now let me tell you about my life, because I am afraid that my tragedy began a long time ago. When I was nine years old someone suggested making love to me because his fiancée had made him jealous. He spread rumors that my dad was having an affair with her and he threatened to tell my mother to divorce him if I didn't let him kiss and touch me. Fortunately, things didn't go any farther than that. He was eventually found out and, three years later, married someone else, not his fiancée who he had supposedly been so jealous of. I left the village and came to Athens. At the age of 15 I got sick. At the clinic they took me to, the doctor there spent the entire first night by my bedside. And many nights after that, so that 25 days later I was madly in love with him. He was engaged, however, and we had to leave each other, which he told me to do if I really loved him, because he didn't want to hurt me. I tried to forget him but it was impossible not to think about him. So much so that a month later my aunt and uncle, who I was staying with, took me to a neurologist. I told him what had happened to me. He, too, advised me to forget about him. So, soon afterward I began doing all the wrong things and ended up where I am today. I started a relationship with some-one else by telephone and also by correspondence. In the end I left him because I saw that nothing could tear me away from my thoughts about the first man. Then I was introduced to a prospec-tive husband. I said yes and got married. Before getting married I had never gone very far with anyone precisely because I was afraid of the evil consequences going too far might have. So my wedding night arrived and I was a complete ignoramus. During our engage-ment our parents occasionally caused us certain minor problems, but my fiancé was good to me and there was no reason to break up with him. My goal was to get married. I was still afraid, after my other disappointment, that it would be easy for my nerves to go to pot again and I didn't want to cause such distress to my family. I got married, and from the very first night certain thoughts began to bother me. We didn't quite sleep together. The next day we went on a trip and that night I became his wife. And again two days later. But after that it began to occur much more infrequently, until two years later I reached the point of consulting a doctor and, on occasion, helping him along with pills. But this situation often caused us to quarrel. In the beginning I thought that perhaps he was seeing someone else. He began ignoring me. Getting out of work and coming home two or three hours later. That would happen regularly all week, and on Sundays. To my complaints in the beginning, and to our quarrels later on, he would answer: I went for a walk, so what? Or: I went to the movies. Or: I had work, what's wrong with that? Or: I was in the local tavern. After the birth of our second child, he took me to a neurologist. I had been bursting into tears at the slightest provocation and feeling on edge after our quarrels, which by then were daily occurrences. The doctor turned out to be the same one who had taken care of me when I was younger. He told him that there was nothing wrong with me and that I needed more attention and care. And he told me not to ask for love from people who cannot give it to me. To look at life from a different viewpoint. To take, as he so characteristically said, and not just to give. And to become less sensitive to many things. I tried to follow his advice. I did what I could. But then last summer I asked my husband if it would be all right for me not to go to the country, as I do every year, because it would be difficult for me to be away from him for two months. He insisted, however, and I went. During that time, an acquaintance of mine informed me that he was leading another life in Athens. That they had seen him in different places. Then everything around me began to crumble. My suspicions, his indifference, everything became clear to me. And a wall went up between us. I could think of nothing else but how to get back at him for the trust I had shown him and my own naïveté, and for all the years I wasted with him. So I fell straight into the arms of another man. Without feeling anything at all for him. Perhaps I was flattered by the fact that he had been after me for three years, without my ever having looked at him. When, however, after the summer vacation, I went back to him—

to my husband—he made me believe in him again. I broke off completely with the other man, even though he repeatedly threatened that he would tell my husband everything. But, Mrs. Mina, he continues to ignore me and our relationship keeps getting worse. I am tired of trying again. If I leave him, I'll be even more unhappy. Because I have the children, what will happen to them? How long must I go on pleading and begging to be understood? Sometimes I even reach the point of talking to him as openly as I am to you. Could he be deliberately trying to make me get involved with someone else so that he can get custody of our boys? Or could he have some secret illness that he is desperately trying to hide by resorting to such tactics? Please answer me, without commenting directly on my letter, because I am a little scared of him. Thank you.

Desperate and Alone

FEBRUARY 11. *The funeral was held yesterday afternoon at the First National Cemetery for the Great Lord Chamberlain of H.M. the King, Dimitrios N. Levides. His funeral was attended by H.M. the Queen, H.R.H. the Prince, H.R.H. Princess Irene, H.M. the Queen Mother of Romania Elena, H.R.H. Prince Michael, the Prime Minister, Mr. I. Paraskevopoulos, former Prime Ministers Messrs. Tsaldaris, Mavromichalis, and Pipinelis, the head of the Center Union Party, Mr. Papandreou, by ministers Messrs. Xanthopoulos-Palamas, Daïs, Stratos, Manos, Karmires, and Zorbalas, as well as by former M.P.'s, foreign M.P.'s, members of the Greek Royal Court, other officials, and members of Athenian high society. Palace guard Evzones paid a musical tribute to him in accordance with the sovereign's wishes. Following the funeral service, the Queen, Princess Irene, and the Queen Mother of Romania took their leave, while Crown Prince Constantine and Prince Michael followed the cortege to the graveside of the Great Lord Chamberlain.*

Lagos, February 23, 1964

Dearest Grigoris—

I received your letter four days ago and was delighted to see that you are well. I would also be most pleased if you would care to send me some of your papers—by surface mail and at my expense—that is, only those pages containing research of yours. Write me if you are open to criticism and I will send you my comments in due course. I will try to contact Mr. Papaleontas, assuming the address is correct. I am already in touch—selectively—with some Greeks, something that of course implies a small, private clientele.

In the local tongue, "come here" is "wah nimbi." In other matters, the sexual customs are the same as in the Congo. I should tell you that a number of my black patients have been bitten by fellow countrymen. They are always asking me for medicine to prevent infection from saliva. You see, it is a local superstition here that a human bite leads to death, and when they get themselves into a fight they really go at it, no holds barred.

I would be most indebted to you if you could send me *Kathimerini* and *Eleftherotypia* from the day after the elections (2/17) with the results. The cost is 13 drachmas by airmail.

With love,

Pericles K.

FEBRUARY 27. *Mariam Iasonidou, age 28, from the village of Itron, Pieria, wife and assault victim of arraigned pimp D. Kyrvorias from Thrace, succumbed to her wounds while being treated at Evangelismos Hospital. Her body was taken to the coroner's to determine the amount and the seriousness of the brutality so as to be included in the brief for the investigation of Kyrvorias still pending by the Eighth Precinct in order to modify the indictment against him. The beastly pimp had lured the poor but pretty village girl into his net by promising her marriage and a comfortable life. Instead, however, he turned her into an unwilling instrument of his illicit operations, and whenever she dared to protest he beat her savagely. His brutal behavior and exploitation of the young woman continued even after he made her his legal wife. He forced her to sell herself for money and to turn her profits over to him, while continuing to abuse her, which resulted in his eventually causing her death. Charges will also be brought against him for causing bodily harm leading to death, in addition to the charges for pimping already on record.*

It has been announced by the campaign office of former min-
ister Mr. Leonidas Dertiles that the votes cast in his favor
during the elections totaled 26,130, not 24,015, as was erro-
neously reported in yesterday's newspapers. This conclusion
was arrived at by a committee appointed by the Prefecture of
Athens, following a reexamination of the voting count.

———

The Royal Air Force soccer team pulled off a winning victory
over the heavily favored Saphrampolis team (Minor League),
with a final score of 4-3 (halftime score, 1-2). Spectators en-
joyed a most interesting and exciting match. The winning
team's goals were made by Mavrikos (2), Vertsones, and Si-
migdalas; the losing team's goals were by Nikolaïdes (2) and
Orphanopoulos. The RAF team played with Doudoumes
(sub: Manegas), Kontopandeles (Papakostakis), Markonides,
Hadzis (Mourikes), Dokos, Marditses, Thomakos, Mavrikos,
Vertsones, Simigdalas, and Arones.

MARCH 4. *The miracle-working icon of the Virgin of Tinos was brought early this morning to Tatoï Palace following initiatives by the Abbot of the Evangelistria Monastery at Tinos. Shortly before 2 A.M., the King kissed the icon of the Blessed Virgin in the presence of members of the royal family, the Archbishop of Athens, and the Abbot of the monastery. The said icon was brought there aboard the destroyer* Sphendone, *which happened to be near Tinos participating in maneuvers, along with other battleships. As had been announced, the* Sphendone *sailed early that morning into the harbor in front of the Naval Academy. The news, which had previously been made public, caused much excitement and crowds of people gathered in front of the Academy to wait for the icon to pass by. As early as twelve o'clock midnight officials began arriving at the Academy. Shortly before 1 A.M., the Prime Minister, Mr. George Papandreou, arrived, along with Minister of National Defense Mr. Garouphalias, Minister of the Interior Mr. Toumbas, Minister of Finance Mr. Mitsotakis, Undersecretary of Education Mr. Akritas, Chairman of the Royal Naval Chiefs of Staff, Vice-Admiral Avgeris, director of the King's Office of Political Affairs, Mr. Hoïdas, chief of the King's Military Office, Vice-General Dovas, and others. Also present were the Archbishop of Athens along with the bishops of Grevena, Ierissos, Gortynes, Trikkes, and Naupaktos. At exactly one o'clock the Viceroy, Crown Prince Constantine, arrived attired in lieutenant's uniform. At the same exact moment the destroyer* Sphendone *approached the wharf, with a landing party lined up on its deck for inspection. The Crown Prince, followed by a group of clergymen, immediately approached and boarded the battleship, while the rest of the officials remained on the wharf. Shortly afterward the Abbot of the monastery at Tinos appeared on the deck and presented the icon to the Crown Prince. The dramatic scene enacted at that moment was unusually moving. Crown Prince Constantine would not let go of the miracle-working icon even for a minute, not even when he got into his car. Riding with him in his car were the chief advisor of his Military Office, Major Arnaoutis, and the Abbot of the Evangelistria Monastery. The car began moving immediately, followed by a car with the Archbishop of Athens. A short while later the Crown Prince, along with the Archbishop and the Abbot of the Evangelistria Monastery at Tinos entered the room where the ailing King lay. By the side of this eminent patient was the Queen, whose eyes filled with tears when she saw the miracle-working icon, a spark of hope lighting up her face. The Crown Prince approached the bed of his illustrious father and the Sovereign devoutly kissed the icon. He was calm and unperturbed. A smile of hope immediately appeared on his lips. A smile engendered by his faith in God—one that seemed to say that everything would turn out all right. Several minutes later the Archbishop left the Palace. The miracle-working icon, however, remained on the King's pillow. As was noted by those in attendance at the Naval Academy yesterday, the Crown Prince was unusually upset. Upon his arrival, he conversed briefly with Mr. Hoïdas, probably about future developments and the course of the King's illness. Mr. Hoïdas subsequently brought Mr. Papandreou up to date.*

Dear Mrs. Mina—

I am 20 years old, married and the mother of a two-year-old child, a boy. My husband has been in the service for several months now. I am living with my in-laws and am having terrible problems, especially with my mother-in-law. She is self-centered, jealous, and, above all, a terrible gossip. I don't dare criticize her to anyone. I put up with everything she does to me and am coming to you, Mrs. Mina, for advice about how I should behave. Dear Mrs. Mina, she always accuses me of not being a good housewife, of having bad manners, of not helping her out. And a lot of other little things like that. She is young, 47 years old, and maybe she doesn't care for the way I do housework. My sister-in-law, her daughter, is 18 years old, in 12th grade, and knows nothing about housework. She runs around a lot, changes boyfriends like she does her clothes and is very very messy. I am from a village and don't do such things but my mother-in-law is still not satisfied. She tries to blame her daughter's faults on me. Every five minutes there she is behind me saying this, that, and the other. I just can't take it, Mrs. Mina. Tell me what to do, how to act toward her. She also tries to control how I dress. I dress simply and stylishly and she can't stand the fact that I am better-dressed than her daughter. She would like me to dress like a forty-year-old woman. My husband wants me to dress as nicely as I can and my mother-in-law keeps coming between us. Is that right? Answer me, Mrs. Mina. What should I tell her, how should I behave with her?

With best wishes,

Young and Bitter

CORFU, APRIL 6. *From our correspondent. High clergy said special intercessory prayers for the ailing King during the opening of the repository of the sacred relics of the Church of St. Spyridon, the venerable protector of the city of Corfu. Prayers were also said in Athens for His Majesty's swift recovery by representatives of the Greek Boy Scouts in the Church of St. Nikolaos and by the Anavryta Boys' School Alumni Association in St. Andrew's School Chapel. Due to the King's serious illness, the National Council of Greek Women, the Athens Merchants Council, and the Piraeus Association have also postponed their annual balls.*

————

ATTENTION ALL: BUY ON INSTALLMENT PLAN!

Call our offices for any construction job. We put up new, ready-to-deliver buildings on your lot. Key in hand. We also finish, renovate, etc. existing buildings. Building permits, blueprints, and land surveying also provided. Unbeatable prices. Guaranteed labor.

CONTRACTORS COOPERATIVE
4 Satovriandou St., 6th floor, Room 11, tel. 536-693

[120]

PYRGOS, APRIL 28. *From our correspondent. The recent spell of bad weather has resulted in frosty conditions throughout the entire Ileia district, causing damage to raisin vineyards and early tomato crops. According to reports, in some areas the damage is as high as 80 percent. In addition, the delay in remunerating raisin farmers who suffered losses due to rain last August has been greeted with indignation. A resolution to this effect was issued by the Gastouni, Lechaina, and Zacharo Farmers' Cooperatives.*

———

MYTILENE, APRIL 28. *From our correspondent. Our fellow Mytilenean, Mr. Erotokritos Pilales, 49, self-employed, visited the local metropolitan and reported a dream in which he saw St. Raphael, who revealed to him that the Turks are planning to land in Mytilene, Chios, and Samos on Saturday, either shortly after the midnight mass of the Resurrection or during the feast of St. Thomas on Sunday. He added that, acting "in accordance with the saint's instructions," he hastened to inform him so that appropriate countermeasures could be taken. Mr. Pilales said that in the past this saint has often foretold things that eventually come true.*

Agia Galini, Crete, June 18, 1964

To: DEME

I hereby submit the required papers and inform you that my wife
Vasiliki is in no way pregnant, at least not now, not yet.

Joey Kalimerakis
Athens

JUNE 26. *A Church of Greece official was asked whether the Holy Synod, or any other church authority, ever intends to deal with the subject of topless swimsuits. The official responded that this will never happen "because the church has more serious matters to attend to." In the meantime, Themis, the first bare-breasted Athenian and well-known striptease artist was arrested last Saturday afternoon on Asteria Beach, Glyphada, and brought before the magistrate at the Misdemeanors Court in Athens, where she was charged with indecent exposure and was sentenced to three months' imprisonment—"to serve as a deterrent," according to District Attorney Mr. Papadogiannis—with the possibility of buying off her sentence at the rate of 100 pre–World War II drachmas per day. The Athenian stripper subsequently appealed this decision, through her attorney, Mr. Petros Giatrakos, and was released.*

The liner Queen Frederika, *carrying approximately 300 passengers, will sail from the harbor of Piraeus (destination New York) today at 12:00 noon. The liner* Patris *will also depart from Piraeus with 1,400 emigrants for Australia at 1:00 P.M.*

July 2, 1964

Dear Mrs. Mina—

I am taking the liberty of writing you about a personal matter. A romantic involvement that has been troubling me for two years. I live in a sheltered environment, with strict parents, and I keep myself busy taking care of the house. Every day that goes by is the same as every other one. I don't go out, I don't have any girlfriends, only my immediate family circle. My mother and brothers. I have no father. And he was the strictest one in the family. Now my brothers have taken his place. I don't care, I've adjusted and I'm used to it. But there's something else that has been disturbing my peace of mind: that much-cursed illness called love. It is two years now since I met a gentleman. The sweet smile on his face moved me so. I've seen him only four times but I really did fall for him. And I began dreaming impossible dreams, which resulted in my thinking about him all the time and getting my hopes up. And the result is zero for me, nothing is coming of it. It's over two years now, what should I do? I don't know. I'm in a dilemma. Should I write him expressing my feelings of love for him? And on the other hand I'm afraid and I wonder what right I have to disturb his peace of mind. And perhaps it will cause him to think badly of me and make fun of me. He's a schoolteacher in our village and I know next to nothing about him. He's not from around here and came here to work as a teacher. But from what I hear, everyone is delighted with him, with his way of thinking. And he's very smart and very well educated. He's a schoolteacher. I'm afraid to talk to my mother, I don't know how she'll react. She has her own ideas— to arrange a marriage for me with someone, but I don't want to do that, not ever. But then again I feel so insignificant, I'm not worthy of marrying such a man. But why do I think that without him my life has no meaning?

To close, I leave you and I thank you, Mrs. Mina. I ask you please not to read my letter and give me away. Just use my pen name. I'll be waiting.

Disappointed, Wounded Heart

JULY 8. *Finding fault with our church leaders is, unfortunately, not a rare event in this country. In other countries where, say, Catholicism or other faiths are established, no one ever disparages a higher, or even a lower, clergyman. Because, according to gospel, "they too have One who will judge them, and unto Whom they must deliver that which was bequeathed to them at the terrible moment of ordination by the holy altar." With regard to accusations directed at the metropolitan of the city of Drama, they have all been dropped after being proven groundless. Because of the public outcry, however, a Synod member moved that the matter be taken up when the Synod reconvenes in October, as the accused cannot really be held responsible for the outcry, according to opinions put forth by other Synod members. It was decided to bring up the matter again during the October meeting when the Synod will be called upon to determine, "on the basis of the rules of holy governance, and of the laws of the State," whether the faithful were made to stumble, and if blame could be attached to His worship, the metropolitan of Drama, Mr. Philippos, who had been exonerated of the charge of "cohabiting with a woman," following a long and painstaking investigation of the whole affair. It should be noted that, a few days ago, during the Feast of the Pennyless Saints held in the church bearing the same name, there was a strong and moving popular outburst of love and respect toward the officiating metropolitan, Mr. Philippos, which continued until the following day. The October Synod meeting will be attended by, among others, the metropolitans of Thessaloniki, Zichnai, Verroia, Kilikision, Mytilene, Arta, Phthiotis, Triphylia, and Karystia. The archimandrite Mr. Theoklitos Philippaios will serve as chief secretary of the Holy Synod.*

Esteemed Sirs:

I kindly request and submit the following: For a long time now I have had a relationship carrying on with Miss Nikolitsa Tsiklitira, age 18, from the village of Lefkon, Thessaly, who was just committed to your DEME School (5 Metsovou St., In Town).

She has been coerced by her brother into emigrating to Australia, and her illiterate mother co-signed for her emigration. Nikolitsa is very upset about having to move to Athens to attend your school, and also by her emigration. In spite of her love for me and me escorting her to have fun at various nightclubs, this has had no success. Some days ago I made her pregnant with her permission so that she will have to stay in Greece and we can be wed.

This would be wonderful for all of us, but I beg you please do not broadcast the above incident because it could dishonor her and cause all sorts of misunderstandings, even murder.

Also could you please keep me informed about this situation? Needless to say, if this young woman does not emigrate, I shall come running to find you and thank you, either in writing or by word of mouth.

Most respectfully yours,

Panagiotis Barlambes

JULY 21. *Following orders by Athens police chief Mr. Kanel-
lakis, police lieutenant Mr. Emanuel Xarchogiannis is being
investigated on charges of "political partisanship." The latter
is on suspension as of yesterday. The day before yesterday this
police lieutenant was seen in the club Skaphida on Zoodochos
Pigis Street in Vyron, in the company of known communists
and center leftists singing and celebrating the electoral victory
of Mayor Georgoutsos. It is a known fact that the above-mentioned mayor was elected on the strength of the combined
votes of the Democratic Collaboration (Center Union plus
United Democratic Left).*

———————

*By common resolution of the secretary of labor, M. G. Baka-
tselos, and the undersecretary of finance, M. Stephanides,
State National Insurance recipients and pensioners suffering
from tuberculosis will receive an allowance for fresh-air treatment. By the same resolution this allowance was increased by
50 percent for tuberculosis pensioners, from 500 to 750 drs.,
and for insured tuberculosis patients from 250 to 375 drs.,
respectively.*

Agios Dimitrios (Brahami), July 29, 1964

Dear Mina—

Hello. I am a girl of 21. I have been in love for the past 4 years with a young man of 25, who happens to also have a sister. When we first met he told me: Lena, I don't want to lead you on because, as I can see, you are from a very good family, you're well behaved but inexperienced about life. I loved you from the time I first set eyes on you, but I won't be able to marry you unless I first marry off my sister. I told him that I'm patient and more than willing to wait for him, I'll do whatever he wants. Now 4 years have gone by, filled with anxiety and worries. Also, Mrs. Mina, he didn't let me go to work. I always did what he said and we were always a happy couple. We would go everywhere together as if we were engaged. But then three months ago his sister got engaged and then exchanged rings with a very nice boy. But as of today he has still not said anything, Mrs. Mina, about us. The days of the year go by so fast we don't even realize it. I often talk to him about getting engaged but he says, don't rush things, we're still young. My parents keep screaming at me and telling me to leave him and to go abroad, where my brothers are, but that's impossible for me. Our relationship has gone quite far and I am in an awkward position. Please give me some advice. What should I do and what should I say to him?

All my love,

Lena E.

JULY 30. *The adjudication of a temporary alimony award to Yola M. Loukanides, to be paid by her husband Neotakis Loukanides, the popular Panathenaïkos soccer player, was discussed yesterday in the presence of chief magistrate Mr. Ioannis Gournas. Specifically, 15-year-old Yola, née Voutsara, appeared in court, along with her proxies, I. Konstanteas and K. Andrikopoulos, and petitioned that she be adjudged temporary alimony amounting to 3,000 drachmas because, as she said, she lacks any other means of support and because the final alimony award will take a long time to be issued. Yola has asked for the above sum because her husband has a monthly income of at least 20,000 drs. from the following sources: (1) the bar he runs on Phokionos Negri Street, from which he earns, according to the young woman, 15,000 drs. a month; and (2) soccer matches, in which he participates regularly and which pay 2,500 drs. per match. Moreover, Neotakis Loukanides, again according to his wife Yola, owns a luxury apartment at 291 Patision Street. It should be noted that Yola married the soccer star in November 1962, following the much-publicized incidents preceding their wedding.*

From Gytheio, August 1, 1964

To: The Board of Directors of the Agricultural Bank
of Greece
Cc: Mr. Panagiotis Kanellopoulos, National Radical
Union (ERE) Party Chairman

Cancellation my work contract via telegram illegal
and invalid because based political reasons. Stop.
Your actions influenced by Center Union agents in
collaboration with United Democratic Left (EDA)
ending in my termination without investigation only
because I belong to ERE. Stop. Am proud I belong to
ERE and adherents Center Union should be ashamed
because party received majority votes due to
illegal contributions and assistance of EDA. Stop.
Will be day of reckoning. Stop. My reinstatement
will take place very soon. Stop.

Antonios Balitsares, Attorney-at-Law

Mr. Adamantios Karamourtzounes, the well-known friend of the poor, has just had a son. In spite of the infant's being only 22 days old, he has begun stepping up his philanthropic activities. Among the items he has received for donation are 5,000 kilos of fish (caught by the fishing vessel Aphrodite*), as well as 10,000 Pavlides chocolate bars. In addition, the travel agencies Horizon and Saronikos have offered the use of two and three motor coaches respectively for the transportation of indigent persons in need of an excursion. Mr. Adamantios Karamourtzounes made use of the five coaches yesterday to organize a trip to Agios Ioannis Rosson for needy pilgrims from the Kaisariani and Tourkovounia districts, distributing a long wax candle to each of them. Today some 5,000 kilos of fish and 10,000 bars of chocolate will be given out in the poorer neighborhoods outlying Athens.*

———

MIAMI BEACH, AUGUST 9. *By special correspondent. As was reported here,* Komsomolskaya Pravda, *the Moscow-based organ of Soviet Youth, in an article on the success of Kyriakoula or Koula Tsopei, recently elected Miss Universe, comments that her measurements are far from ideal. Our Miss Universe ought to have a smaller waist and curvier hips.*

IOANNINA, AUGUST 12. *From our correspondent. By cable service from Preveza, it is reported that 15 gypsy women were apprehended while bathing in their birthday suits in the area of Monolithi, Kanalaki. As soon as they noticed Port Authority officers approaching, the above-mentioned ladies immediately fled. In other news, it has been announced that in the town of Preveza more than 15 topless bathing suits were sold in the past few days.*

Then boat was 13 hrs. later

Dear Mrs. Mina—

This is the third time I am writing to you. Thank you for your two previous answers. They were very helpful to me. But now some other things have happened in the meantime and I'm up a dead-end street again. Everything's chaotic. I feel all alone and more than anything, I feel guilty. As I wrote you, I am 26, with a much older husband who has health problems (mainly his lungs). I married him for love. He had been after me for a long time and I was flattered by his love. I was looking for a way out, because I was an only child with a strict father and an unhappy childhood. And, as you said in your answer to my second letter: "People like that never grow up emotionally." I really feel that's true. I feel immature, in spite of my age. It's hard for me to take the initiative, and when I find myself stuck in a situation, I'm afraid to make any decisions. That's how it was then too. He was unreasonable from the start— and I knew that—and we could never agree on anything. But while on the one hand he had become extremely tiresome to me, on the other I still saw marriage as my salvation. So, when he raped me one day, I had no other choice. I absolutely had to marry him. And that's exactly what happened. I trusted him and he had no respect at all for my wishes. He behaved atrociously toward me. And we began having quarrels from the first day we were married. I couldn't take being with him and he did everything he could to annoy me. For example, I would be asleep and he would come and caress me with wet hands. I took it all patiently. In the meantime my nerves are shot. I start crying and screaming at the slightest little thing. During the next few years our two children were also born. For them and them only am I being patient, even though he assures me that he, too, is only staying with me because of the kids. In reality we are two strangers. As if that weren't enough, some time ago I almost lost one of my babies. He had contracted tuberculosis. After some medical tests, my husband turned out to have bilateral tuberculosis, according to the diagnosis. Both lungs had been affected, that is. The doctor recommended moving him to a sanitarium, but he wouldn't hear of it. He said that now there is medicine and he can be treated at home. In the end, after we all insisted, he was forced to go.

He stayed for six months, though it was hard for him. Now he is almost well. He goes to his office—he's an insurance agent—but I still sleep in a room with the children. I don't sleep with him, I'm afraid. And my life has become even more dreary and boring. Recently, as I wrote you, I met a young man. We got involved. He is polite and reliable. He had been separated from his wife for three years. And then there are the children. His marriage was the result of pressure from his parents when he was still in the service. He never loved his wife, but now, after a trial in court, she has managed to make him go back to her. Because if he were to go to jail, his career would be ruined. He went back to her, with a heavy heart. They sleep in separate bedrooms. He is begging me not to break up, to stay with him—something that I want, too. But I feel guilty, and when I'm by myself I cry. Once upon a time I despised women who came between married couples, no matter what their problems were. Now I'm one of them too. When I go to church with my children, I tremble in shame. On the other hand I feel such a deep love for this person. He is so honest and shows me so much understanding. Believe me, I am unhappy. I don't know what to do and sometimes I think my mind is coming unhinged. Should I continue seeing him or resign myself to my fate? I know that you can't give me an answer, but tell me anything, I need to hear something. Answer me under the same pen name: "Chloe."

With my deepest gratitude,

Angeliki Voskopoulou

SEPTEMBER 1. *There is a strong likelihood that the wedding ceremony of His Majesty King Constantine and Princess Anna-Maria, originally set for Friday, September 18, may be postponed to either Saturday or Sunday. The reason is that, according to Greek Orthodox tradition and church law as set out by pan-Orthodox councils, weddings are expressly forbidden on Friday, a day set aside by the church fathers for fasting and prayer. This position is already embraced by a large number of ranking clergy who are in agreement with His Blessed Holiness Msgr. Chrysostomos, the Archbishop of Athens, a firm devotee of the incontrovertible and irrevocable spirit of the Constitution of Orthodox Christianity.*

September 14, 1964

To: The Department of Emigration to Australia
DEME Athens

The undersigned party, Magdalini Vlachopoulou, daughter of So-
tirios, wishes to be informed regarding her application to the
DEME School in Ioannina. I sent in my application forms on
July 17, 1964, and I have already had my physical examination and
consular appointment in Patras.

Respectfully yours,

Maggie Vlachopoulou

SEPTEMBER 23. *Korina-Koula Tsopei, Miss Universe of 1964, has been in Greece since 4:30 yesterday afternoon, She flew in aboard an Olympic Airlines plane, accompanied by Bobby Johnson, Miss USA, Mrs. Rose Bonefield, Mrs. Toula Mekra, and Mrs. Bouly Antenucci. Immediately upon exiting the plane, thanks to the efforts of the police, who were able to maintain exemplary order, she accepted a gift of flowers from Olympic Airlines and proceeded down the stairs, followed by Miss USA, who was also given a bouquet by a stewardess. Flowers were also presented to her by two young girls from the municipality of Kalamaki, whose mayor, Mr. Smaragdis, wished the two beauty queens a warm welcome. Finally it was the family's turn to be greeted. Korina threw herself in her father and mother's arms, then kissed her brothers and sisters. The two beauty queens proceeded to the visitors' lounge, where they faced the first onslaught of journalists and photographers. Questions began to rain on this modern Aphrodite who, with the utmost composure, answered them all without exception. Q. Do you intend to work in the movies? A. Not for the time being.—Your impressions of the welcome given you in Greece?—My impressions are excellent, and my feelings about coming home after a three-month absence are impossible to describe.—What places did you visit after your victory?—Aside from a number of places in the United States, I visited Canada, Brazil, Japan, Formosa, then came home.— One Athens newspaper claimed you gave an exclusive interview immediately following your victory as Miss Universe. Which Greek newspaper did you give an interview to?—Following my victory, I gave an interview to only one Greek newspaper: Apogevmatini.—Where were you received with the greatest enthusiasm?—In Canada, and particularly in Toronto by the 25,000 members attending the AHEPA congress.— Of all the offers you were made, which one was the most unusual?— One from a man who wanted to make me happy, but was 70 years old.*

At this point Miss Bobby Johnson, Miss USA, gave a word of greeting, in Greek, to those gathered. "I'm very happy to be visiting Greece. It's a dream I've had for years, and now it's fulfilled." After these words of greeting, which were received with applause, Miss Johnson was asked her opinion concerning the selection of Miss Tsopei as the 1964 Miss Universe.—It was the best possible choice.

Korina became the center of attention once again as she answered a pointed question:—I would prefer the man I marry to be Greek. Besides, isn't there a saying to the effect that one should prefer a shoe from one's own village, even if it is patched?

The same opinion concerning a Greek husband was shared by the charming Miss Johnson, the only difference being that she says she does not know any Greek.

At 5:00 the motorcade was already underway with the two beauty queens in limousine convertibles that had been put at their disposal. The pageant committee led the way, with a movie crew and an American TV network camera following. Miss Universe, Korina-Koula Tsopei, stood in the flower-strewn blue limousine behind them, waving left and right to the cheering crowds.

Miss USA, Bobby Johnson, in the second limousine convertible, also greeted the people gathered at the airport. A Traffic Police honor guard escorted the two beauty queens' automobiles. They were followed by cars carrying their chaperones, Korina's parents, Greek National Tourist Organization representatives, photographers, and journalists. NTO motorcycles brought up the rear of the parade, with hundreds of other cars following.

The motorcade followed the seaside avenue to Athens. Mrs. Zisimopoulou, the assistant mayor of the Palaio Phalero municipality, welcomed the beauty queens, as did Nea Smyrni municipality mayor, Mr. Papathanasiou. Following a route including Syngrou, Amalias, and Vasilisis Sophias Avenues, the procession reached the Athens Hilton. At Hadrian's Gate, as well as at many other locations along the way, crowds of people cheered the two beauty queens, who immediately retired to their rooms to get some rest. (Please read our special column concerning the reception held in their honor by the NTO as well as the dinner given by the mayor of Athens, Mr. G. Plytas.)

September 28, 1964

Dear Mrs. Mina—

Hello. I've taken the liberty of writing you once again. I'm the girl from the village Doxato in the province of Drama, who wrote you that I loved someone who was in an automobile accident, etc. It was under the pen name "Desolate Creature." I imagine you answered on your radio show, but an unfortunate incident made it impossible for me to listen to it. And I didn't get to hear your answer and the advice I needed so badly. Mrs. Mina, please could you possibly answer me again? Because the situation has remained the same, even though a lot of time has passed since then. I have to tell you I can't act any differently, I like him too much. If you do not find my letter—my first—in your files, I will write you again. I'm sorry I'm asking you to answer twice about the same problem.

Greetings,

Desolate Creature

SEPTEMBER 29. *The First National City Bank branch office in Athens had its Grand Opening at noontime yesterday. Greek bank presidents and vice-presidents, American Embassy rep-*| |
resentatives, industrialists, and entrepreneurs were in atten-dance. The bank's vice-president, Mr. Leary, spoke briefly during the ceremony, emphasizing, among other things, the fact that this bank, confident of the upward trend of the Greek economy, established itself in Greece with the intention of assisting private enterprise in this country, and of contrib-uting, in close collaboration with other banking institutions, to the promotion of more general developmental planning.

Sampatiki, November 12, 1964

Honorable Sir—

Greetings. I received your letter in which you say that in order for our emigration to go ahead, our son Vasileios should come and have a physical examination) I want you to know the following: When our son found out about our plans he got off his ship in Australia, in order to join the family there. To speed things up and wait for us there. Here is his address: Mr. Vasileios Koudounes, 36 Leonards Ave., West Leederville, Perth, W. Australia.

Please let me know if you need more information.

Respectfully yours,

Dimitrios Koudounes

LARISA, NOVEMBER 16. *By special correspondent. The Larisa Court of Appeals has upheld the sentence condemning Mr. Rodolphos Pamboukis, editor in chief of the newspaper* Voice of Thessaly, *to 45 days' imprisonment for using the press to defame Mr. Gervasios Aspiotes, canon of the metropolis of Karditsa. The newspaper had written that last July the canon was at the Pteleos beach bathing in the presence of women and that this is considered scandalous behavior by the church and its believers.*

This court decision makes it acceptable, by implication, for clergy to go swimming, provided of course that they do so in a bathing costume and within the bounds of decency.

———

We extend to our son and brother, Demosthenes D. Toufexis, and the lovely Miss Palmyra V. Lambrakis, who plan to be married on November 18, 1964, in Perth, West Australia, the warmest fatherly and brotherly wishes for a happy, rosy future; and together with our beloved in-laws, wish our children a long life together.

The Dimitrios Toufexis family

December 9, 1964

My dear Mrs. Mina—

Good day. I am a terribly desperate young woman. I am 26 years old, I am from the provinces, and I am engaged to a man 9 years older than me. This man is from the city. I have been engaged for 15 months, plus 3 months apart, that makes 18. I've been wanting to write you for a long time, but I was waiting until Christmas to see if anything happened. Mrs. Mina, during these 15 months we were a happy couple, I could even say we were in love, although it did not start out as a romance, because our engagement was arranged. The matchmaker was his first cousin, who has known me ever since I was a little girl. We are friends, and he is from the same village as I am. Before getting engaged, or rather years earlier, when I was a very young girl, I was in love with someone my age, and we had a relationship for about five years. During all those years I only went out with him three times, and he kissed me. Nothing more. And only toward the end. He later got married. The cousin who introduced us knew about this relationship. It was a mistake that I never mentioned this to my fiancé and let him hear it from someone else. I explained to him how things stood, but he refused to understand. There were times when he said it was okay, and other times when he was angry he had found out about it from other people. As a matter of fact, he found out about it through an anonymous telephone call, and that's not all they told him, they even said I'd been the other young man's "girlfriend." This is how bad things had become, to the point where he couldn't take it and was getting even angrier. And not only that, Mrs. Mina. My mom and my mother-in-law had a fight, and my mother-in-law went to a neighbor, who told her a lot of things about me. And since then, my mother-in-law will have nothing to do with me, nor will my fiancé. They won't even come to our house. During the next few months I decided to go to their house myself, twice. The first time was with my brother, without anyone asking us to go. We first went to his office and then to his house; his parents were there, too. He and my brother started fighting, so my brother told me to take off the engagement ring. I took it off and told him, let's go.

At this point both my in-laws told me to put it back on. I did, but I told them I wasn't marrying *them* so they had no right to tell me to put the ring on. Then my fiancé told me to put it on. He said that if I didn't, I wasn't leaving his house.

The second time he asked me himself to come, so I went. He had called me on the telephone. His parents were not in, but they found out from a neighbor, and came barging in, my father- and mother-in-law. They started yelling, but I said nothing, just sat there crying. They kept telling him: "We don't want a bride who has already been kissed. Take her and get out." They said all sorts of nasty things about me. Then he started telling me he doesn't want me anymore, and that I'm not good enough for him.

Mrs. Mina, don't tell me to leave him. Just tell me some way I can win him back. Don't tell me to forget him. In spite of all he's done, I still love him. And if he comes back I will love him even more. I am going out of my mind, and I think that I will go crazy, Mrs. Mina. And the gossip is driving me insane. They come and tell me right to my face that my mother-in-law said this or that, or that my fiancé came to the village and didn't come to my house. Things like that and a lot more. Mrs. Mina, there are twelve people in his household: he has a married brother, two unmarried ones, a sister who is divorced, my father- and mother-in-law, plus four nephews. Two of them are in Athens, that's where they live now. When our engagement was being arranged, they said that we would go and live somewhere else by ourselves when we were married. Then he said that we would all live together. If he does come back, should I tell him I cannot live there with all of them?

Georgia

DECEMBER 17. *In regard to the controversial question of the repatriation of fugitive communist civil war guerrillas, the Department of National Security for the Interior (DNSI) has given its answer: "The majority of repatriated individuals are in ill health, elderly, and reformed to the point of having become true exponents of anticommunism." This statement, made by the minister for public order, Mr. Polychronides, was the most recent development on a subject that is extremely troubling to the majority of law-abiding Greek citizens. As usual, the minister did not venture to give any figures or details on the schedule for these repatriations, limiting himself to a single reassuring statement: that he intends, very soon, to provide extensive information on the subject. We nevertheless invite Mr. Polychronides to state whether he actually believes that those being repatriated are truly reformed Communists or mainly ailing and elderly people. This by reason of the fact that the above category is no more than 10 percent of all repatriated individuals.*

Kastri, January 21, 1965

Dearest husband Nikolas—

We are well. The children are well too. It's a struggle, but somehow I manage. Except for the field over at Chouni. It's the fourth year we've let it lie fallow, it's such a pity, when you used to keep it so lovely everybody admired it. If you're not back to plow it before Easter, I will hire people to come and do it, and let people talk if they want to. I have nothing else to write, so pay close attention.

Your wife,

Chrysanthe

JANUARY 28. *Mr. A. Angelousis, undersecretary for public works, has announced that the draft bill legalizing previously unlicensed construction of buildings throughout Greece is now ready and will soon be submitted to the House of Parliament. This bill will legalize buildings erected as late as March 31, 1964, with the exception of buildings in public squares and streets, which in any case will be demolished in order to free public space. Owners of illegal buildings will be obliged to pay a fee before they can obtain titles of ownership. The fee will vary according to the value of the building, but it will most certainly be payable in long-term installments. Thus, owners of property valued at up to 100,000 drachmas will be reimbursed approximately 5 percent of the value of their property. Other legislation measures provide for the creation of construction police whose main job will be the prevention of illegal construction. The draft bill will also provide for the removal of kiosks from main city arteries, and it determines that from this date on, in every new apartment building, it will be obligatory that an area measuring 2 x 1.5 meters on the ground floor be set aside for the incorporation of the nearest kiosk.*

February 4, 1965

Dear Mrs. Mina—

I have been going with someone for the past two years. Our relationship has not progressed beyond the point of no return, fortunately. And I say "fortunately" because this person is making me unhappy. Whenever we go out with a group of friends, to a taverna or a coffee shop or anyplace at all, he always starts staring at some strange woman. He usually sets his sights on someone flashy, heavily made up, with a nice hairdo or sexy clothes. At such moments I don't exist for him. The others in the group don't realize what he's up to because they're not concerned by it. But I am, and it's really killing me. When we go out alone and I voice my complaints to him, he says that everything I'm accusing him of is only in my imagination, that I have a sick mind, that I'm just jealous. I have to admit, because I am honest, that I do get a little jealous. With an emphasis on the words "a little." But not in a sick way, not obsessively. It's my pride that's being stepped on more than anything, my self-esteem, because the women he looks at aren't any younger than I am. Without wanting to sound conceited, I have a pretty face and a nice figure, at least that's what my girlfriends tell me. Moreover, I know myself quite well. I am 42 now and he is 54, but please don't mention our ages on your show, for many reasons. When we're alone he tells me that he loves me, tells me not to leave him, but usually when we're out on a date we do nothing but quarrel. I get mad and ask him, as nicely as possible, to please be more considerate toward me, and if he wants to flirt, he shouldn't do it in front of me, or at least not every time we go out. We break up and then something happens and we get back together again. My mind tells me to get rid of him, but my heart doesn't agree. I try my best not to think about him or go out with him, even though I am 42. But when I hear his voice on the telephone, even though I am very negative in the beginning, in the end I give in and go running happily to meet him. Remember that when we're alone he is kind and gentle with me. Until we go out again somewhere with our friends and he starts the same thing all over again. You made me cry, I said to him one day. And his answer was: You're

[148]

sick. He never has any complaints about me because I never give him any reason to. I don't look at other men, wear gaudy clothes or a lot of makeup, I'm not at all loud. I do wear red, of course, but on me (with my blue eyes, blond hair, and white skin) it's not in bad taste. Please do not mention this either on your show. And now I have stopped calling him again. I'm making myself scarce, but I keep thinking about him. I had two other failed romances. My first boyfriend was much older than I was. I was twenty, he was fifty. He was always running around with other women and because he was more experienced, he really took me for a ride. Many years later I met another man. We were both in our thirties. We fell in love, but it only lasted for twelve months. In the end I had nothing but heartache from all three of them. I don't behave badly. So why are they so unstable, so unfaithful, so superficial? Now I'm alone again and I feel sad and very bitter. I have not given up my other interests, of course. I don't work, I stay home and do housework and in my free time I knit or embroider. I apologize for not expressing myself well. And for any mistakes I might make. But I'm very upset. When I'm not out with my friends, I smile and make the best of my life and my situation. When I go out and he's there, I stand there without talking to him or trying to be nice to him. Like a stranger. But inside I hurt. Because I think that I am still someone worth loving. I haven't yet reached that blissful state of not caring. And that's what's so hard, Mrs. Mina.

With my deepest gratitude,

Ioulia L.

VALPARAISO, CHILE, FEBRUARY 9. *By special correspondent.*
A construction worker yesterday noticed a strange luminous
"object" in the sky that was emitting colored beams of light at
a high altitude. The worker stated that it was a blue disk
surrounded by a bright orange halo. A short time later two
journalists from the newspaper El Mercurio *noticed the same*
phenomenon above the sea. The object, which has been clas-
sified as a flying saucer, remained motionless for about 10
minutes. It then began moving and emitting pink and violet
rays of light. This phenomenon was observed over Chile by
other people as well. These people have noted that this object's
shifting colors, speed, and abrupt changes in direction rule
out the possibility of mistaking it for an airplane.

———

IOANNINA, FEBRUARY 9. *From our correspondent. Unidenti-*
fied vandals entered the military cemetery of the village of
Doliana yesterday and destroyed 14 crosses on the graves of
soldiers killed during anticommunist civil war operations.
They also caused damage to the ossuary. It is obvious that
these are communists emboldened by the tolerant policies of
the current government. An investigation is underway.

February 21, 1965

Chrysanthe,

I did understand your letter, but did you, who wrote it, understand what you wrote? Or do you think I came here to have fun and pass the time of day?

When I wake up at five in the morning it is pitch dark outside, and when I leave work at five it is pitch dark again. Not only that, but I was stopped and threatened for breaking union standards by working so many hours overtime. I put in twelve- and fifteen-hour days, and don't even have time to think about you. So who am I working for, Chrysanthe? Please give this some thought; not to mention that I'm on the verge of ruining my health. So try and be patient, as I am, because if there is no home for me to return to when I get back, the fault will be all yours. I have nothing else to write; kisses to you and the children.

With love,

Nikolas

MARCH 13. *It has been announced by the Holy Archdiocese that reports in today's morning newspapers concerning pressure exerted by the government, following the death of King Paul, for the creation of a church anthem specifically mentioning Queen Mother Frederika, are unfounded. The sole body authorized to create such an anthem is the Holy Synod of the Church of Greece. Exercising this authority, it composed Encyclical No. 1289/2200/817, dated September 9, 1964, and circulated the following text to all Church of Greece clergy: "Lord God protect our most devout King Constantine, our Christ-loving Queen Anna-Maria, and their most devout heir Irene, together with the most devout Queen Mother Frederika. Protect them, O Lord, and grant them a long life."*

Nikolas, Nikolas. I do think of you killing yourself at work, but I don't want you to come back to me an invalid. And I don't want to end up like your aunt either, lonely and pining away for thirty-two years. Just remember what you told me when we got married, that you'd never leave me alone. What use is the money you send me to buy shoes and a purse when I lie in our double bed like a log?

If you are not back by Easter, Nikolas, I'm going to have a third child anyway, I don't know with who, but I'm telling you, really.

The children send you their greetings and kisses and so do I, your wife.

Chrysanthe

Melissa Publications has issued Vols. 12 and 13 by
the renowned Sexual Therapist and Founder of
Sexual Therapy in Greece

* * *

GEORGIOS K. ZOURARES

* * *

MEMBER OF THE BERLIN INSTITUTE FOR
SEXUAL RESEARCH.

1. *Your Sexual Life:* Masturbation, abstinence, self-restraint, promiscuity, loss of sexual libido. This classic describes the factors that lower the sexual urge, the dangerous role of masturbation, self-restraint, and promiscuity in all of their forms and manifestations. The book presents scientifically, and in the light of scientific truth, the serious problem of youth, which is the problem of sex education. *Price: 60 drachmas or 3 dollars.*

2. *The Sexual Libido:* Impotence, frigidity, and sexual perversions. The book, unique for its kind, contains a thorough description and explanation of human sexuality, a complete analysis of the male and female urge and potency, the latest advances in therapy, the cure for frigidity and impotence. It describes how the sexual urge works, and it discusses and analyzes sexual aberrations with compassion, without stigmatizing unfortunate sufferers because of the excesses caused by their condition. *90 drachmas or 4 dollars.*

Sensational books, both instructive and fascinating

Dear Mrs. Mina—

I am 19 years old. Three months ago I exchanged vows with a boy
from my hometown. He stayed there for 15 days after we made our
vows and then he left. He's a sailor and he had to leave. Our engagement was arranged and I still can't understand how I agreed to
marry him. Now that I'm alone I realize that I don't love him and
I am very unhappy. I told my parents and they said no, you will
not break it off with him because he's a good person, he's better
than you. They have given me an inferiority complex and all they
talk about at home is him. About their son-in-law and what he did
or what he's going to do, so you understand how hurt I feel every
day. Please give me some word of advice about what I should do.

Thank you,

A desperate listener

KALAMATA, APRIL 29. *From our correspondent. Twenty-eight-year-old Syriani Kanellopoulou, from the village of Eudokimon, Ileia, in retaliation against her lover and fellow villager Euth. Iliades, alias Kokkalis, who left her in order to marry someone else, arranged a meeting with him during which, in the course of an intricate sexual act, she caused serious injury to him using a razor blade on a sensitive part of his body. The victim, hemorrhaging and in terrible pain, was taken to the city hospital. Iliades, alias Kokkalis, was planning to be married tomorrow to a young woman with a large dowry from a neighboring village. The assailant admitted that her intentions were to render him impotent.*

Preveza, May 2, 1965

Dear Commissioners—

Hello there. I had stomach surgery, but I am completely well now, and I am sending you the hospital paper that says so. Read it and if I pass let me know so I can prepare whatever I need to and not spend money for no reason.

Dalakas

SEASIDE APARTMENTS

Anavyssos-Phokaia
Kilometer 52 on Sounion Highway
Paved road, sea frontage
5-year installment plan, also cash down
1, 2, 3 bedroom apartments

Under construction, within city limits, spacious,
clear view, all around
(apartments facing sea to be sold first)
Water—electricity—transportation—shopping
Lot and building contracts final

Avlonitis Suburbs

18 Akadimias St., corner of
Char. Trikoupi St., tel. 627-611

JUNE 6. *It has been announced that the King will be traveling today to Corfu for what will probably be a two-day visit, during which time he will be briefed on the latest developments in the Armed Forces as well as on conditions in general. Sources indicate that at 10:30 A.M. the King will receive Mr. Garouphalias, the minister of defense, who will bring His Majesty up to date on occurrences of sabotage against the 164th Field Artillery Squadron stationed in the Evros River area, as well as other matters regarding the army. It should be noted that ranking members of the United Democratic Left cabled the following query to the House of Parliament: "We hereby charge that Private Athanasios L. Karinos, from Arta, enlisted in the 534th Infantry Regiment, Company 3, Kabyli, Orestias, has been brutalized and beaten three times daily for the past ten days. The Karinos case is not the only one in that particular unit. Signed, Officers Brillakis, Ephraimides, Kyrkos, and Skopoulis."*

Ministry of Defense officials who were asked about published reports concerning the theft of firearms (three revolvers and a number of cartridges) from a training base in the Peloponnesus stated that no such incident had been reported to the Army Chiefs of Staff. In response to these allegations, the minister of defense, Mr. Petros Garouphalias, has ordered, via telephone, that the charges be investigated anew and that base commanders file their reports with the Army Chiefs of Staff.

Dear Mrs. Mina—

I am a regular listener of your wonderful program. A serious problem has been bothering me lately. I am 25 years old, married for six years with two children, ages four and eight months. My husband is 37 years old. Two weeks ago my husband cheated on me. Unfortunately I happened to witness it firsthand, and it was with a widow who is his age or maybe even older. They spend a lot of time together because of my husband's job. She is a saleswoman and he is a buyer. It was lunchtime, the shop was closed, and they went inside so the lady could get paid. He was carried away by her talk, that's what my husband told me. But I saw him get up from his seat and make the first move. And even if we believe his version, that he was excited by her dirty talk (she told him, in effect, that men make advances to her and that she, being a widow, can't say no), don't you think, Mrs. Mina, that he gave in very easily? And if another such occasion arises, won't he do the same thing again? Tell me, how can I trust him after seeing all that with my own eyes? Now he's on his knees to me asking me over and over to forgive him. I have and we've gone on living as though nothing happened. All that for the sake of our children. I don't know if you can call that love. He takes care of me, he's a good provider, he gets jealous if I so much as look at another man, even after all that's happened. When he found out that I was thinking about getting a divorce because of that incident, he cried and said he couldn't stand it. He even promised me that he was willing to go to confession. From now on I'll show you through my actions how faithful I can be, he tells me.

That's all well and good, Mrs. Mina, but wasn't he all promises and words of love before? How can I trust such a person from here on in? And how can I forget that vile scene? It's impossible for me not to relive it at least two or three times a day. And what should I do now? Please give me some advice.

I'm crying—hurting—suffering

Please don't mention the background to my story. I'll understand from the above three words. But there is also another problem: The merchandise we buy from that lady is necessary to run our shop. My husband says we should buy it through someone else. But I am afraid that she will try to see him again in some roundabout way. Once she realizes that we need her. My husband is leaving it up to me. I told him: This whole thing has cost me a lot. If the alternative is ruining my health then let's just not sell her type of goods. What do you think, Mrs. Mina? Bear in mind the fact that she is the sole source of that merchandise in our town.

Ailing Angelos Stasinopoulos, accompanied by his wife, flew to Budapest yesterday aboard a Malev Hungarian Airways plane. Stasinopoulos is suffering from hyperkinetic syndrome following a mental breakdown; he will undergo brain surgery in two stages at the hand of the renowned Hungarian neurosurgeon Professor Zoltan and his assistant, Professor Toth. The expenses for the two operations, as well as Stasinopoulos's stay in the biggest hospital in Budapest, were underwritten by the "friend of the poor" and well-known philanthropist Mr. Adamantios Karamourtzounes.

June 11, 1965

To the Editor,

I would be obliged if an official government representative would deign to answer the following questions:

First: If the Officers Associations for the Defense of National Ideals (ASPIDA) conspiracy is so insignificant that it comprises only low-ranking members of the military, as the Government claims, then why were high- and top-ranking officers called for questioning and summary reassignment?

Second: Is it true that more than ten depositions made by officers of Cypriot origin confirm the existence of a politician who both organized and is currently running ASPIDA?

Third: How does the Prime Minister explain the fact that ASPIDA had at its base, both here and in Cyprus, officers of the Central Intelligence Agency (KYP), a service directly under the Prime Minister's jurisdiction?

Fourth: Does the Government assume the responsibility toward the Greek people of verifying the fact that in actuality only four petty officers are implicated in the conspiracy? Awaiting your response, I remain

Respectfully yours,

Demosthenes Papaephstratiou

Colonel, Communications Corps, inactive duty
4B Metropolitou Germanou Karavangeli St.
Nea Smyrni

KALAMATA, JUNE 14. *From our correspondent. Passengers on the Patras-Pyrgos-Kalamata train witnessed a most unusual sight. As the train was approaching the Alpheios River, the passengers sighted a peasant crossing the river, stark naked. Due to the slow speed of the train and the length of the bridge, the spectacle remained in view for quite some time. A number of passengers initially thought the naked peasant fording the river was the embodiment of the god Pan.*

June 14, 1965

To: DEME

Dear Sirs—

Greetings. I received my latest papers about a physical examination on August 18 in Patras. It is a great pleasure for me to be emigrating through you. I want you to know that I am not well off financially. In the first place, I will be leaving by myself. I do have an invitation from my sister, who has been living and working in Melbourne for the last six years. My family consists of my wife Dimitroula, née Papasiachami, and our two small children, ages four and three. Angelikoula is four, Nektaria is three.

    Please reply immediately and let me know. And I am asking you again about my wife and children, should I bring them along to the doctors? Because they will be leaving after I do. We are braiders by trade, both of us.

Konstantinos Manthopoulos

MILAN, JUNE 17. *By special correspondent. A Milan civil court today confirmed the separation of "bed and board" between Maria Callas and her estranged husband, Mr. Giovanni Battista Meneghini, citing responsibility on both sides. It is well known that in Italy there is no divorce, just "bed and board" separation. In its verdict the court makes reference to the celebrated diva's relationship with Greek shipping magnate Mr. Aristotle Onassis but declares itself of the opinion that it is merely a friendly and social relationship, thereby rejecting Mr. Meneghini's petition that his wife be deemed responsible for the separation because of this relationship.*

———

LARISA, JUNE 20. *From our correspondent. Ioannis Makrinos, a rural policeman from the village of Skiti, Agyia, has sued Michaïl Efthimiou because the latter insulted the crown on his officer's cap. In other news, police arrested I. Chelidones because he insulted a law enforcement officer by saying, "The Corps of Gendarmes is illegal and ought to be disbanded."*

Acharnai, June 21, 1965

To Our Dearest Mrs. Mina on the *Woman's Hour* program—

You say such wonderful things and I listen to you every day. I am a young schoolgirl, age 15, but my heart has been wounded by the arrows of a tall, handsome boy. I am madly in love with him, and he is with me. My parents have somehow found out about it and won't permit me to go out at all. And I am suffering. My girlfriends say he's playing me for a fool, that he's a good-for-nothing who just wants to have a good time with me. What should I do? Should I believe my girlfriends or him?

Red Poppy

CORFU, JUNE 22. *From our correspondent. It was an emotion-filled 24 hours for Queen Anna-Maria. Early in the day she felt a "pain" that was surely the first sign of the happy event to come. Constantine was standing next to her on the veranda of the Mon Repos Palace. He could tell what had happened by the Queen's expression and movements. Smiling happily at her, and with his usual sense of humor, he said, "It seems the baby is in a hurry." The physicians, Messrs. Doxiades and Koutipharis, who hastened to the palace soon afterward, determined that everything was normal and that the Queen's overall health is excellent.*

MRS. DAPHNE: MEDIUM

Prizewinner in telepathy for her successful experiments under Mr. Tanagras, long distance between Athens and London-Tübingen-New York. High hypnotic suggestibility and psychometry. Will perform all experiments. Impressive results. Office hours: 9:00 –1:00 and 3:30 – 6:30, 32 Kypseli St., Athens, tel. 812-278.

Gavrovo, June 29, 1965

Dear Mr. Consul who I don't know—

Please excuse us for not showing up when you and your committee came to Trikala. I did come but we didn't catch you there in time, because the announcement you sent us came on the 29th of the month, today. The mailman was not making deliveries, he was on vacation and we knew nothing about it. Anyway, I apologize for that. And I would like you to please tell me if there is a committee in Athens so I can go before it. Or when you will be coming to Trikala again. Don't get the idea I do not want to emigrate, and I am truly very sorry for putting you to the trouble of answering me a second time.

Thank you and good-bye,

Kavalares, Ioannis

MYTILENE, JULY 4. *From our correspondent. Forty-year-old Evangelia Damianou, mother of five and resident of the village of Pefki, was brought to the Vostaneion Hospital with an ax wound to her head. According to current information, her injury was caused by her estranged husband Michaïl, who visited her at home last night and threatened her with a knife. In the ensuing struggle she wrested the knife from his hand, but he seized an ax that was lying nearby and struck her. This dramatic scene took place right in front of the couple's children, who watched in terror as their parents struggled.*

Dear Mrs. Mina—

What I am concerned about is my rebellious son, who just turned
14 and is driving our family crazy. First of all, his father is not alive,
it's been four years since he passed away. We live with my daughter,
who is 9 years older and married, with a little girl. As she loves him
and it was she who brought him up because I was out working, I
don't want him to talk back to her or to be disrespectful toward
her. Something else, equally serious, is that he smokes, and not just
an occasional cigarette with his friends, but regularly. When we
became aware of this we tried to give him advice and to point out
the terrible consequences, without success. In any case we had been
telling him for a long time how bad smoking was and how harmful
to one's health, with myself as the prime example of someone who
suffers terribly but cannot quit. What's more, he doesn't even pretend not to smoke with other people, it's only in front of me that
he doesn't dare to smoke yet. I tried being nice to him, then strict.
I even slapped him. And because his sister gets mixed up in all this,
they quarrel and he uses language with her that I don't care to write
about. He's no good in school, either. He hates it and he has had
to do the same class over for the second time this year. He has no
plans for the future. Everything is confused in his mind. First he
wants to be an engineer, then a radio operator. Now he says an
electrician but in ninth grade where he is now I don't even know if
there is such a possibility. And he wants to get a summer job now
too. Fortunately he is not lazy, he's hard-working, he just can't
settle down at anything. Because he finds the wages too low. And
he looks for short-term jobs. When I say something, he doesn't
listen to me. Every now and then I can see some conscientiousness
in him, like a few days ago when he got paid. He came home and
proudly gave it all to me. I don't know if I did the right thing
letting him keep 100 drachmas for his allowance. He is earning
300 drachmas a week now, but he says if he gets a raise I should
give him more. And our family is not that well off for him to be
asking for so much, if indeed it is too much. Also he has been
staying out till all hours lately. No matter how much I yell, he

rarely gets in before 11–11:30, sometimes even 12. I don't know how to handle him. Sometimes when I'm nice to him it works, but the next minute he forgets it all again. If I hit him he gets even worse. If I'm strict he won't listen. Please, Mrs. Mina, answer me. Is there another solution besides patience which I am fast running out of? This letter was written by my daughter.

Regards,

M.D.K.

LONDON, JULY 7. *By special correspondent. The* Daily Sketch, *a newspaper selling over 5,000,000 copies daily, in its column on Greek affairs, quotes sources to the effect that as soon as the Queen has delivered, there will be a meeting in Corfu between the King and the Prime Minister in search of a permanent resolution to the government crisis that has just erupted. The cause of the crisis is attributed to the involvement of members of the Prime Minister's entourage in a conspiracy within the ranks of the Armed Forces. The newspaper reiterates news already published in Athens concerning a rift between the Prime Minister and the Minister of Defense and also comments that the King has strongly opposed the Prime Minister's plans for a takeover of this ministry.*

TAM-TAM

Save the bottlecaps.
Gifts of 500,000 dr.
You, too, can take part in this grand competition.
Entrance forms: 57 Sokratous St. and 53 Syngrou Ave.

Dear Mrs. Mina—

I am 19 years old. Some time ago I met a young man 25 years old. We have been living in the same neighborhood for two years. This past summer I saw him all the time, he lives a little past our house. I've been out with him several times. He stopped by on his way to some relatives and two or three times I went with him. He asked me to go to secluded places and I refused because I don't know much about him. He treats me very nicely but I don't know what he's like underneath. He got mad when I refused him. But that's not my problem. He had given me a phone number—to call him when I had made up my mind. I called him twice and then he told me not to call him again, because he didn't want to keep bothering his next-door neighbor, because he was using her telephone. But I called him anyway and he got mad. He met me by chance in the street and told me that I shouldn't have done that. And he went off. Now he goes by without speaking to me. He drives past on his motorcycle and sometimes honks at me or looks at me. But he doesn't talk to me. I don't know what to do, I'm really confused. Can you help me find the words to make him understand that he shouldn't get so upset about such little things? He has a younger brother who comes by and I see him. Is it right to talk to him? I mean, should I tell him to tell his brother that I want to talk to him? And is it right for me to talk to him when he's not talking to me?

A friend from Ano Liosia

JULY 23. *The National Student Association of the College of Commerce and Finance handed the minister of education, Mr. Iakovos Diamantopoulos, a communique stating that the governing board of the Association expressed its deepest regrets at the death of their fellow student, Sotiris Petroulas, and indicating that he was the victim of the anarchist element whose aims are to drive the country toward bloodshed. In addition, the minister of education, Mr. Diamantopoulos, made a statement expressing his grief and emphasizing the fact that this student fell victim to unruly demonstrators. He also mentioned that he would recommend that the family of the deceased be awarded a pension.*

Dear Mrs. Mina—

I am 19 years old and, for the last 7 months, engaged. When I was 14 years old I met a young man who was 27. From the beginning of our acquaintance he asked me to become his. Of course I didn't want to, but 5 months later I did without even realizing it. My problem is now with my fiancé, who is 25. When he met me and told me that his intentions were honest, I didn't hide anything from him. He led me to believe that it didn't bother him and he told me not to worry about it. But I can't forget about it. I love him so, I love him more than anything and I'm afraid that later on all this will build up inside him and he will throw it up at me during some quarrel or other. What do you advise me to do? As for breaking up, it's out of the question. Girlfriends that I have talked this over with haven't given me a precise answer. I am impatiently awaiting your opinion and I thank you.

Maïra

ROYAL COURT, JULY 25, 1965. *H.M. the King arrived this morning from Corfu by plane.*

H.M. the King attended a critique of war games finals at the Naval War College, following which he had the pleasure of awarding the graduating senior naval officers their degrees.

H.M. the King met with the Prime Minister, Mr. G. Athanasiades-Novas, for a working session. H.M. also received the Minister of National Defense, Mr. Stavros Kostopoulos.

H.M. the King returned to Corfu by plane in the afternoon. From the Office of the King's Chamberlain.

———

The body of an unidentified young woman, about 25 years of age, was washed ashore yesterday in the vicinity of Votsalakia, Castella. She was fully dressed but barefoot. Her shoes were found on a rock. It was clearly a case of suicide. Her body was taken to the Piraeus Hospital.

My dear sister Faní—

I hope my letter finds you in good health. I wish you all a Merry Christmas, you and your children and your grandchildren. And now I will answer you, dear sister, concerning what you wrote me. It is not possible for me to go out and to get that power of attorney, and, second, I have signed a quit deed as did our brothers and sisters, and everything has been left to the three of you for quite a few years now. Eleni sold off her share because she, too, needed a house where she could stay; Argento wanted a dowry, all well and good. Now why do you want to start dragging everything up again? As far as I know, you shouldn't have any complaints because you got more than we did; you got the other plot of land and the yard in the back, and you built there without the slightest intervention from the township. Now, dear sister, if I did get the power of attorney—which I can't—all the old problems will be brought up again and we'll have to involve Eleni and start dividing up shares again. I don't want either a share or money. If a paper renouncing my claim to my paternal property is all you need, I will sign one immediately and send it to you. But I won't grant power of attorney to anyone. As for Argento, she's in the wrong, she's stubborn and doesn't listen to anyone. And now she's off there by herself. Let her do whatever in God's name she wants, she can go become a queen. It's not true, however, that her brother-in-law tried to lay claim to her property, and his wife didn't say anything, either. Up until last year she was paying Eleni rent and Argento has the receipts. Don't let Satan manipulate you, dear sister, by bringing all this up again after all these years. The house belongs to you, to your children, our father's grandchildren. No one will bother you. Fix it any way you like, do whatever the children like, and let them be happy and enjoy it. Kopanitsas will not object. I had a dream that I probably shouldn't write you about. I saw our old nanny, who is my aide and companion in all circumstances, and who brought me up from the time I was young until I went away. And she said to me: Marigo, don't be deceived into signing a power of attorney. I won't do it, dear sister, I won't go against the wishes of a dead person. As far as our brother's wife is concerned, whatever Jim had, his house, his shop, his things, it was all in his son's name, all for our Giorgos. She lives far away, in another state, with her elder daughter from her first marriage. I am sending you her address so you can write to her, and do whatever in God's name you see fit. But even if you write her, how will she be able to read what you say in your letter when she is barely able to say hello?

My greetings to Ilias and lots of kisses to all your children and grandchildren.

Your sister,

Marigo

August 6, 1965

To the Editor,

I kindly request that you publish this letter. The political crisis in our country during the past 15 days or so, plus the destructive division brought about by the former Prime Minister Mr. George Papandreou, have also directly contributed to the frustration and indignation of all of us law enforcement officers who, guarding the streets day and night in the face of immediate danger to our lives and in a constant state of physical and emotional exhaustion, struggle to maintain the very order that this arsonist of public peace and this preacher of division relentlessly attacks in his speeches. Hundreds of policemen have been taken to hospitals with wounds caused by rocks, bottles, and other objects thrown at them during the bloody and riotous disturbances fomented by Mr. Papandreou with the assistance of the United Democratic Left (EDA), whose intent is to do away with all idea of law and order. It is imperative, therefore, that the former Prime Minister be prevailed upon to stop encouraging unruly demonstrations so as to restore peace to our country and offer some relief to our policemen, a great many of whom have had their health seriously impaired.

With many thanks,

Zoïs Ioannis Kytronias

Police officer

A 34-year-old construction worker, Dimadiros Stavrou, and 36-year-old Eleni Karabotsou, wife of Athanasios, were arrested at Stavros, Agia Paraskevi, because they were caught in the act of adultery at the latter's home. The two were arrested following charges brought by Karabotsou's husband and were referred to the District Attorney's Office.

Dear Mina—

It's been 15 months now that I've been living in a terrible state of turmoil. First of all, let me explain to you that I am 47 years old and my husband is 52. We have been married for 25 years and, unfortunately, are childless, in spite of all our efforts time and time again.

When I was 30 someone "left" a baby, only a few days old, on our doorstep, but I didn't keep it because the doctors were still holding out hope for me. My husband wanted to keep it. He was doing pretty well at work, with a gas station and spare parts shop, but now he's been on a disability pension for two years because of a heart condition. The only property we have acquired during our marriage is our house, worth practically nothing. And that wasn't easy, because my husband wasted a lot of money on booze, women, etc. In spite of my tears and complaining I never managed to make him change his ways. As for me, I was and still am the perfect wife.

I am very meticulous in carrying out my duties as a wife and homemaker, but unfortunately, I get nothing back from him. But I still love him, and above all I feel sorry for him, being so sick. I am writing all this to you, Mrs. Mina, to help you to understand.

And now on to what is bothering me. For several years now, I have occasionally broached the subject, politely and almost as if it were a joke, of his putting the house in my name, after his death, of course. And if God saw fit to take me first, the house would belong to him. He would refuse to even discuss it, saying that he had supposedly asked a notary public and that no papers were necessary because he had no other close relatives who could be his beneficiaries. And I believed him. But one day I went myself to a notary public and he told me that, unfortunately, at any time I could easily be excluded by even his most distant relatives.

When I told my husband this, in a nice way of course, and then asked him to provide me with some security whenever he was feeling up to it, do you know what he answered me? "Are you crazy, why should I leave you my house? I'm going to leave it to Neni." Neni is his cousin's daughter, age 18. Now you can imagine the state I'm in. This went on for a month. He only came home to sleep and he stated categorically that he would never leave me the house. Finally, I was forced to bring an uncle of his and his wife, who both like me a lot, from Xanthi, and I told them what was going on. And after they talked to him, he gave his word and agreed to go to a notary public.

Now he claims and insists that there was never any name but mine in his will. One of the witnesses says the same thing. Another one is not really clear about things. As for asking the third witness, they try and pretend they've forgotten his name. Meanwhile, one month later, the master himself went off to Switzerland to be examined by some doctors. And he stayed at my sister's. She put him up, she's been there since 1958, married. And my sister, whom I'd written to asking her to sound him out, asked him one day and he told her: I made a will because I wanted to settle whom I would leave our property to after our death. Now that word "our" is very upsetting to me, Mrs. Mina, and continues to be so. So then he gets mad at my sister and ends the conversation immediately. And he calls her all sorts of names. I, however, am living through a terrible time, and my nerves are on edge. I cry all the time, but I don't pick any fights because I think of his condition. I feel slighted and very insulted if he has really written off all my sweat and blood to his niece. My doctor said that I'm going through menopause, and that I want to leave him, but my conscience won't permit it. If he were well, I definitely would.

And now, Mrs. Mina, after reading all of the above, what have you got to say? What conclusions can you draw? Has this person really made his will fairly, as he insists, or has he pulled a fast one? I ask you please, when you have a chance, please talk about this situation. Show me a way so that I, too, can understand him. Only please send me the answer in writing, even if it's just a word or two. I don't want to tire you. I absolutely do not want to hear it on the radio, although I listen with great interest to your programs and especially to you. I have my reasons. Write me the truth. Even if it is disappointing, don't hide it from me.

I thank you from the bottom of my heart,

A sad listener

PARIS, AUGUST 11. *By special correspondent. A pale and tearful Odile Rodin, wife of Porfirio Rubirosa, escorted him to his final resting place. The notorious playboy was buried in the cemetery of the French township of Marnes-la-Coquette. There were no last rites at his funeral. Instead, Odile received her friends' condolences at the cemetery chapel. The widow of the deceased Casanova is 26 years old, while the deceased was 56.*

———

ROYAL COURT, AUGUST 10, 1965. *H.M. the King received Mr. Stephanos Stephanopoulos, who reported back in the negative concerning his mandate to form a new government. From the Office of the King's Chamberlain.*

A BIOGRAPHICAL SKETCH
OF THE NEW PRIME MINISTER

Mr. Ilias Tsirimokos, son of the veteran liberal statesman Ioannis Tsirimokos, was born on August 2, 1907, in Lamia. He married Argyro Gheka. He studied law, political science, and economics in Athens and Paris. He has practiced law in Athens since 1931. His political career began in 1936 when he was elected M.P. for the regions of Phthiotis and Phokis on the Liberal ticket. He played a leading part in the resistance by founding the Union for Popular Democracy (UPD) in 1941. He participated in the Resistance Government (R.G.) as justice minister (secretary), and as minister of finance in the government of National Unity during the liberation. Between 1945 and 1953 he served as secretary of the Socialist Party (S.P., Greece). In 1950 he was elected Athens M.P. on the Socialist Party ticket. He was one of the charter members of the Liberal Democratic Union (LDU). In 1958 he was elected Athens M.P. as an independent, but with the support of the United Democratic Left (EDA), at which time he founded the Democratic Union Party. As a founder of the Center Union, he was elected to the Athens seat in 1961, 1963, and 1964. He was Speaker of the House of Parliament in 1963. He was also active in journalism, publishing the magazines The Battle *(from 1941 until 1952) and* Politics *(in 1959). He has authored numerous books.*

LA CORUÑA, SPAIN, AUGUST 20. *The Associated Press. The 19th track and field championship of the Athletic Federation of NATO Countries opened to an audience of 20,000 spectators at the local Municipal Stadium. During the shot-put finals yesterday Abatzis was ranked 5th with a throw of 15.28 meters, while our record holders Marselos and Mesimertzis participated in the preliminaries for the 110-meter hurdles and the 1,500-meter race, respectively. Both of our athletes qualified to enter the finals.*

September 15, 1965

Dearest friends—

Could you please have your office send us the necessary papers so that we can emigrate to Australia? My marital status is: a widow with one male child, one year old. I am a resident of the village of Axo Milopotamou, where I live.

Name and Address:

Maria, widow of Stergios, Zagalakis
Rethymnon, Crete

ROYAL COURT, OCTOBER 11, 1965. *H.M. the King received the Prime Minister, Mr. Stephanos Stephanopoulos, for a working session.*

H.M. the King received Lieutenant General Mr. I. Pipilis, the departing chairman of the Joint Chiefs of Staff, who presented Lieutenant General Mr. Tsolakis, the new chairman of the Joint Chiefs of Staff, as well as the departing chairman of Army Chiefs of Staff, Mr. I. Gennimatas, who presented Lieutenant General Mr. Gr. Spantidakis, the new chairman of Army Chiefs of Staff.

By high command, H.M. the King's Chamberlain called on His Excellency the Chinese Ambassador and conveyed H.M.'s congratulations on the occasion of China's national holiday.

From the Office of the King's Chamberlain.

NOVEMBER 28, 1965. *Stavros Niarchos, the Greek shipping magnate, spent a day of bliss yesterday in St. Moritz with his fourth successive wife, apparently unperturbed by reports from Greece that his marriage is invalid according to Greek law. The 56-year-old Greek tycoon has successfully evaded any encounter with journalists since his unexpected marriage in Mexico six days ago to 42-year-old Charlotte Ford, daughter of the multimillionaire car manufacturer Henry Ford II. Mr. Niarchos's secretary, however, flatly denied accusations that this marriage is illegal according to Greek law and stressed the fact that announcements to this effect were made in Athens by a spokesman for Mr. Niarchos.*

The validity of the Greek magnate's marriage was challenged by his former brother-in-law, Mr. Konstantinos Goumas, in a letter to the English-language newspaper Athens News.

To the very dear staff of the *Woman's Hour* program—

Greetings. I would appreciate your attention. I was married in 1951 against my wishes. My mother chose the bridegroom and as I was only 17 at the time what could I do? Soon our troubles and worries began, because my husband is much older, we're 15 years apart. And as you can understand, he is insanely jealous. At the age of eighteen I brought our first child, Eleni, into the world. Today she is thirteen years old. Fifteen months later I had a boy, my Argyris. Six years later I gave birth to a little girl, who was born in good health, but 7 months later I lost her. And then our quarrels got even worse, I ended up with a heart condition. My husband didn't care at all about anything, he thought I was pulling his leg. And I was pregnant, too, in my last month. Until one day the doctor came and said if she doesn't get to Pireaus she's going to die; my blood pressure was down to 70. And after they told him that, he took me to the hospital, left me there, and went off. In the hospital I needed blood and the doctors asked me if I had any relatives. I said no, call my husband. But unfortunately he didn't come. But some other blood donors came and saved me and my little girl, who was born three days later. Luckily for me, however, an uncle of mine came and got me and took me back to the village. Two years later I gave birth to another child. Imagine what a heel he is, he never lets me relax for a minute. And he keeps asking for more and more things, like having intercourse from behind, I mean. I don't know what to do, he has no limits, he won't go to work. He says if you don't come with me, I won't go. Please help me. The children are hungry, they have no clothes, and the holidays are coming up. Eleni, age 13; Argyris, 11; Dimitra, 5; Giorgos, 3. I'm a mother, where is there a job so I can go and work?

Panagiota Her. Manolou

I will close my letter with these soothing words: I wish you a Merry Christmas.

Unhappy

PYRGOS, JANUARY 3. *From our correspondent. Nineteen-year-old infant-killer Paraskevi Gouzoules, daughter of Ioannis, a resident of the village of Aithria, gave a detailed description of how she committed the crime, assuming full responsibility for her actions. A reconstruction of the infanticide took place at 11:00 A.M. in the presence of gendarme officers and attorney general of the Amalias region, Mr. Phakos. The perpetrator admitted that on the previous Tuesday night (after Christmas) she had given birth to a baby, the product of her illegitimate affair with Stylianos Kokkinos, a serviceman in the Mountain Military Engineers Corps. Gouzoules stated that Kokkinos had raped her near the River Pineios as she was grazing her sheep: "The soldier was bathing in the river, and after bathing came and assaulted me." Her allegation is, however, patently false, since the conception of the child cannot have taken place in the summertime. Furthermore, there were no MMEC units in the area between March 20 and 30, which is when the infant-killer must have become pregnant. It can be concluded that some other person must have been responsible for her pregnancy.*

After giving birth, she wrapped the child in her undergarments and began walking in the direction of the water well about 40 meters away from her house. The infant began to cry and while she was trying to stifle its cries, she dropped it and hurt its head. She picked it up, carried it to the well, and threw it in, still alive. She then returned to her house and remained in bed until her arrest. The reenactment confirmed the coroner's report issued by the surgeon, Mr. Doukas, which indicates that the baby drowned after being thrown into the well alive. Traces of blood were also found at the spot where the murderess said she had first dropped the baby and also on the protective ledge around the well. The baby's body showed bruises caused by the fall as well as marks on its neck, indicating earlier attempts at strangling it. The infant-killer was transferred yesterday afternoon to the examining magistrate of Amalias for arraignment and pretrial detention.

He loves me but I don't love him

Dear Mrs. Mina—

I am 21 years old. I was born on June 1, 1944, and I come from Macedonia. As you can see from my letter I don't have much of an education, I stopped school after sixth grade. Mrs. Mina, I have been in Athens for 8 years and have learned a good trade and am very happy with my work, I'm a hairdresser. But for about 5 years now a young man of 25 has been in love with me but I'm not in love with him. All my friends tell me to marry him and that I'll learn to love him later on. He is a good person, without any exaggeration, almost too good. Tell me, please, what to do. He has kept this up for five years now. I thought that when he went into the army he would forget me. The opposite happened. He is so good that he would do anything for me. I mean if I married him there would be nothing I couldn't have. One day he went and told all this to a lady who is almost like a mother to me; he said if he doesn't marry me he will kill himself because I am the first and last woman he'll ever love. Before he went into the army he told me that too. I told him then that I don't love him but feel only friendship for him. And then he started to cry. What can I tell you, I felt so sorry for him that if he'd been out of the service I would have married him just to keep him from doing anything crazy, and me from feeling guilty. Mrs. Mina, I listen to your radio show every day and, judging from the advice you give, I know what I should do. I have tried many times to find the right man for me but in vain. Because all they wanted was to have a good time and nothing else. Perhaps all this will make you think I'm a flighty young girl. No, you mustn't believe that. Because everyone tells me I should marry him, time's passing, and I'll end up an old maid.

Mrs. Mina, tell me what to do. Will I learn to love him in time? And how should I behave toward him if I say no, so as not to hurt him?

I will wait anxiously to hear your reply on your wonderful program.

Maria (pen name: He loves me but I don't love him)

NAUPLION, FEBRUARY 14. *From our correspondent. The testimony of a Kalamata woman has revealed a remarkable instance of the survival of the practices of ancient Magi priests. During interrogation at a trial pending before the Appeals Court of our town, the woman in question stated the following: "The plaintiff and I went to the priest of the village Skarouchi, who can cast spells, and she asked him to help her keep her husband under her control. The priest gave her a liquid to pour over the marital bed and asked for an additional 80 drachmas in order to prepare an amulet made out of one of her husband's soiled handkerchiefs." It should be noted that, in order to obtain this money, the plaintiff sold eiderdown bedcovers, overcoats, and other articles of clothing for trivial sums. In spite of all this, the spell had no effect, and the couple's separation was officially finalized in court.*

To our dearest and most respected parents—

Greetings. We received your letter after all this time. Well, dear parents, you should know that we too are well. Theodora is fine and so am I. You wrote that the rain ruined your grapes, but don't worry, God is great and He helps people. But you didn't mention anything about Kallio, where she's going and what she's doing. Is she by any chance going to Athens to work? Don't do it, Father, don't send her to Athens by herself, keep her there with you and when luck comes her way she'll grab it.

There is a boy there who's been in love with Theodora since junior high school, I know all about it and so does our sister Kalliope. He's a very nice boy and very hardworking. He lives by the harbor just past Uncle Antonis's and he has a sister and a brother, both married, in America. Theodora won't issue him an invitation if he doesn't come and ask for her from you first, but if he does come, we really should hang on to that boy because, I'm telling you, he's a very fine boy and will make Theodora happy if she ends up with him. Really, Daddy, I want us to get her married, because Karouzakis here went and waited for her outside her factory and when she got off work one night he beat her up because she isn't interested in him. I went there and if some other people hadn't intervened, I would be in jail today. I went there intending to fix him but good, and if he bothers her one more time I'll kill him, I've thought it over, that son of a bitch, I'll fix him so he never sees the light of day again. He also went after Katzourbos's daughter and she moved out of the tailor's and went to live on her own, because the tailor's sister was trying to take advantage of her and was asking him for money, too. Things have been happening here that I can't write you about, but tell Katzourbos that he's destroying his daughter by sending her to stay with people like that. Karouzakis just wanted to sell them a line and get them into bed, and she warned them about him, told them not to take up with him, but they didn't listen, and when Marika saw how bad things were, what trouble was in store for her, she upped and left. And now he goes every night and stalks her because he wants to kill her for telling on him. But tell Katzourbos for me, please, tell him just how his in-laws are treating his daughter. But what can you expect from people with no children? I have no time now, or paper, to write you any more, and I'll write you the rest of this in another letter. Send our greetings to everyone, to Kalliope, Giorgos, Marina, Athina, Chronis, and Giannakis and also to yourselves, especially from Theodora and from me, with love.

Irini

MARCH 5. *The trial of soldiers K. Matakis and D. Bekios of the 117th Field Artillery Squadron, stationed in Orestias and accused of sabotage, has been in progress since yesterday before the Military Court of Appeals. The two men had been condemned to 15 and 4 years of imprisonment, respectively, by the Standing Military Tribunal of Thessaloniki, both for causing extensive damage to state property, and the former for abandoning his post as a guard.*

This case of sabotage at the above-mentioned base, located on the Turkish border, is now quite well known. As stated in the indictment, the sabotage is the work of an organization that has extended its reach even outside the army. At their arraignment in Thessaloniki, Mr. Gotsis, Prosecutor for the Crown, stated, among other things: "I regret that the law prevents me from sending both of these traitors to the execution squad. Without a doubt, their actions were motivated by communist theories and ideas."

Five witnesses were examined at the trial before the Military Court of Appeals yesterday, and it is expected that the verdict will be announced later this evening.

Oreini Serres, March 8, 1966

To my favorite radio show *The Woman's Hour*—

Greetings. I hope this letter will reach you like all the others. Dear Mrs. Mina, I would like you to help me. As you did once before when you gave me advice. I am 17 years old. I am not like other girls, who run around with boys. I am poor and well behaved and here is my tragedy: I am in love with someone very, very rich, but he is not interested in me, he doesn't take any notice of someone so insignificant. He was here in our village on vacation but now he's gone, only I can't forget him, even though I know that it is impossible for a high-born man like him from Kolonaki to even look at a village girl like me. I try and avoid thinking about him, but every night he's there when I sleep and I often dream about him. Do you perhaps know, Mrs. Mina, why he's still in my dreams, since I know very well that he doesn't love me? You will tell me it's because before I go to sleep I think about him, that's why. No, Mrs. Mina, I have stopped thinking about him for some time. But I have endless dreams about him. I am very strong-willed and want to forget him, and I will. It's not worth crying over him, I'm not meant for him, I know that. He wants to marry a girl like himself, someone modern, with boyfriends, a classy woman from Kolonaki. Me, I'm nothing like that. I may have a nice personality and good looks, I'm actually pretty cute, but he is high society. Please answer me, dear Mrs. Mina, give me some advice.

From an adoring listener,

Insignificant village girl

Forty-two-year-old gentleman, honest, in good health, at-
tractive, with respectable income, wishes to meet young or
mature lady (may even be older than he), principled and
possessing cash or real estate affording comfortable life to-
gether. Write to newspaper: Ta Nea, *attn. P.E.N.*

To: The Official Bureau of Emigration

Gentlemen:

I received your letter of November the 8th in which you express regret for the rejection of my application by the Australian government. I too wonder why I was rejected, since they do not know either who I am or what I do. I am no liar, thief, or criminal. Last year you wrote me that I do not fulfill the requirements set by the Australian authorities, but they answered that it was you who rejected me. Whom should I believe? And to whom should I address myself to find a solution to my problem? I wrote to my M.P. and the letter wound up somewhere else. I do not know if this is my fault or if there have been accusations made against me of a political nature, but I am neither for nor against anyone politically. If this is the case, gentlemen, I would like you to inform me so that I can set things straight. My patriotic conscience is clear. Between 1947 and 1949 I fought against the communist guerrillas and was decorated with two medals for valor and the War Cross, 3rd Class. If I have been in error, to err is human, even Christ himself said "there is no one without sin." I am asking you to please help me emigrate. I have already written you the reasons why I want to leave for a few years. I am not asking for money or for anything difficult. I am asking to go there with my family and work, not to be supported by the Australian authorities. It is up to you to decide my fate. If there is anything I can do, write to me and I will come to your office. I am a reasonable person and will do anything you recommend. I send my greetings and wish you all the best.

Yours respectfully,

Panagiotis Manolopoulos

MUNICH, MARCH 17. *By special correspondent. Police here have placed 35-year-old Greek laborer Dimitrios Kotsyphas from Megara under arrest in connection with the slaying, on February 27, of his fellow countryman Demosthenes Karle, also a laborer, from Corfu. According to sources, Kotsyphas confessed to stabbing Karle to death with a knife in his sleep because 19-year-old Brigitte, with whom both men were in love, had shown a preference for Karle, 11 years his junior. The young woman is still in the hospital after suffering a nervous breakdown when she was informed what had transpired.*

———

BLACKOW

Potency at every age. No drugs, no long treatments, simple and completely natural method. Sexual insufficiency and impotence as well as frequent urination and cramps can be treated with the Blackow invention. An important scientific discovery by Robert Blackow, Associate Professor of Anatomy. Ask for detailed brochure.
"Blackow," 51 Stadiou St., 6th floor, room 12, tel. 237-662.

To Mr. Consul:

We are honored to report to you, as director of the DEME service, the following and unfortunate grievances: Through your agency, numerous poor and probably destitute young women have emigrated to Australia to find employment as unskilled workers and save their earnings so they too can live better lives. They therefore left parents, brothers, sisters, and relatives behind and have moved to far away and unknown places where we would like you to know they have no other company except Almighty God. Unfortunately I, Ioannis Pol. Sigountakis, a resident of Skopi, Siteia, Crete, have two daughters in the state of Melbourne, Australia, sent there through the DEME service: Theodora and Irini Sigountaki, who might be mere names to you but who are in your records, as are other young women from our village. A certain good-for-nothing named Ioannis Em. Karouzakis has also emigrated there. He comes from a dishonest and irreligious family whose members are born troublemakers, looting anything they can lay their hands on in churches, breaking up families, deceiving married couples, and slandering innocent youngsters. It has now been a year since that punk Ioannis emigrated to Australia through DEME and headed for Sydney, where a young woman from our village has been residing for two years, a sweet girl by the name of Nenaki, and he proposed to her, asked her to marry him, and her parents put their trust in him and swallowed all his devious propositions and were preparing for the wedding when he, after squandering her savings from work, skipped town at the last minute, just before fulfilling his obligation. Well, he has now moved to Melbourne, where there are other girls from our village, including girls he is acquainted with from all over Greece. As you can see from the attached letter, written by my daughter Irini, he tries to abuse these girls, beating them up in the middle of the street for his own pleasure and satisfaction. Also living here is a friend of his who is just like him, Georgios Siphis Tsikoudakis, a man of similar character and mores, with the same bad behavior and manners as Ioannis. He too asked for the daughter of a certain Michaïl Pasparakis and, after living with her for quite some time, walked out on her for no reason. His parents used to do similar things and it seems that they have inherited this deceitfulness, so the two friends have been corresponding about Tsikoudakis going over there too, about meeting there, where they will keep on beating and robbing people at random. Well, it so happens Tsikoudakis is coming by your office the day after tomorrow so he can leave and emigrate. Mr. Director, Sir, I report all this to you and I beg you with tears in my eyes that some measures be taken concerning these girls in Australia. Try and put yourself in their place, or imagine that your own children are there in such a situation and can find no protection anywhere at all. We think about them, about their fears, their tears and their terrible anguish, and no one to turn to with their complaints. Because of all of the above, I take it upon myself, as a parent and family man, like all of us, to report these goings-on, and ask either that those vagrant youths be pursued by your agency or, if this is impossible, that our girls be returned to us so they do not have to spend their days in fear, pining away over their fate.

I tearfully report the above to you, dear Mr. Consul and director of DEME, and I the undersigned send you our greetings.

Ioannis Pl. Sigountakis (father of Irini and Theodora who have emigrated to Australia)

ROME, MARCH 29. *By special correspondent. New escort for Soraya. An athletic Italian and well-known playboy, Sato Magri of Naples, has been her inseparable companion for the last three weeks. It is widely believed that this is the latest romance of the melancholy former empress. For the sake of this new beau, Soraya abandoned the attorney Peter Robert Haaf, her steady escort all last winter.*

Dear Grigoris,

I sent you an Easter card with best wishes and the request that you pick up something from the Bank of Commerce (Aeolou & Sophokleous St. Branch). Not having heard from you, and because the bank (Foreign Accounts Dept.) has informed me you never appeared to pick up anything, I gather you did not receive the above-mentioned card. You might be interested to know that it pictured a naked black beauty and I assume that some Post Office employee (most likely the neighborhood mailman) became infatuated with it to the point of breaking his service oath.

You probably read in the newspapers about the coup that took place here. In a single night the prime minister, the ministers, and their chief advisors were massacred, so we now have a dictatorship. And the cause was last year's "fraudulent" elections.

We keep hearing uneasily about the mess Greece is in—especially the devaluation of the drachma, which immediately affects all those people like myself who send our meager savings to our home country for the future. Now, of course, all our excess earnings are sent and deposited elsewhere. I hope to be in Athens on vacation in about twenty days. So do write me where I can reach you. You must have already received a small package I sent you through Mr. Papaleon.

Stay well,

Pericles K.

*Three bullets and two people in a pool of blood was all that re-
mained in the shabby room of thirty-year-old plumber Nikiphoros Tzinieris. With him was twenty-five-year-old* GIOULA
*Glass Works employee Ekaterini Kalogerea. Probable cause:
abandonment of one by the other. For once, however, it was
not the man who raised a criminal hand. In the wake of the
recent epidemic of crimes by husbands and lovers against de-
fenseless women, the "weaker" sex has been fighting back. It
was the glass worker who perpetrated the tragedy in the early-
morning hours, at exactly 2:15* A.M. *in the Korydallos suburb
of Piraeus. Following her crime, the perpetrator turned the
handgun on herself and fired twice at her heart. Only seconds
before, she had tiptoed in, so as not to be heard by anyone
in the house, to Nikiphoros Tzinieris's room and workshop,
putting the revolver to his temple and executing him at almost
point-blank range. Both were taken to the Piraeus State Hospital where, in spite of the doctors' protracted efforts, Tzinieris succumbed to his deep wound while Kalogerea struggled
desperately for life until late last night. In just fifteen words,
spoken with difficulty from deep in her wounded chest before
she fell into a coma, the young heroine of this double tragedy
revealed, in brief, the motive behind her dramatic act: "He
was my boyfriend. I loved him. He didn't treat me right. I
killed him." Her confession was confirmed by the victim's
mother. "She wanted to kill my son," she wailed. "She had
made another attempt too, just a short time ago. She fired
three bullets into the fireplace. Nikiphoros was not harmed. I
found the burnt bullet shells." The brothers of the unfortunate
shooting victim have kept silent regarding the deeper motives
of the love tragedy. They nevertheless confirm the fact that
Kalogerea was pressuring their brother to stay in the relationship. "Nikiphoros had a heart of gold," his younger brother
stated, "and he tried, in a gentle manner, to persuade her that
the tender friendship that had developed between them could
not go on forever. He could not possibly know what was in
store for him, that his youth would be lost so soon to the*

grave." Neighbors are guarded when speaking of this double tragedy. Some have gone so far as to maintain that the two young people did indeed have some sort of relationship but that it did not seem to be heading toward a happy outcome. Someone else claimed that there was nothing between the two except mutual fondness, which was stronger on the part of Kalogerea toward the plumber. The one person stating that he knew absolutely nothing was the perpetrator's brother, the police sergeant of the Piraeus Security Police. He was the first to come upon the nightmarish scene with the two blood-soaked lovers, and it was he who saw to it that they were taken immediately to the hospital. It was the policeman's own revolver that Kalogerea used against the unfortunate plumber. Her brother was fast asleep when she crept quietly out of bed and took the gun from a nearby table. She then walked barefoot out of the room, closed the door softly behind her, and proceeded to the end of the courtyard to the Tzinieris family's apartment. She went directly to her lover's room. There was just enough light from the street lamp across the way so that she could avoid making noise and spoiling her plan. Her victim was easy to see in the light coming in through a crack as he slept, unsuspecting, following a hard day's work. With her fingers steady on the trigger, the young Glass Works employee approached the head of the bed. Not wanting to waste a second bullet, she pointed the revolver directly at his temple. There was only a little blood at first, followed by more, spurting out of his mouth, indicating that the man was not simply asleep. He was already dead. The murderess herself could do little else at that moment. She had no other way out, and no choice. She shot herself in the chest with the same weapon and fell on the floor beside the bed of her victim. She was in such furious haste to end her life, and to pay for her crime on the spot, that she used a second bullet on herself, narrowly missing her heart. The initial reenactment in the plumber's bedroom and workshop corroborated the dramatic scenario referred to above and also the move-

ments of the perpetrator. How it was possible for this young woman's heart be filled with such hatred that she could bring herself to kill her beloved with such criminal deliberation is something no one has yet been able to explain. The killer was not yet in any condition to make a statement. Was it insanity brought about by rejection from the man she believed to be the sunlight in her life? Or was it the neighbors' laughing and talking about her behind her back, seeing that Nikiphoros had no intention of marrying the young woman? Had the victim promised to marry her and then gone back on his word in the last few days? Or was there some devastating secret casting its dark shadow over the two young people's relationship, a secret that perhaps will never be revealed? As yet no one knows.

Oh, Mrs. Mina, for some of your wonderful advice! My son is going out with a girl 9 years older than he is. And he wants to marry her. They have been going out for 4 years, and my son, who is quite well educated, clever, and also a fine, sensitive boy, tells us that he and his girlfriend are perfectly suited to each other. And what's more, she is a very nice girl, serious, well mannered and well educated.

I have met her and I am of the same opinion. But I am worried by the age difference. He is 28 and she is 36–37. And she looks older. Not always, but she does look older. Can such a marriage work out in the long run? Won't they both develop psychological problems? And won't they be bothered by what people will say? Will their love be strong enough to make it through? Should I tell my son it's all right, what do you think? After listening to all my reservations, he remains undecided. Has he simply gotten used to this girl's company, or does he perhaps feel sorry for her?

Please tell me your opinion, but without mentioning their exact ages so they won't realize it is them. Especially the girl, who is in a very difficult position. Answer me under the pen name "A Mother." I thank you again.

Artemisia Achtari
28 Octovriou St., Brahami—Agios Dimitrios

IOANNINA, MAY 24. *From our correspondent. A family trag-edy occurred yesterday in the village of Alamana in the Ypsi-loi Kedroi region during a sudden spring storm, which hit at 3:00 P.M. Dimitrios Sphyris, a 50-year-old shepherd, and his 24-year-old daughter, Yakinthi, while watching their sheep under a tall tree where they had taken cover, were struck by lightning and killed instantly. Villagers who ran to their as-sistance found them completely charred. From their posture of embrace and Yakinthi's missing undergarments, it appears that father and daughter were engaged in an incestuous sexual act. Many sheep were also killed by the lightning bolt.*

Iosif Belekos
Manhattan Hospital
New York, N.Y.
USA

May 24, 1966

I, the undersigned, Iosif Belekos from Cheimara, Northern Epirus, ask the above emigration organization to please inform me how I might be able to return to Greece. Long live Greece.

JUNE 4. *The newest and largest aircraft of the U.S. Air Force will land today at Hellenikon Airport. The C-141 Star Lifter is bringing 37 members of the U.S. War College to Athens. The C-141 troop carrier is the first to use jet propulsion and is a virtual colossus, capable of carrying 140 persons. This figure does not include its eight-member crew. It has four jet engines and is able to attain a speed of up to 880 kilometers. It is 48 meters long, longer than the distance covered by the Wright brothers on their first flight.*

To my dear cousins Kleomenis Andreades, primary school teacher, and Miss Mary P. Iviropoulou, kindergarten teacher, who exchanged vows to be married, I wish a speedy wedding.

Ioannis Vayias

Dear Mrs. Mina—

I am 19 years old and have a problem with my father. I have no mother and have been living with my aunts since I was 2 years old. As far as I can remember, my life with them was happy. The same holds true today. From time to time my father considered asking for me back, but his financial affairs were less than flourishing. He had a one-room apartment and of course I could not stay there with him. Now that I am out of school I wanted to go twice a week to look after him. He lives in the center of Athens, Heroes' Square (Psyrri), but I never had his exact address. I finally managed to find it out through an acquaintance of ours, a lady—who only gave it to me after a lot of coaxing from me—and I went there. He received me coolly, not exactly coolly but not like a father, either. He said let's discuss this. I sat down next to him. And he told me that I was now old enough not to need my aunts anymore and that the best thing for me would be to say good-bye to them and go and live with him. Of course, his proposal upset me. It wasn't exactly easy for them to raise me to be the 19-year-old girl I am. And during all those years he had only contributed 100 drachmas a month, although he collected 300 drachmas a month for me from the Social Security office. I told him that and then he began in a roundabout way to make accusations against my aunts. Finally he told me that I am not his child and that my mother was a "licensed" prostitute. I got angry and slammed the door and left. The next day they telephoned me from the local police station. My father had asked me to appear in front of the officer on duty. There I learned that my father had quite a lot of property and that contractors had been hired to construct apartment buildings on this property, to be ready in March 1968 at a cost of 4 million drachmas. If I went to live with him, he would transfer ownership of them to me; if not, he would disinherit me. I said I was not interested. I said I would gladly go to his house twice a week to look after him. But that I wouldn't live with him. And let's say I did go, where would I sleep? I left the police station and the same nonsense went on for three more weeks. His constant pressure on me to move in with him made me into a nervous wreck. I'm on pills—Bellergal, Valium 2—three to four pills a day. And as if all that weren't enough, he had me summoned to the Central Security Police headquarters to prove to me that my mother had a prostitute's "license." Of course, they found no such thing and I was furious. I told him we would go to every police station in town to check this out and that if there was nothing against her, and I was 100 percent sure there wouldn't be anything, that I would sue him for defaming the character of a dead person. That more or less calmed him down and he has not bothered me for a month. I hope things don't go any further. I would like to know from you whether I behaved correctly and how I should behave in the future. I am writing you from the country; I'm staying here with my aunts. I will be back in Athens at the beginning of October. Please, I beg you, write to me if you can. If not, telephone me at 718-793 so that we can meet. Any place. I could also come to your radio station.

With thanks,

Estrelita

P.S. He bases his suspicions that I am not his child on my facial characteristics. I have green eyes. He is dark-haired. And so is my mother, in the photographs. But if he believes that I'm not his child, why does he want me to come and live with him in a one room apartment? He's 45 years old.

JUNE 9. *According to a statement issued by the Panhellenic Confederation of Farm Produce Growers, the government measures on wheat policy announced yesterday are unsatisfactory because a large number of small producers are still unprotected and because individual farmers with small lots are also excluded from such protection by being treated as large businesses.*

Moreover, when Mr. P. Kanellopoulos, head of the National Radical Union (ERE), was asked by reporters whether the "recall" of minister Mr. D. Vourdoumbas from Mr. Stephanopoulos's cabinet was related to the wheat issue, he avoided giving a direct answer, stating, "We may have withdrawn Mr. Vourdoumbas, but we have not withdrawn our confidence in him."

TYPALDOS COASTAL SHIPPING

Lines for the interior:

m/s Angelika: *Every Monday, Wednesday, Friday, 6:00 P.M., for Chios-Mytilene.*

m/s Kriti: *Every Saturday, 6:00 P.M., for Kythnos, Seriphos, Siphnos, Kimolos, Milos.*

m/s Lemnos: *Every Thursday, 11:00 A.M., for Syros, Paros, Naxos, Apollonia, Donousa, Aigiale, Kouphonisia, Schoinousa.*

m/s Aegeon: *Every Tuesday and Saturday, 12:00 noon, for Paros, Naxos, Kalymnos, Kos, Rhodes.*

All routes: Same ports of call on all return trips.

THESSALONIKI, JUNE 17. *From our correspondent. The brazen fetishist and Peeping Tom who, at about 11:00 A.M. the day before yesterday, caused such a disturbance among the tenants of the old apartment building on Karaïskaki Street near the School for the Blind is still at large. There is information to the effect that two female students at the Midwives' School had taken the bus home, and as one of them stood in the kitchen preparing lunch, she was suddenly frightened by the sight of a strange man's head in the window, staring at her and moaning. The young woman cried out for help and, having mistaken the Peeping Tom for a "Lover's Lane" killer, passed out. Her sister and their two brothers, with whom they shared the apartment, rushed into the kitchen, awakened by the cries. The stranger, however, had disappeared. The young woman, having come to in the meantime, related the whole incident to them. Her two brothers ran out into the courtyard in search of the pervert, but to no avail. Instead they found two undergarments belonging to one of the sisters that had been removed from the clothesline where they were hanging and on which our sick Peeping Tom had consumed his passion.*

Later in the day, one of the young ladies' brothers made an official report of the incident to the Central Security Police. Investigations are underway to discover the identity of this pervert.

Dear Mrs. Mina—

I have a little boy 8 years old from my first marriage—I'm divorced. I am now remarried. My second husband loves my little
boy a lot. As for my first husband, I will spare you the details. He's
not the slightest bit interested in anything. My problem is the following: I am pregnant, in my fifth month. What I am afraid of is
that my husband might stop loving and caring for my boy. And
also that my little boy might start feeling jealous due to the arrival
in our house of the new baby, which we are expecting in a few
months' time. How should we handle things, both myself and my
husband, in this case?

Best regards,

Ioanna P.

AUGUST 15. *Following the summer break after the end of the last soccer season, today is the first of five decisive days for the Panathenaïkos Athletic Club (PAO), during which time the Yugoslav coach Mr. Bobek will be arriving from his country, the training period of the team will begin, and, more importantly, decisions will be made concerning the fate of those players whose acts of insubordination were so widely publicized. More specifically, Mr. Bobek, who will be returning from his country by car, will be at Kamena Vourla this afternoon. Soccer players Sourpis, Domazos, and Oikonomopoulos will arrive earlier to greet their coach, at the head of a large number of PAO fans who are expected to arrive there by chartered buses for the same purpose. Later in the afternoon they will all drive to Athens in formation.*

Dear Mrs. Mina—

I am 17 years old and have been going with a boy my age, a class-mate from school. We liked each other from the first moment. I let him see everything in my heart, just as it was, and offered him all its treasures. I let him know how much I needed him. He was happy that he was the first man in my life. But he quickly got tired of my being so naïve and asked to break up, saying he was bored with me because I am a child. During our relationship another man, age 23, an architect, began taking a marked interest in me. When he graduated from the Polytechnic School and went into the army, he never stopped writing me letters and declaring his love in a variety of ways. But I always hurt his feelings by my indiffer-ence. My mother, who knew about the architect, told me he would make a good husband for me and that I should try to like him. Under her influence, I began writing to him and encouraging him. In reality, however, I am still suffering because my "first love" con-tinues to be uppermost in my thoughts. My problem is the follow-ing: How should I act toward the architect? He loves me, I'm sure of it. My own best interest tells me I will be happy with him. Is it right for me, when I don't care about him, to pretend that I do? What do you think? Is there a chance I will come to love him? Is there any hope?

With my heartfelt thanks and greetings,

Gilda

NOVEMBER 3. *The Holy Synod of the Church of Greece, during its meeting yesterday, examined the cumulative inquest record of Athanasia Kriketou, a visionary also known as the Aigaleo Saint, and concluded the following: It is a case of a very clever charlatan who, completely lacking in spirituality, pretends to be talking to the Virgin and receiving revelations from God. She is a psychoneurotic suffering from obvious religious delusions, calling herself "the light of the world," preaching that those who believe in her will have their sins forgiven, and threatening unbelievers with hell and the like. She exhibits intense "dermatosis," a well-known ailment in pathology, and she deceives and exploits the religious sentiments of gullible Christians. She preys on the entire region of Attica. She has accumulated large sums of money and maintains an affluent lifestyle in the company of her blinkered followers. As a result, she has become a stumbling block for any right-thinking Christian. In order to protect Christians from Athanasia Kriketou's charlatanism, the Holy Synod has decided to bring her records to the attention of the court in authority with the request that the provisions of the law as it stands be upheld and that the scandalous activities of the Aigaleo charlatan be brought to an end.*

My dear Mrs. Mina—

My greetings and thanks for your speedy response to my urgent questions. Of course you may not remember what I wrote you; still, I must tell you that your advice, even though it was not needed—and you will see why—was very sound and to the point. I confess that even I never expected things to turn out this way. To fill you in briefly, I will remind you again what my problem was. I was going to get married, but my fiancé's personality was completely unsuited to mine. He had changed my life for the worse and I felt unhappy, bitter, and fearful. I had become listless and unenthusiastic, just another "Pale Poppy." I was like a wind-up doll to him, obeying his every wish, whether it was for the good or not. It was then that I desperately asked for your help and you did help me with your advice, although it came a little late. As you told me then, you felt sorry for me being in such a relationship. That's when I put my foot down. I spoke to him gently, I really tried, and in a nice way I let him know that he could change if he wanted to. I told him both nicely and (why not) threateningly that I was tired of being around him. I began at that time, without realizing it, to free myself from the bonds of fear. I grew strong—who says you're any better than me? That's how much I rebelled, in a certain sense. What's more, because I'm rather cute and everything, I broke down his resistance. He was really shaken up and began to straighten out. I told him, if you want to continue, you'll have to choose between your nasty behavior and me. And a miracle occurred. Now he is kind, attentive, he treats me nice, and all the things which made him so unbearable have disappeared. But now, Mrs. Mina, there is something else—it's me. And once again you have to help me. I said above that I didn't need your advice, not meaning to insult you, of course. And now I really need to hear your wise and useful words. I don't want to tire you so I'll come right to the point. Well, all this time it's been so tiring, I think something has died inside me. I'm worried. I don't love him like I did before, something's changed and he knows it too. I often feel bored around him and want to get away. Tell me, is this something passing or is it just my nerves? Help me once again, help this "Pale Poppy"—I use the same pen name. I don't know what to do to feel the same with him as before and I'm upset about all this, and I think I can't go on with him. You will say I'm spoiled, because now that I got what I wanted, I'm tired of it. I don't know, Mrs. Mina, the only thing I know is that I'm really sick of it. And I'm bored. I anxiously await your advice, always so good. I thank you very much. I sincerely mean it when I write you that I respect and love you. Also, please convey my warm greetings to the director in charge of your wonderful program.

An old, true friend and admirer

Pale Poppy

NAUPAKTOS, DECEMBER 29. *From our correspondent. On the third of next month Vasiliki (widow of D.) Voskines, 29, and Diamantis G. Matas, 72, will be tried here in town in Criminal Court, the former on charges of homicide with intent, the latter for moral complicity. On November 5, 1959, Vasiliki Voskines, using a hunting rifle, shot and killed her husband Dimitrios, at the instigation of her elderly lover and codefendant.*

As was revealed at the inquest, the two defendants have carried on a relationship for the past 14 years, a relationship which also happens to be incestuous (Matas is Voskines's mother's first cousin).

In other news, on the 20th of this month, the Preveza Criminal Court will be hearing the case of K. D. Soutis, 25, from Samoti, accused of raping 70-year-old Theodora (wife of Michaïl) Panarites.

———

ROYAL COURT, DECEMBER 28, 1966. *In the presence of H.M. the King and of the Prime Minister, Mr. J. Paraskevopoulos, His Grace the Bishop of Kernitsa, Msgr. Chrysostomos, swore in Mr. K. Chourdakis as undersecretary of national defense. From the Office of the King's Chamberlain.*

Iosif Belekos
Manhattan Hospital
New York, New York
U. S. A.

January 4, 1967

To: The Department of Emigration from Europe, No. 1 Sophokleous Street, 3rd floor, room 14, tel. 523-525

I kindly ask the above organization how I can return to Athens.

Iosif Belekos

Athens, Greece

JANUARY 7. *The Feast of the Hallowing of the Waters was celebrated yesterday with particular solemnity in the presence of H.M. the King, the Prime Minister, and government officials, the highest command of the Armed Forces, the diplomatic corps, and municipal authorities. The King, in admiral's uniform, arrived at the site of the ceremony in a car with a transparent top and became the object of fervent acclamations by thousands of people. As soon as the King took his place on the large platform that had been set up in the space fronting the Harbor Clock, with Prime Minister Mr. J. Paraskevopoulos on his right, the service began, officiated by the Most Reverend Metropolitan of Piraeus, Msgr. Chrysostomos, who also tossed the crucifix in the water amid sounds of ships' sirens and the ringing of church bells.*

———

Middle-aged gentleman, Law School graduate without license seeks employment as in-house attorney's assistant. Promises growth in clientele. Telephone 451-360, afternoon hrs.

Dear Mrs. Mina—

I always listen to the good advice you give out, which is why I decided to write to you about my life, too. So let me start right off with the pen name "Flower of Thessaly."

Mrs. Mina, I am, without exaggeration, a pretty girl and a kindhearted, sensible girl. But it's been my luck to have nothing but setbacks. I had a love affair when I was 15 and after we split up he left to go abroad. Then I got involved with someone else, broke up with him too, and continued going out with other people. Now I'm all alone like a leaf in the wind. Everything I loved, I lost. I am tired of my life, Mrs. Mina, because not one of my boyfriends ever came to ask my parents for my hand. They lied to me. And I feel so let down and so angry too. You can't imagine what I've suffered and how hard it's been. I mean, really, what have I done to deserve all this? I have finally started dating someone who wants us to keep going out but I don't believe in words any more, only in actions. We write to each other and he says that we can meet whenever and wherever I want. But the village where I live is a very tight-knit community and there is talk about me. And I can't get away from my parents very easily. Also, someone else I knew from before who I'd gone out with just once turned up and has been asking me to start going out again.

Mrs. Mina, how will it all end the way things are going, and how will I find the right person for me? I want you to give me some advice because I've been through a lot and I'll do whatever I need to do. And then there's the problem of my parents, they keep me under close watch and won't let me see anyone. My mother says that none of the boys I dated asked to marry me, and the same will happen now. And I am completely disillusioned.

Mrs. Mina, I hope you will answer me soon and can give me a good solution.

Many thanks,

Flower of Thessaly

FEBRUARY 15. *A new "tax" will be levied on hundreds of thousands of residents of Athens and Piraeus who use the trolley or the bus for transportation. The Electrical Transportation Company announced its decision to raise trolley fares by 20 lepta for the Kypseli, Patisia, Ampelokipoi, Pangrati, and Kallithea routes, as well as for the Electrical Subway Depot, Kastella, and Neo Phalero routes. This sudden increase in trolley fares will be followed, according to all indications, by an increase in bus fares, for bus proprietors invariably follow on the heels of the ever-insatiable Electrical Transportation Company.*

———

LAMIA, FEBRUARY 19. *From our correspondent. Nikolaos Manikas, 59, a resident of Ampelos, Phthiotis, while working on the roof of his barn, was swept away, along with a piece of metal sheeting, by a gust of wind over a distance of about 70 meters, resulting in his death. Before crashing, surprised by his unexpected and fatal leap, he shouted, "I'm flying, I'm flying."*

Dear Mrs. Mina—

I am 17 years old. Nine months ago I met a young man of 22 who was in the service. The young man is a neighbor of ours. One day he took me aside and confided to me that he loved me, and that if I wanted he would come and ask my parents for my hand, after completing his military service, where he had only 5 months left. Our relationship lasted four months. In the meantime I had not felt anything for him but just plain friendship. During those months I never gave him a positive answer, that is to say, a yes or a no. We went out as friends and not as lovers. Finally, after much thought, my heart spoke and told me to say yes, because I had begun to love him. This happened very slowly, without my realizing it. I fell in love with him because of his good character and the sensible things he said. It was obvious that he was not trying to lead me on. I felt certain of that because of his behavior toward me. He was affectionate with me and I wanted affection above all else, which I never got from my parents. Oh, I forgot to tell you that my parents did not treat me well at all. They used to beat me, and they still do, brutally. He welcomed my answer with unspeakable joy. But a girlfriend of mine advised me to tell my parents about it too, and because I knew how reasonable she was, I told my mother. My mother listened to me and was very understanding. But I made a terrible mistake. When I heard his brother's car outside our house—we're neighbors, you see—I went outside and told him: Tell your brother, now that he's in the service, to come and exchange vows. And when he gets out, we can get engaged. He knew about our relationship and answered that there was nothing to stop us. When my sweetheart came to spend the weekend with me and I saw him he was very angry with me. Why did you do that, why did you go outside and talk to my brother, and at eleven o'clock at night no less? he said. We had it all arranged between the two of us. And I answered him angrily: Why shouldn't I have told him, since they were going to find out about it someday? Without saying a word, he fixed a date to see me. I begged him to cancel the date because now that my mother knew about it she wouldn't let me out of the house. But he insisted and I said yes. When I told my mother about it she got very angry and threatened that if I didn't tell my father about it she'd tell him herself at once. So I was forced to tell my father everything. At first he listened to me without speaking, but when I had told him everything he took off his belt and began beating me without pity, mercilessly and brutally. Then he went to find the young man and his parents. But the young man wasn't at home and his brother spoke for him. He told him not to shout and that his family knew about our relationship and had good intentions. It has been five months since then. I am living in torment. I can hardly eat, I don't talk to anyone, and I stay locked in my room. When I go out on my veranda he comes out too, he's out of the service now. He looks at me with a sad look, as if to say, why did you do that, when you knew I loved you? He stays there for hours, until late at night, chain-smoking. Every once in a while he smiles at me, I think, as though he were trying to say, take heart. A friend of my mother's, seeing me sad all the time, keeps telling me: What can we do, poor girl? Well, I suppose I'll have to go and tell him that you love him, so as to break the ice between you so you can start all over again. Mrs. Mina, what do you advise me to do? No matter what, don't tell me to forget about him, that's impossible. If I find out he doesn't love me I'll put an end to my life. I don't want you to make light of what I'm writing you because I am capable of doing it. I am up a blind alley. Please reach out your hand and help me out of it.

All my love to you,

Appaloosa

MARCH 12. *A number of photographs from the Adults Only* movie Five Women in Heat *posted outside the Pantheon Theater were deemed indecent. The person in charge of the theater was arrested and sentenced to four months in jail by the Summary Misdemeanors Court.*

March 18, 1967

I received your reply and the information I asked for. Thanks for the help but as for your advice about emigrating to Australia, it's not for me. Not right now. Nothing further.

The interested party:

Dionysios Komborozos

MARCH 20. *Due to declining health, the philanthropist Mr. Adamantios Karamourtzounes was admitted on Friday, the day before yesterday, as an emergency patient at the clinic of Dr. Bandouvas. Mr. Karamourtzounes has been ill for the last two months but, in spite of his doctor's advice that he get some rest, he continued working and even intensified his efforts to help needy patients go abroad.*

MARCH 21. *The "Beirut-Tangiers Chorus-Girl Trade" Affair: The trial of 36-year-old Dimitra Arvanitaki before the three-member Misdemeanors Court in Athens ended yesterday in her being sentenced to 14 months' imprisonment. She was charged with "procuring and deceitfully inciting people to emigrate," while the four "artistes" Nikolitsa, Evangelia, Agape, and Theodora, who were indicted for violating Royal Decree No. 195/9/3/1958, prohibiting the emigration of artists to countries in the Near East and North Africa, were acquitted.*

The "rose ballets" about to be sent to Cyprus for "artistic engagements" and subsequently farmed out to white slave markets in North Africa were broken up. This "merchandise" never arrived at its destination.

Nikaia, March 23, 1967

Dear Mrs. Mina—

I am 15 years old. I have finished elementary school. I went to junior high school and did one year but flunked out of my second year. I went back, didn't pass Physics and Mathematics, and again was put back. It is now impossible for me, a girl 5'8" tall, to go back into the Seventh Grade, for the third year in a row. What I mean is, I don't know how to say it, I feel embarrassed. My mother and my father tell me I should become a seamstress or a hairdresser but I'm not interested in such things. I want to become a designer but I heard that they require a Junior High School diploma for that. Is that true? Or, at least, can you find me something else better suited to me and which I could do in a few years—three or four—so as to earn a living by working with my hands? I would like you to explain a few things to me, like, for example, that to do this you need this and to do that you need that.

With my greetings and respect,

M.P.

Dear Mrs. Mina—

Once I wrote you about my problem and you told me over your lovely program to write you again and be more specific. I made a mistake and my father went to my sweetheart's house and yelled at him. Since then I have been very unhappy. Unlike my father, who is incapable of understanding, my mother has stood by me like an angel during the difficult time I was and still am having. Mrs. Mina, the same day I sent you that first letter, a few hours later, I saw my sweetheart with another woman. I was with my mother. When I saw him I fainted. But he, too, when he saw me, hung his head down in shame. After that, every time we ran into each other in the street he would stop and try to talk to me but I would act indifferent. Even though it hurt me, because my pride had been wounded. Now I regret having done that, I mean avoiding him. You answered me that I should either send him a letter telling him I had had a change of heart or have my girlfriend talk to him. In fact, my girlfriend is friendly with his family. But the problem, Mrs. Mina, is whether he will agree to talk since he is now involved with someone else. Mrs. Mina, because my mother is also unhappy with my father, she doesn't want me to have to go through what she went through too. Which is why she told me to write you, and tell you for her that she is on my side. And if there is anything that is in her power to do, she is determined to do it. She told me to write you and ask you to answer us as to what she herself can do to help make me happy. And also, how she should deal with the situation in the event that my father doesn't go along with us? Mrs. Mina, help me to get through this difficult situation, so that it has a nice, happy ending.

My love to you,

Appaloosa

P.S. I am anxiously awaiting your reply. If it is convenient, send it in writing. Here is my address:

Rania Hydra

29 Mitropolitou Tyrolois St., Volos

I enclose a stamp for your answer.

ROYAL COURT, MARCH 31, 1967. *H.M. the King received Prime Minister Mr. I. Paraskevopoulos, who submitted the resignation of his government.*
In the afternoon, H.M. the King received the head of the Center Union Party, Mr. G. Papandreou.
In the afternoon, H.M. the King received the head of the Greek Radical Union (ERE,) Mr. P. Kanellopoulos.
By high command, H.M. the King's Chamberlain went to Hellenikon Airport to convey His Majesty's greetings to H.E. the Indonesian president, Mr. Soekarno, who arrived in Athens today.
From the Office of the King's Chamberlain.

APRIL 21. *Patriots and arts lovers packed the Orpheus Theater yesterday as drama teacher Mrs. Zanantri's theater group, Poetic Art, gave a performance celebrating the anniversary of the National Rebirth. It was a moving performance, both for the artists on stage and the distinguished audience alike, given the fact that every new work created by this brilliant poet and writer has captivated the public for many years. A huge tableau depicting the historical events of the year 1821, framed by silver-plated artificial laurel leaves with two white-and-blue standards on each side, was the only decor on the stage and set the mood of grandeur for this solemn occasion.*

Oresteias, April 24, 1967

APPLICATION

To DEME: I kindly request you to send me the regulations according to which I may be absent from Greece.
Comments:

    a. How do I go if married?
    b. How do I go if single?

The applicant,
Demosthenes Mylonas

IOANNINA, APRIL 26. *From our correspondent. Despite continued good weather these days in and around our city, temperatures remain low for this time of year due to snowfall on the Pindos, Mourgana, and Nemertsika mountains.*

A pack of wolves decimated 10 cows and 17 sheep and goats belonging to cattle farmers in the area of Gyromerion, Philiates.

ROYAL COURT, APRIL 26, 1967. *In the presence of the King and of Prime Minister Mr. K. Kolias, the Most Reverend Bishop of Kernitsa, Msgr. Chrysostomos, swore into office Messrs. I. Tsantilas as minister of transportation, Spyros Lizardos as minister of finance, and G. Georgakopoulos as undersecretary of commerce.*

In the afternoon H.M. the King attended a meeting of the Ministerial Council.

The King and the Queen, Queen Mother Frederika, and Princess Irene attended the Holy Week Vespers of Christ the Bridegroom at the Tatoï Palace Chapel.

From the Office of the King's Chamberlain.

Dear Mrs. Mina—

I have listened to you so many times on your show *The Woman's Hour* giving advice to friends seeking your help. And there have been many times when I understood from the answers you gave to their letters just how useful they must be.

Mrs. Mina, I cannot find a way for myself out of the dilemma I am now in. So I decided to ask for your help. I am certain that your experience will help me to find my way again. I have been involved for a year and a half now with a young man who works in our village. I am 19 and he is 25 (years old). Until a few months ago everything was going fine. I loved him and he loved me just as much. But now he has changed. And while I thought I knew him well, I now see in his face a completely different person. During the whole time we were involved I often asked him to get engaged, if only to put a stop to all the gossip about us. I must admit that whenever I talked to him about getting engaged, his mood would quickly change and he would always make the same excuse to me. That he had responsibilities to his family, to first marry off his sister, and that if I loved him I shouldn't pay any attention to what people said. I was patient and I waited. Until a few months ago, when another girl joined our crowd. She is from our village but she was away for a long time and now that she is back she is openly flirting, right in front of me, with my sweetheart. When I made some remark to her she said it was he who had first asked her to start going out. Then I made a decision, Mrs. Mina, and I sat down and wrote him a letter asking him to please make his position clear. Whether he loved me or the other girl. If he didn't love me he should tell me so. When he got my letter he came and found me. Do you know, Mrs. Mina, what he said? That it was all my fault. If I wanted him to love me I shouldn't talk about our future at all. It's up to him, he said, when to make up his mind. After that he started the same thing all over again. Sometimes he says he loves me and sometimes he won't even turn to look at me. And in fact he often says he doesn't know me, in front of my girlfriends. I am certain that if we go on like this much longer it will kill all my feelings and that will make me hate men. I was the most proper girl in the village and everyone liked me. I never gave anyone any reason to say anything bad about me. I had a lot of boys flirting with me but I never trusted any of them or fell in love. The only one I loved was him and I was capable of doing almost anything for his sake. Oh, Mrs. Mina, is it possible for him to love me and not to want to hear anything about getting engaged? Is it possible for him to flirt right in front of me with one of my girlfriends and at the same time stare at me intently? Can he possibly love two of us? And if so what should I do? Should I leave him? But I love him, Mrs. Mina. And if I stay, won't every day be like killing off my feelings one by one? Help me before it is too late, Mrs. Mina.

Desperate Dolce Vita

P.S. I didn't write you that he is a technician and quite well off. I'm an embroiderer, I'm not well off but I'm not poor either.

MAY 10. *During today's meeting, the Holy Synod unani-mously voted the following: (1) To bless and congratulate the National Government on having undertaken the governance of this country. (2) To convey, through two Synod members, its wishes for a speedy recovery to His Blessed Holiness, the ailing Msgr. Chrysostomos, Archbishop of Athens. (3) To ex-press in writing its solidarity with the reverend metropolitans whose areas were so severely damaged during the recent earth-quakes and to take up a collection in every church of the country, the proceeds of which will be sent to the earthquake victims. Also that the reverend priests set aside a comparable amount from their monthly stipend for this purpose. (4) To set aside the amount of 100,000 drs. from a Clerical Funds Administration account for the same purpose. (5) To issue a circular to the reverend priests urging them to contribute in any way they can to the most magnificent celebration of Re-serves Day.*

———

HELP NEEDED: *Housekeeper from islands, 40–45, with experience and references, all household chores, for three persons. Monthly salary 3,000 drs. Fully electric home. Telephone 716.463, 10 A.M. to 2 P.M.*

Dear Mrs. Mina—

Forgive me for bothering you again. This is the third and last letter
I am sending you. I did as you suggested. I didn't send him a letter,
but I went and talked to him in person. A good friend of my
mother's told me not to tell him that I panicked and told everything to my parents and to say that it all happened in spite of me,
that is, without my knowing anything. About my father going to
their house, etc. I am writing you the conversation we had:

—Hi, G. I came to ask you to clear something up for me. And
to answer a question I am going to put to you.

—Ask me whatever you want and I will answer.

—Did my father come to your house and yell at you?

—Yes.

—Do you know that I knew nothing and only found out today from a few words my mother let slip?

—How is it possible that it wasn't you who told them, and if
not, then who did?

—A girlfriend. We had an argument and she got back at me
by telling everything to my parents.

—Great, so what do you want from me now?

—I came to tell you that I wasn't the cause of our separation.

—Well, if you knew nothing, how come you didn't come and
talk to me all this time?

—Didn't I try telephoning you, but they always said you
weren't home?

—How could they have told me about my other phone calls
and not say a word about yours?

—Only the people who took my phone calls know the
answer.

—And how can I be sure it was you and not someone else?

—Of course, since I'm not the only woman in your life.

—I told you that I don't have just one girlfriend but two or
three. Now will you tell me what you want with me?

—I want to ask you if we can start over again from the
beginning.

—After all that's happened, how can we find the courage to start over?

—I have the strength, I don't know if you do.

— Okay, let's say we start over. Won't your father do the same thing again, making a spectacle of us all in front of the whole neighborhood?

—You can't tell, only time will tell.

—All right. I'll answer you in two days.

When the day came, Mrs. Mina, he didn't go in from their balcony even for a second. He kept looking at me, intently, lost in thought. In the evening when we met, I said to him:

—Did you think it over?

—Yes.

—And what did you decide?

—That we should stop things here. Forget me, as I will try and forget you.

—You mean I have to pay for my father's mistake?

—And who do you think should pay for it: Giorgos? We can't go on. If anyone sees you and tells your parents, you know what will happen. And, anyway, you're from a good family. What do you want with a bum like me? (That's what my father called him).

—So is it my father's opinion of you that counts or mine?

—When I'm being accused everyone's opinion counts. So, we have nothing else to say. Good-bye.

— Good-bye. I wish you luck.

He smiled and waited until I turned the corner.

Mrs. Mina, I still have one hope, that perhaps in this way he was trying to test the strength of my love. He can't be such a hypocrite as to have spent the whole evening so lost in thought. He can't have been wearing a mask. Please send me your answer in writing. What else should I do?

Appaloosa

NEW YORK, MAY 23. *Reuters. Mr. Teddy Teenling, the British designer of tennis fashions who was the first to promote lace underwear for women players at the Wimbledon championship, firmly ruled out topless styles for tennis yesterday. "I am afraid," he stated, "that young women will not feel comfortable playing bare-breasted and their game will suffer as a result. We will therefore use tops with lace necklines, which create the same effect and are much more exciting." Mr. Teenling, introducing the new line of tennis wear at a press conference, wore a white suit with a double-breasted jacket and gold buttons, a red shirt, and a red and white polka-dot tie.*

Mr. Teenling, who is 60, explained that the new tennis apparel is sexy but practical. He gained notoriety in the fashion world when Gussy Moran showed up at Wimbledon wearing lace panties.

-----

14 DAYS TO AUSTRALIA

On the newly built 28,000-ton Ocean Liner
GULLIELMO MARCONI

June 10 Departure from Piraeus
for
FREEMANTLE—MELBOURNE—SYDNEY

Tickets and Information
at Travel Agencies and Emigration Offices

THE HELLENIC AGENCY, LTD.,
47 MIAOULI WHARF.

Dear Mrs. Mina—

My parents made me marry someone whom I neither liked nor disliked. I agreed because he was a very nice boy, even though he comes from a slightly lower-class home than ours. In the end it turned out that my husband was also morally inferior to me. I know, Mrs. Mina, that you will think I'm stuck up and very selfish when you read the things I will write. But I'm not. Let me tell you a few things they say about me: "If you told me that you were from a good family, that you didn't come from a village, and that you had graduated from junior high school, I would believe you." As you can understand, just the opposite has been happening. From the first day I married, I saw what a humble life I would be leading, and I got a job immediately. It is six years since then and we have two girls, ages four-and-a-half and eight months. We're doing well, Mrs. Mina, in our jobs. We are both factory workers, and with some cash I received as a dowry we own a two-story house today. Everyone sees us as a well-matched, happy couple. Only I know how much difference there is between us, especially in spirit. Unlike me, he has nothing nice to say about anyone. And I don't care so much what he says about other people as about my own family. My parents live very far away and whenever they come for a few days, they always leave feeling bad, having understood that he doesn't want them around. And the same thing happened with his mother once when she came to see us. You don't know how hurt I get by his words, by his low-class swear words. The first few years I used to lock myself up and cry, cursing the fate that brought him to me. Now I have changed my tactics and I swear back at him and I have realized that it's better, because then he shuts his trap, as they say around here. But I am not happy with this state of affairs. I was hoping for a proper husband who would respect and appreciate me, as I do myself and other people. I should tell you, however, that he has no other faults. Now you will be wondering how we are raising our children with both of us working. We work separate shifts, first one of us and then the other. And I decided to write you last night when I got home tired at ten o'clock and he started screaming at the baby for crying and not letting him sleep. He said he didn't love it because it took after me and my mother, and he threatened to kill it. But I have to tell you something else. After saying all that the night before, in the morning he told me to go and pick out a washing machine that he had arranged to pay for. That's how he always acts, as though nothing has happened. I often put aside my anger and forget about it all. But this time it will take me days to get over it, and I believe that if I didn't have my village upbringing, worrying about what people will say, we would have separated. We live in an industrial town near Athens. He lived here before we were married, for eight years. But he hasn't become more civilized in anything. He lived alone. These are the things I wanted to write you, Mrs. Mina. Things I can't say even to my mother because I am afraid of sending her to her grave unhappy. I thank you in advance for the reply you will give me. Tell me your opinion about all of this, if my thinking is correct or not. I will accept and adhere to your advice. Let me tell you what we look like. He is kind of sad and grumpy. I am the opposite, strong-willed and determined in life. But I didn't pick a person able to understand me. I try not to let all this go on in front of our eldest daughter, who understands everything. And after all that, he says he loves me, that it's just the way he is. And if I don't like it I can ask for a divorce,

Greetings to you,

Your listener K.E.

JUNE 18. *Eight hundred detainees on the island of Gyaros arrived yesterday in Piraeus. The Ministers of the Interior and Public Order stated, in answer to questions by journalists on this occasion, that the number of detainees discharged from Gyaros has now reached 3,300 out of a total of 6,130 political prisoners. Therefore only about 2,800 persons are still in detention. The two ministers stressed the fact that a large number of prisoners are also expected to be discharged soon. Moreover, when the Minister of the Interior was asked specifically about former M.P.'s in exile, he repeated the categorical statement that only 13 former M.P.'s are still being detained and that fewer than 20 others are awaiting trial in criminal matters. A number of them have engaged in antigovernment activities and systematically undermined the state machine using tactics of old-style, hard-line party politics. Three former M.P.'s should also be added to the above detainees because they have continued their political activities despite explicit injunctions under martial law.*

At the Panathenaïkos Stadium
Today August 3, 1967
the spellbinding international clash of giants

professional wrestler and Greek Man of Steel

SPYROS ARION

fights against the Russian Giant

GYORGY KORIENKO

in an all-out, life-or-death battle of giants

2nd match
Our legendary champion

THEODOROS MEGARITES

against

ATTILIO

3rd match
Two on Two
The Incredible

KARPOZILOS Jr.

and the Outstanding

KARYSTINOS

against

JOSEPH TANUSH (Arab)

and

KING KAY (English)

Stadium doors open 5:00 P.M.
Wrestling begins at 8:30 P.M.

To: DEME

Hello.

Can you please give me information for the subject of emigration? I am going to emigrate but I don't know what I should do or what qualifications to get. My first choice is Canada or Germany, and I would like to know everything in detail about these two countries.

If you want information about me, I am: Nikolaïdes, Plastiras; resident of Panagitsa, Edessa, Pella Prefecture; age 22; born 1945. I have fulfilled my military service obligations. I am a certified stone mason; I attended the Pyrgos Vasilisis Trade School at Agioi Anargyroi in Athens in 1961. Right now I am working as an assistant bulldozer operator at the Kastraki Hydroelectric Plant. Education: some elementary school, that's all, because I did not know my parents, they died for our country in 1947, and I have had to struggle all my life against poverty. This is why I want to put my trust in you and ask you to advise me, like your own child, what to do in this case? Is it better for me to stay here or go abroad, and which country would be best money-wise and culture-wise? All I'm sending you right now is this letter from me because I don't know if I need to send money. If I do, make a note of it on the schedule you send me so I know. Please answer me as soon as you can, quickly.

Greetings to you,

Plastiras

THESSALONIKI, OCTOBER 24. *From our correspondent. After combing the wooded eastern side of the Kedryllia Mountains all night long, three gendarme detachments discovered the hideout of the kidnappers of Gialta Isaakidou, a young woman from Mesagros, Langada. The kidnapper, Anastasios Madravilias, surrendered to the detachment while his accomplices, his brother Antonis and his friend Paschalis Païrides, escaped arrest. The kidnapped woman reported that the kidnapper "respected" her completely; she also appeared fully inclined to accept a marriage proposal from him.*

FOR SALE

Between Kalamos and Lavrion. Charming, prime seaside lots, planted with pine trees, from 5 to 500 acres. Our ownership. Clean titles. Contracts final. Easy payments. Antonopoulos, 5 Gladstonos St., tel. 631-012.

To my very dear Mrs. Mina—

My greetings. First of all, let me send you my love and my respect, and the same to your program director with his good sense of humor. You are all to be admired for your wonderful program, which has so many listeners tuning in, myself among them. Now I would like you to help me with some problems that have been on my mind for a long time without my being able to find a solution. I don't know how to begin, but as you will see it is about my character, which is so weak it's unacceptable. I am 24 years old and until now I spent my time having fun, flirting—harmlessly—and had a wonderful, happy life, without a thought for the future. I was very self-centered and sure of myself, I knew when boys liked me. I was rebellious too, with plenty of faults. But I'm honest, that's one good thing about me. Recently I got engaged to someone 11 years older than I, but he is quite nice, serious, has a good job and position, is well educated, because I have only done one year of junior high school, which is hardly anything. Anyone else in my place would be completely happy, because here in the village it is difficult for a girl to find someone with a job. This is what has happened with me. On top of this, my fiancé has very good prospects. He has a terrific car, which is a big temptation today for a woman. No, don't think the worst, that I'm after his car, etc. Because even though I am not very rich, I do have my dowry. And I have never lacked anything. My father, thank the Lord, makes a very good living. And something else, Mrs. Mina. I chose my fiancé, I mean we love each other, and he adores me. I am his queen, Mrs. Mina, I know that but . . . This "but" is something I can't explain. And what is this feeling that never lets me be happy? Now I am getting ready for the wedding, sewing myself dresses, fixing up our house, but . . . What is it that's keeping me from feeling happy? Then again I sometimes feel tired of this life. Sometimes I love him like crazy and sometimes I feel bored with him. Sometimes I get jealous of him, or I nag him. And the main thing is that very often I think of my old life, how wonderful it was compared to now and I miss it. I miss the time when I had fun without serious thoughts and actions. I know, you will call me scatter-brained, but I always liked change and I get bored very quickly, and the worst thing of all is how often I just say to his face: I'm tired of you and your seriousness. Or: You're so mature but me, I'm just not. And then I feel sorry for him, because he loves me and he is honest with me and he makes me feel guilty. Then I think about all he's done for me, all the gifts (gifts are proof of love). He treats me like his baby. Dresses, jewelry, never leaving me without cosmetics. Also, he rejected offers of arranged marriages from his own circle, and all for me. And I'm so ungrateful. Settling down like this has changed my life, Mrs. Mina, and me. And I still can't get used to the idea of having a family with the man I have chosen. And whom I love, really I do. And then the idea of being cooped up with a child to care for scares me. His job, I'll have to go away from my mother and so many other things . . . so many. They scare me and make me unhappy. What do I want, what do I need? I don't know. And our relationship is going from bad to worse, I'm always nagging at him, about every little thing. About the way he dresses (which I liked at first). And he puts up with it all. He understands that I've grown cold and often just pretend. That's awful, Mrs. Mina, it really is. I beg you to help me. You may say whatever I need and deserve to hear, as long as you can get me out of this difficult position. I will be waiting anxiously and I thank you in advance.

Summer Storm A.M.

DECEMBER 14. *The Revolutionary Committee has, by proc-*
lamation, and due to extraordinary developments which
threaten the established order and security of the state as well
as the King's unjustifiable failure to carry out his duties, ap-
pointed Lieutenant-General George Zoïtakis as Regent; he
was sworn in by Msgr. Ieronymos, the Archbishop of Athens
and All Greece, and has taken up his duties. The Regent sub-
sequently delegated the formation of a new government to
Artillery Colonel George Papadopoulos.

The Panhellenic Association of Families of Gendarmes Killed in Action wishes to inform you that the special performance of the play I'm Proud To Be Me, *by Theodoros Synadinos, scheduled for Sunday, January 14, 1968, at 10:30 A.M. at the Hadzichristos Theater, is postponed for reasons beyond our control. Please excuse us for the postponement of the above special performance. You will be notified when a new date has been set.*

Respectfully,

PAFGKA

Dragani, January 19, 1968

Please send me the supporting documents to enroll in your school. The interested person is me, Vaios Tsakirides, for my daughter Aroritsa, so she can emigrate to Australia. Because I have my son there too, who also attended your school.

I ask you please to send me the papers so we can fill them out.

Sincerely yours,

Vaios

Dragani Village, Paramythia, Thesprotia

As of tomorrow, February 8, 1968, Constitutional Amendments Nos. 8 and 9, covering loyalty and professional competency of both civil servants and state agency employees, as well as control of political partisanship at the expense of colleagues, are rescinded. There will be no extension of the validity of these two amendments. This decision by the Prime Minister of the National Government, concerning the right to a review of decisions on the basis of the above amendments, will continue to be in effect after February 28, as the Prime Minister's circular has indicated.

———

POLYKRITI SKOUFA

Excellent, licensed, Tarot Card reader accurately foretells past, present, and future. By appointment only. Tel. 722.178, 9–1 and 4–6.

Agioi Anargyroi, February 17, 1968

My dear Mrs. Mina—

I am fifteen years old. I have been engaged for a year. Before getting engaged I was in love with a young man for five whole years without his being aware of it. When I saw that nothing was going to come of it I began dating. I went out with all sorts of people. I met a 24-year-old man who loved me from the bottom of his heart. I too began to like him a little, even though I was still burning with passion for the other young man. I ended up getting engaged to the young man who loved me so much. Now a year has gone by and I am preparing for the wedding, which will take place in July. But recently I found out something very disturbing. The young man I was in love with before getting engaged also loved me but was afraid to tell me about it. You can understand what a dilemma I am in now. I am afraid that if I break up with the young man who loves me deeply, he might do something crazy. On the other hand my heart keeps telling me to go with the man I love. I don't know what to do. Please help me.

Torn between two loves

P.S. I forgot to tell you that the young man I was and still am so interested in is 18 years old. And he says that if I break off my engagement, he and I will get engaged.

Alpheiousa, April 5, 1968

To: His Excellency, the Prime Minister of the
National Government
Athens

We, farmers Alpheiousa community Ileia, following
life-saving announcement cancellation farming
debts, profoundly moved, raise voice in deep
gratitude, pray for Your health and wish Your
noble goals advancement Fatherland attained. Rest
assured glory of Greeks gratitude of farmers—until
recently so desperate—will forever follow you.

My dear nephew Kostakis,

It's been several days since I received your letter and I thank you for your kind thoughts. I did not reply immediately because Vivika was here for a month, and she must have given you our news, and added some of her own besides, no doubt, such as saying something about Nikos having taken the girl he plans to marry to Greece with him. I never believed a word of it, but people here are so impressionable they swallowed it all. Never mind. I was stupid and I got upset, but Nikos knew what he was doing. He met a nice girl and he is going to live his life as he sees fit. I haven't met her yet. I will visit them in July. They are not able to come because they work and go to school. As my brother-in-law and his wife have written me, she is a wonderful young woman. She writes to me in English and my nephews explain it to me. She is trying to learn Greek, and they will have a Greek wedding. I'm sure everything will work out just fine for them. Let's not forget that many Greek women, especially the ones from villages, are enough to horrify most Americans. We spoke to Vivika here about all the things we hadn't been able to tell her, but she seems to be having problems with her husband. We talked to her about you and said that she should come to see you and try and stay on good terms with you, because she is not to blame for what happened. The day before yesterday she wrote us that she did come to visit you, and that you have now made up. You should all be there for her, like brothers, Kostakis. Stand by her. Because the other ladies, Ioanna and Sonia, are against her. If you believe that the things they're saying about her husband are true, then help her. Not by giving her money, she doesn't need any because her father left her some, but with advice and with love. As for him, someone should really go and talk to him. She may be a little simpleminded, but she loves her father's side of the family. She has a kind heart, and Vasilis should help her, I mean medically, too. During the five weeks she was here she was so tense she couldn't sleep. Her husband wrote to her every day, and that made us realize that he's a good man. And it really confused us. I kept saying maybe he's like that Giagoulogiannis who committed such terrible crimes but seemed so meek to everyone. And everybody laughs at me. Kostakis, write and tell me what you think. I will keep it in confidence and won't write a thing about it to her. But even if what your Sonia is saying about him is true, you shouldn't let her get a separation. Sonia is just imagining things. Aunt Marigo has sent you a few little presents through Vivika. Has she given them to you? A nightgown and a bathrobe for Kiki, some shirts for you and for Vasilis, some fabric from Rhodopi for your mother and some for Maria, and a few small dresses for Eleni's little girls, one slip each for Eleni and Maria, and two dark blue bedsheets with two pillowcases from the priest's wife. I wrote your mom before Vivika arrived, and she didn't answer. I don't have the time to write to her again, but writing to you is almost as good. It will be Easter soon and we'll be very busy with housecleaning, etc.

Greetings to everyone, and we wish you all Happy Easter. The Negroes here are in an uproar, because their leader was killed. Let's see what happens now.

Lots of love,

Aunt Argento

Kingdom of Greece
Municipality of Piraeus

ANNOUNCEMENT

To whom it may concern: the new style of tables and chairs on city squares and sidewalks will be as follows:

1. Eastern (Prophitis Ilias, Castella, etc.), Western (Kalavryta Square, Phreatys, Callipolis, Hadzikyriakeion), and Central sections, including the Electric Subway Station area:

a. Armchair-type chairs: White frame (plastic-coated), back rest, plastic webbing, white or tan; seat cushion, pastel color (according to taste), same colors for all chairs of any given establishment (but different for individual establishments).

b. Tables: White, plastic-coated tabletops, same color as seat cushions—50 cm. in diameter, 60 cm. in height.

2. Other sections of the city:

a. Standard-type chairs: White frame, Formica back and seat (optional), light color (not loud).

b. Tables: same as 1b (Difference: Height and diameter to be determined by owner of establishment), tabletop to match seat.

3. Restaurants and similar establishments:

a. Chairs: same as in 1 or 2 above, depending on location.

b. Tables: same as 1b; square, 80 cm. x 80 cm. in dimension; light colors, according to taste; tabletops to match seats in each establishment.

Samples of the type of chairs and tables described above are on display at the Municipality Building. For additional information: Piraeus City Hall, Makra Stoa 15, 4th floor, Dept. of Taxes, Fees, and Privileges, tel. 412-384.

> *In Piraeus, April 11, 1968*
> *The Mayor*
> *Aristides Stephanos Skylitses*

Katerini, May 7, 1968

Dear Miss,

I received your letter today informing me that I should come as specified to your offices on June 16 for a new medical examination so that I can emigrate to Australia. I would like you to know that the young man has changed his mind and, for this reason, my trip is canceled. The young man who had invited me there. So do not contact me again.

Respectfully,

Frederika Vasileiou

MILAN, MAY 13. *United Press. Princess Soraya, the former (and occasionally) sad-eyed empress of Persia, was immortalized by the irreverent lens of a devilish photographer as she was kissing a married man. This is a double, or rather a triple, scandal because the kiss took place at a swimming pool, where she was of course in inappropriate dress, or rather appropriate undress. It was revealed that the happy man—at least until the naked truth was revealed—is the well-known Italian movie producer Franco Indovina, who had encouraged the beautiful princess to go on the silver screen in the past. Indovina is married and has two daughters. The Milan magistrature has ordered the confiscation of the magazine* Gente, *which published the most impressive photograph of the 1968 summer season, with the caption (and afterthought): "Soraya's Kiss: Cool or Hot?"*

From The Regent's Household

ANNOUNCEMENT, JUNE 12, 1968

His Excellency the Regent, Lieutenant-General Mr. G. Zoïtakis, on board the warship Pyrpoletes, *carried out an inspection of the naval fleet sailing in the Saronic Gulf.*

Dearest Mina—

I am twenty-four, attractive, and well educated—in two months I
will be getting my B.A. degree. I come from a family of seamen.
Until three years ago I had a steady relationship, which began before I was 15 and ended unhappily when I was 21, after it had begun
to have something official about it and after we had begun sleeping
together. I say "something official" because our families knew
about it and we were going to get engaged. It was he who left me,
to get married. I was unhappy for a long, long time but I finally
came around. It was then that I got involved with a new young
man, age 28; he was very poor but was a good person with strong
morals. He had been taken out of the country as a child during the
so-called child-snatching years of the civil war, and grew up behind
the Iron Curtain. He was raised and educated accordingly, and
when he finished high school he was admitted to a university. In
March of 1966 he came back to this country and transferred to the
university here in order to continue his studies; he is studying
physics. However, because of his indigence, he has run into unbe-
lievable difficulties. His parents, who are old and come from a barren village in Florina, were also among those abducted and have
returned here with him. All this is very well documented. So you
understand, Mina. He works to make ends meet and, unfortunately, because he does not know the language well, he has difficulty with his studies. However, he is moving forward and nearing
completion, he needs two more years at most. When he was behind the Iron Curtain he had been in love, but she got married.
He never told me all the details. He behaves very decently toward
me, always taking into account what I want, but he rarely shows
me his feelings. And this is what causes me concern. I can say for
certain that my behavior toward him is perfect (concern, love, and
affection). I told him right from the start about my affair and we
never said another word about it. He is a man of integrity, but still
I do not feel completely sure of him. During the 14 months we
have been going together he has never once said "I love you." Nor
shown any feeling. Nor said a sweet word. And as for tender ges-

tures (like, for example, putting his arm around me when we're out together or stealing a kiss in a darkened movie theater), there are none. Of course, I've never asked him if he loves me. Because I would feel ridiculous at such a moment, since I really believe that he doesn't love me. He once told me: I only believe in tangible things; God and love are intangible. They don't exist. You can understand how I felt. I was insulted and began to cry. What was I anyway, some silly cow? And after he calmed me down I told him: You may not be able to touch love but you can feel it. And a person can get hurt when she feels indifference from someone she wants to give herself to. A few days later he gave me a gold bracelet. I have also given him many such presents. Of course, he still holds back his feelings and the sweet talk every woman is dying to hear. Now he's gone to his village for ten days and I miss him terribly. All his friends respect me and talk about me in a way that indicates that he considers our relationship to be one that is leading up to marriage. I can see that clearly. But two months ago he confessed to me that when he lived behind the Iron Curtain he had been hospitalized for a nervous breakdown. He did not tell me the cause, and out of consideration I did not ask. Could it have been his disappointment in love? Here, at any rate, when it is exam time, he gets very nervous and anxious about failing. When he does fail some test, I notice that he has a tendency to run away from things, to become very upset, to want to be alone and to have headaches. When he told me about all this, I cried right in front of him. He tried to make light of my being sad and started joking around. I told him: everything passes. We two will make everything right again. A week ago in his apartment—he has given me his key—I found his health booklet from the Iron Curtain country among his things. It contains information about his illness and treatment, but I can only make out a few words and I want to get it translated. I know this is not right, but I don't want to make him feel uncomfortable by asking. I am afraid he has some serious illness that can be passed on to his offspring. That is my story. I have completely forgotten about my other young man, even though we were very much in love and even though he was considered quite handsome. As for today's young man, his face still shows traces of the ordeal he went through, but I no longer pay attention to external qualities. I have matured. It is enough for me that he is an unusual person. I do miss, of course, those silly little things that lovers do to reassure each other. A tender kiss when one least expects it. A spontaneous caress, a special word, anything that will show his feelings for me. And not just when we are having sex. Sometimes I try, very discreetly, to get across to him exactly what it is I crave. Then he tries a little, and soon goes right back to his usual inexpressive self. Then he starts yelling: I may not be good with words, but can't you understand from my behavior? He thinks his behavior says it all. He has often expressed a desire, when he is finished, to go back to the place where he grew up. To see his friends. Also, he often makes fun of anything Greek. I have explained to you what my problem is. And another thing, he has often said he has doubts about the emotional stability of women, i.e., one should never trust them, or one never knows what to expect from them. Please give me your opinion. If you could answer me in writing, I would be terribly grateful.

With the utmost Respect,

Anatole Dimitriadou

Poste Restante, Central Post Office (Tsimiski St.), Thessaloniki

Nea Moudania, July 13, 1968

To His Excellency, the Prime Minister of the
National Government
Athens

Historical milepost incalculable national
significance outstanding new constitution of
beloved country enacted by Your Excellency,
distinguished son New Greece, brilliant leader
Revolution. Stop. Giant step toward political,
social, economic progress. Stop. Resounding
slap enemies Rebirth, abroad and at home. Stop.
Your enlightened thoughts leading Greece to
A c h i e v e m e n t   o f   N a t i o n a l   goals under
Revolution. Stop. God bless Your labors and protect
trailblazers National Uprising April 21.

Andreas Papaleonardou

National Telephone Company employee
Nea Moudania

Rachi, August 1, 1968

Dear DEME—

Hi there. I want you to know that I got your letter and that I was very pleased. You write that I should go to a school and learn English. For about five months. All right, my dear DEME, why can married people go to Australia without studying English while single people can't? I want to go without learning the English language, all right? Can I still go? Answer me yes or no. I have a brother in Australia, a first cousin, a brother-in-law, and friends, and these relatives of mine can teach me English over there. I have nothing else to write you. I close this letter with all my heart, and I am expecting your answer.

Good-bye,

Asprogerakis, Apostolos

In Thessaloniki, August 15, 1968

The Board of Administrators of the Thessaloniki Bar Association, having convened an emergency meeting following the announcement of the cowardly assassination attempt on Your life, in addition to its congratulatory telegram upon Your narrow escape on the 14th of the current month through Divine Providence, expresses its repugnance at this heinous criminal action and demands that the perpetrator and other known moral accomplices, all of whom are paid enemies of the Fatherland, be punished accordingly.

My dear Maria,

Your letter arrived yesterday and I couldn't get enough of the news in it. Do you think there's a romance developing between Nikos and Ismini? I sure hope so, if it's for their good. I was happy you had so many visitors on your Name Day even though it was in the middle of the summer. You will get my present in December, when we're planning to come there on vacation. Oh, and thanks a lot for the magazines too, but you shouldn't have spent so much money on postage. Gerasimos says that next time you shouldn't put them in an envelope, but roll them up instead so it shows that they're printed matter, and you'll pay much less. I started reading them and intend to go through them "cover to cover" until I receive the next batch. They take a long time to get here, over a month. Imagine, the last issue of *Gynaika* hasn't even arrived yet, nor has the *Pantheon* of July the 26th. In any case, please charge me for your expenses. I wrote to Vasilis too. He was worried and phoned us to say that in case things didn't work out all right, I should take the children and go back. I wrote him that I had to go see a doctor three times. Because I was really suffering badly from depression, not so much because of homesickness as because there's no way I can keep myself busy with anything. You have no idea, Maria, how slowly the hours go by when you keep looking at your watch. It's become a nightmare, I wake up in the morning thinking that I have nothing to do. My doctor has prescribed tranquilizers for me but they don't help much. So starting today, Gerasimos is taking me to work with him. He has started showing me how to use the equipment, the telex machines, etc. I hope I do all right. It's not difficult and at least I can forget myself. Tell Vasilis that I'm doing better now, and just the thought that I'll be working soothes my nerves. I also hope to gain some weight, because I have already lost six pounds. I weigh 108 now. Right now it's our lunch break. I'm writing you from the office. Write to me as often as you can. Your letters and the news you send cheer me up. I wrote Mom yesterday. I'm glad Dad's feeling better. Tell Rhea that I will answer her letter tomorrow. How is Zoe? I had my coffee cup read and they told me there's going to be a wedding. Who'll get married first, will you or will she? I'll be expecting the good news. The kids send kisses. They think of you and speak about you every day. Because there are no other children to play with at home, and Athens is all they talk about when they're together. I will stop and let Gerasimos write something too.

Love and kisses,

Chara

Maria, thanks for the tie. The girls at the office tell me it's very sexy. Poor things, if they only knew how appearances deceive! Please ask Giorgos to find out how much the Canon Auto Zoom 814 and 1214 movie cameras cost there. Write me.

Love and kisses to everybody,

Gerry

GREECE-AUSTRALIA LINES, LTD.
HEADQUARTERS IN PIRAEUS

OCTOBER 25
GREECE-AUSTRALIA

On the Safest Greek Ocean Liner

"PATRIS,"

25,000 Tons
Speed: 18 Nautical Miles

COMPLETELY VENTILATED
PARTIALLY AIR-CONDITIONED

Travelers accepted to first- and tourist-class
one- two- three- and four-bed staterooms

Freight carried in both
regular *and* **refrigerated** *holds*

Tickets and Information at all travel agencies

GENERAL BROKERS: ELMES,
ELECTRIC RAILWAY BLDG.

PIRAEUS, tel. 41-651, 40-636, 42-639, 47-322

THESSALONIKI, OCTOBER 27. *From our correspondent. Geor-gios Bakos was brought in yesterday for questioning to the Fourth Police Precinct, where he defended himself concerning the vicious murder of his wife.* Last Thursday, in the presence of their mutual acquaintance Dimitrios Stais, Bakos struck his wife Ermioni with a metal pipe on the head and killed her. In his defense, Bakos claimed he committed the act be-cause he was pathologically in love with his wife. "When I sensed that she would soon be out my life, my mind stopped working. I believed it would be unbearable without her. She provoked me into the argument we had, and without realiz-ing it I picked up the pipe and struck her."

Following his statement, the police investigator and dis-trict attorney agreed that he be placed in pretrial incarcera-tion, and he was therefore jailed. It should be noted that the murderer, at the time of his assault, cried out: "You whore! You put this dress on to seduce my friend."

Thasos, November 13, 1968

Dear Mrs. Mina—

I am a regular listener of your lovely show, and I am resuming our correspondence for the third time. I don't know how to thank you, Mrs. Mina, for your precious advice. I send you many, many thanks. I am a girl from Thasos, a 17-year-old girl. Alas, Mrs. Mina, I feel so lonesome, and so sad. My 17 years have gone by with so little joy and so much unhappiness. I can't stand the loneliness, the unfairness. My parents make my unhappiness worse with their harsh words. They treat me so heartlessly my sad eyes brim over with hot tears. Their behavior toward me changed when I refused to marry the suitor they chose for me. How could I agree, dear Mrs. Mina, without loving him? How can a household be built on any foundation but love? If you remember, Mrs. Mina, it was about this very subject I asked your advice. ("Sad Green Eyes.") Your answer was not to do it, and I agreed. Let's hope I won't regret it. I've heard it said, Mrs. Mina, that there's no such thing as love, that it changes like fashion. Tell me, is this true? Listening to the radio is my only comfort. But they forbid me to listen. They speak to me so coldly it breaks my young girl's heart. I mustn't read any magazines or do any needlework, everything I do is all wrong to them. Believe me, Mrs. Mina, I have desperate thoughts sometimes. The sea across the way is so near. Sometimes I feel the urge to just close my eyes one fine morning and lose myself in the deep blue sea. There in that vast expanse of sand, to bury my sadness, my sorrow, and all my beautiful dreams. I'm tired of this kind of life, Mrs. Mina. It's hell. The clouds of sadness are so big they overshadow my poor heart. What should I do? Why don't my parents show a little understanding? Why do they keep saying I have someone else, that I have other hopes? It's not true. Oh, if you only knew, dear Mina, how happy it makes me when I hear you on the radio. Especially when you talk about me. I get teary-eyed at the thought that someone is talking about me. Mrs. Mina, do not be offended if I address you in familiar terms. I consider you a good friend, because I have no girlfriends. Could it be, Mrs. Mina, that I was wrong to turn him down? He's a good person, and he's rich. And he just got engaged. But I don't regret my decision, because I want to feel love in my heart for the man I marry.

Greetings and thanks,

Melancholy and Lonely

P.S. Am I perhaps just exaggerating and dreaming? Yes, Mrs. Mina, I'm quite a dreamer. I fly high in my dreams, and when I land I am terribly disappointed. I am sending a few flower petals with all my love for your wonderful program.

Monday, November 18, 1968
A Panhellenic Presentation

The People's Own Beloved
Nikos Xanthopoulos
In a Dramatic, Legal, and Social Colossus

THE TRAMP'S HEART
(Suitable for All Ages)

Aphrodite Grigoriadou, Manos Katrakis
Anestis Vlachos, Eleni Zafeiriou

Klack Films
Movies for the Entire Greek Family

NAUPLION, NOVEMBER 19. *From our correspondent. There is an APB out on Dimitrios Kaisaris, age 30, who, last night, after entering the home of Grigorios D. Vasileiou in Manesi, Argolis, as the latter lay sleeping with his wife, climbed into their bed and proceeded to fondle the woman. Thus rudely awakened and terrified, Vasiliki G. Vasileiou began to scream, whereupon the brazen intruder fled after jumping out of the window.*

DECEMBER 21. *By royal decree (Official Government Gazette, No. 439), the following individuals, for reasons of antinational activities abroad and other miscellaneous offenses, have been stripped of Greek nationality: Pavlos and Vasiliki Tsirogiannis, Ethymios Stagias, E. Pasias, Maria, Victoria, Parthena, Cleanthis, Kyriaki, Sara, and Sophron Karypides, Iro Papadopoulou, S. T. Stavrou, S. T. Karatzios a.k.a. Barbanasis, Chr. Ghekas, I. Ghekas, Georgios Mitropanos, Effie Polymenides, M. Maropoulos, Polyxeni Papaïoannou, A. Vellis, Chr. Karatsos, B. Angelides, Anthoula Photopoulou, and Ath. Boulasis.*

JANUARY 23. *By joint decision of the Vice-President of the National Government and of the Minister of the Interior (Official Government Gazette, No. 16), the following 18 Greek subjects living abroad have been stripped of their Greek nationality on grounds of antinational activities: P. Gavriilides, Gr. Vasilopoulos, P. Gagouzis, Milt. Malatetsis, Eucl. Xanthopoulos, Urania, wife of Nik. Paraskevopoulos, Eugenia or Ginia, wife of Geor. Photopoulos, Laz. Damos, Geor. Gagoulides, Daphne Maropoulou, G. Siaperas, G. Giannides, Ekaterini Vamvatira, Apost. Antoniou, Chrys. Spathopoulos, Cosmas Milentses, Moschos Moschides, and Char. Theodorides. By the same decree, the names of the above have been stricken from their respective county and community records.*

What should I do?

Dear Mrs. Mina,

I am 13. I never wanted to experience love this early, and I'm not even sure if it's the real thing. I met him last year. I mean, I first spoke to him last year. He lived near our house and we used to see each other almost every day. But as fate would have it, we couldn't go on, at least not like that. My brother caught us together, and after giving us advice, told him to stay away from me. I must tell you that neither of us tried to blame the other in order to get off the hook with my brother. Anyway, we stopped for a week. In the meantime, my brother, my sister, and my brother-in-law were watching us, or at least they said they were. I then enrolled in a foreign language institute, and every day, though very afraid, we saw each other, sometimes down at the entrance, sometimes at the bus stop. He is 19 but has done only one year of high school. He is now working, and he also plays soccer. He believes that he is doing something with his life by playing soccer. My brother caught us again and gave us the same advice. And once again we stopped, but only for a week. The third time, when my sister caught us, I got a beating, and they threatened him too. But we still kept on, this time by phone, he gave me the number where he works. I called him every day to talk to him and not once did we say words of love. I don't know, maybe he's not the type. It's been almost a year since last May, and I still don't know him well. I don't know what he's really like. I called him again today and told him very tactfully for the second time that we should break up. Because we can't go on like this, constantly afraid of being seen. I said the second time because I had brought it up once before, and he answered: "Well, if you've really thought it over . . ." This sentence is still ringing in my ears and makes me have my doubts about him. Anyway, the next day he came by school and kept signaling me to call him, which I did. And he said that we shouldn't stop talking to each other, at least not on the phone. When I asked him why, then, he had accepted my decision the day before, his excuse was that he had been upset about his work. But those are not the words of a man who's upset, now, are they? This is what makes me think he doesn't want to lose his "silly little fool." That's what I call my-self ever since we moved out of his neighborhood, because I don't know what he's doing behind my back anymore. He never tells me any of his problems, unlike me, because I tell him everything. Without, of course, having ever said "I love you" to him. Because I don't know if I love him. His behavior makes me have doubts. My family just won't leave me alone, everyone keeps trying to make me understand that I'm still young and that I have my whole life ahead of me. I know they're right, and I swear that had I not met him, I would never have let them say all those things to me. They even called me a tramp. Why? Why did they call me that? Is this relationship wrong? It is love in all its purity. If it is love. He's never asked me to become his, or talked about making love. Nor have I ever asked for anything like that. He never touches me ei-ther. You will say, how can he touch you if you don't see each other? We do, Mrs. Mina, we see each other once a month and arrange to meet near the same place. I should tell you that my family keeps me very cooped up and I never go anywhere. And I have no girl-friends. They tell me they'll be bad for me. I feel so stifled, I cry every night. They tell me I'll stop being a good student. I don't believe it myself. When I study—I'm in my second year of junior high school—I don't think about anyone, not even him, even though I spend all my free time thinking about him. And I'm a good student. Ever since my first year I've had good grades, and they haven't gotten any worse since I met him. Why doesn't my family understand this? They say they're afraid he'll be bad for me. I've tried telling them that he's not what they think. But he hasn't tried to make them believe in him either, or make them see that his intentions are good, if they really are. Nor has he said anything to me. Should I be the one to make the first move? Should I tell him how I feel, although he must have guessed from my behavior? Or should I tell him one more time that we have to stop? When we spoke on the phone today I hinted at this and said of course I would make things clearer the day after tomorrow when we planned to meet. But then I went back on my word and begged him not to meet me. He said that he'll go to our meeting place, and that if he doesn't find me waiting for him there, not to phone him again. In other words, he's trying to force me into going. I am thinking of calling him tomorrow at home (his family knows about our relationship) and asking him to postpone it for a while because something has come up at work. The purpose of this is for me to get your advice first. I must tell you that I usually go to our meetings half an hour before class because, as I said before, I am not allowed time to be out on my own. I know that my letter is long and complicated and tiring for you. But I needed to write all this down for you. I just remembered something that may help you with the advice you give me. When I asked him why he chose me out of so many other women he could have gone out with, women who might have given him anything he wanted, etc., he said: Because you were the most serious girl I had ever known. Tell me how to go on from here, or shouldn't I go on? And why is he behaving like this? Should I make inquiries about him, or should I listen to my family, who I think are trying to protect me? But from what? Please, help me. I am writing this letter in secret, so please don't mention anything too obvious, otherwise my family will realize it's me. Give me your advice on either Thursday, Friday, or Saturday. I have class in the afternoon during the rest of the week.

My Best Regards,

Ersi

THESSALONIKI, MARCH 18. *From our correspondent. In the village of Arnisa, Diamantis Mitsinas, age 38, brought home a mine he had found in a field on his property, which he placed in the fire in order to remove from it a metal band that his son insisted on having. The mine exploded, fatally injuring him and injuring his son, Theophanes and, less seriously, a three-year-old boy, S. Papadopoulos, who was also present. Mitsinas succumbed to his injuries en route to Thessaloniki.*

––––––––

Ioannis Christopoulos, son of Dimitrios, resident of Tripolis, in memory of his wife Aphrodite, née Charalambos, daughter of Angelos, or Charalambaki, resident and grocer of Tripolis, on the first anniversary of her death, in place of a memorial service, hereby expunges from his Accounts Receivable ledger all customer debts under the amount of one thousand drachmas.

Johannesburg, March 31, 1969

My Dear Loukas,

Getting a letter here means a lot to me, especially from people in my family. Although in the beginning there were moments when I didn't think I would be able to live in this country, I have now got myself into a certain routine and feel better. In any case, I must keep taking the pills the doctor prescribed for my nerves. I am worried about the children's schooling. They will forget their Greek. They only get one hour of Greek a week, and that not regularly. In English they are doing fine. Write and tell me your opinion. Maria says as long as they get an education, it doesn't matter what language it's in. Is there a book you can send me that I might like? Not too hard; I've finished the novel *Pantheoi*. Anna also loves to read; I bought her something from here, but there isn't much of a selection. Konstantina has not learned to write yet. But she told Anna to write and tell you what she wanted. Gerasimos is well. There's so much for him to do until the office is running smoothly that I often feel like we're loading him down with extra worries until we all get settled. Our greetings to Kalliope, if you still see her.

Love and kisses from all of us,

Chara

Dear Uncle Loukas,

I read your letter today. I like South Africa. And let me tell you why. First of all, there's no school on Saturdays. I read a book called *In the Years of Slavery,* by Alexis Daphnomilis, and I liked it a lot. I want you to send me a book, for my age level, about the Byzantine period. I have already read *The Castles of Morea.* Konstantina wants you to send her a book with pictures and fairy tales.

Kisses from both of us.

APRIL 6. *An end to rumors. The shipping magnate Mr. Stavros Niarchos has no intention of marrying Maria-Gabriella, the daughter of the former king of Italy, Umberto. A communique to this effect, issued by Mr. Niarchos's offices in town, states: "With regard to Mr. Niarchos's family situation and his probable future plans, Mr. Stavros Niarchos wishes to make it known that according to law and to the regulations of the Greek Orthodox Church, he is and remains the husband of Mrs. Eugenia S. Livanou. Any other reports are completely unfounded." As is well known, the Greek magnate had been married not only to Eugenia Livanou but also to Charlotte Ford. The news of his impending marriage to the Italian princess was first published in the Italian newspaper* Tempo *and was quoted from an American source. In addition, the former queen of Italy has categorically denied these reports, describing them as mere figments of the imagination.*

The conversation between Tarzan, Major Blake, and General Yates continued for some time over the two-way radio. General Yates, despite his initial objections, was finally persuaded to give his approval. From that moment on they began planning how Tarzan would make his way into the midst of the savages. Major Blake clarified the following information for the General. "Tarzan is only asking for a helicopter to take him to the land of the Moto-Moto tribe. The nurse's life hangs on the speed with which he can get there before the savages kill her." The General had no other objections. He agreed that they dispatch an army helicopter immediately. Still, although he agreed with Tarzan's point of view, he was afraid that by the time he reached their territory the savages would have killed the unfortunate nurse.

At that point Blake picked up the receiver and said: "General, Tarzan wants to avoid violence, and is asking to proceed as he thinks best."

"In other words, he wants to meet the savages alone, without an armed escort?" the General asked, surprised.

"Yes, General," Tarzan replied. "I know the Moto-Moto well and I am not afraid of them. The only person accompanying me should be the helicopter pilot. I hope to return with the nurse. A military attack on the savages' village is exactly what our mysterious enemy is waiting for in order to turn all the tribes of the jungle against us."

The General's reservations were beginning to give way over the telephone.

(To be continued)

CALENDAR

*(Sunday: Day of the Healing of the Blind Man.
Day of the Holy Martyr Theodotus of Ancyra)*

Sunday, June 7, 1969.

Theodotus was accused of pulling the bodies of martyred holy virgins out of the lake where they were drowned and giving them burial. For these acts he was brutally tortured. In the end his torturers were ordered to decapitate him. Sunrise is at 5:02 A.M., sunset at 7:46 P.M. The moon rises at 3:05 A.M. and sets at 4:33 P.M.

Dear Mrs. Mina—

I am 16. I spent the summer vacation in Athens because my parents decided this is where I should go to school, provided, of course, that I wanted to. I am staying with an aunt of mine who is young and has two small children. At some point during my four-month stay with her I met a young man, age 25, from a good family and gainfully employed. This young man is a cousin of my uncle's and, from the moment he saw me, he took an interest in me. He spoke to my uncle about his interest in me, and my uncle spoke to me. Now, although he knows nothing about it, I know everything. All about his good intentions. He often asks my uncle's permission and takes me out, in a group with lots of people, and we have a good time. But he has still not spoken to me about his feelings. I don't know why. My family met this young man and they liked him a lot and would like to see something happen between me and him. I'm worried though because this young man is not my type, which makes me very unhappy, as I am touched by his attention. My uncle's work is such (he is a waiter) that it prevents him from being home early. So, while we sit there waiting for him all by ourselves, I mean my aunt and I, this young man often comes over and stays for several hours, until very late. And of course when he stays as late as 12 midnight, he is unwelcome. Now tell me, Mrs. Mina, what kind of man could he be when it never occurs to him that he might be intruding? Is it possible that it's his interest in me that makes him want to stay at our house so late? And when he does talk to me about his feelings, what should I say to him? How should I behave? Is it better to wait a little longer? Tell me what to do.

With my gratitude and admiration,

Pen name: Angela—Thessaloniki

JULY 26. *The Federation of Greek Schoolteachers, during an extraordinary meeting, having received information about the anti-Greek activities of Panteios School professor and bank employee D. Karagiorgas, has issued a statement condemning his antinational and inhumane actions and requesting that he and others bearing responsibility for or moral complicity in his actions be duly punished.*

The Educational Publishing Company
PENTAS

*is offering you a unique opportunity to embark on
a successful career*

as a Journalist, a Lyric Writer, a Musician

IN TWELVE LESSONS BY CORRESPONDENCE

*Equip yourself with qualifications that will prove
valuable both now and later in your life.*

A Little Time—A Little Money—Goes a Long Way

PENTAS
*Educational Publishing Company
15 Paparrigopoulou Street, Postal Zone 124, Athens*

Gerakion, July 28, 1969

Dear Mr. Director,

I should like to bring to your attention through the present letter the following, for the sake of improving efficiency in the civil service so that we all may contribute to the world-saving mission of our National Government:

a. If an indigence certificate was ever issued to George Epam. Magaziotes or his brother Ioannis for the purpose of emigration, such a certificate is false and void of all legality because, as the priest of the parish where they live, I know that they are not indigent.

b. The said brothers happen to be good-for-nothings, evil characters, and communist sympathizers opposed to the regime, and it would be a good thing not to permit them to emigrate for fear of their spreading this contagion to other countries as well.

The above facts are for your records.

With the utmost respect,

Vasileios Ramazanes

Parish Priest, Church of St. Gerasimos

GENTLEMAN, around 60, tall and in good health, dark hair and complexion, attractive, owner of respectable 30-year-old business and furnished apartment fully equipped with electric appliances, including washing machine and TV set, divorced, with divorce decree in his favor, no obligations, seeks tall, slender, young woman, not more than 30 (thirty) years old, of strong moral character, demure, attractive, for immediate matrimony and creation of stable, happy family. Tel. 531-768, or write Mr. X. M., P.O. Box 312, Syntagma Square. Cypriot or Muslim women from West Thrace also acceptable.

her friend the policeman. He came and laid siege to her in my own home. In 1953 I also caught her committing adultery with another man and I forgave her. We made up and went home in each other's arms. We had a good life for 14 years. We had two children. No one bothered her again and now this policeman comes along and seduces her. An acquaintance of mine brought him along as a friend and he began flirting with her. I was away and he talked her into it. He also blackmailed her and was taking money from her. He had her anytime he wanted her. That's why she became desperate and killed herself. I'm innocent. I believe she killed herself. It was eating away at her, getting her down, she'd just sit there and sigh.

—So where did she find the pistol?

—I don't know where she found it.

—How about the man who says he gave it to you?

—I don't know him. I have no idea. Bring him here and see if he recognizes me. I haven't even got money for cigarettes.

— Then where did your wife find it?

—I'm a cobbler, I never fought in the mountains. Her brother did, though. Maybe he had pistols. I don't know. Maybe he's a false witness who's been told to say he gave it to me.

So you believe your wife committed suicide?

—Yes, I really do. She was depressed. I recorded a conversation she had with her boyfriend. She was telling him she would commit suicide. I have the tapes to prove this. Even our daughter says so, about her mother's boyfriend.

—Did she have any reason to commit suicide?

—She did, love was the reason. She was tormented by being in love. She had really fallen for this guy. And he was blackmailing her, too. She was always sighing. I'm innocent. I intend to tell everything in court. My wife was fine for 14 whole years. Until the policeman came and stole her away from me.

A large swarm of bees made its appearance yesterday in the center of Athens, surprising all present. Initially flying along Pireos Street, the swarm entered Omonoia Square, then went along Dorou Street, carefully investigating inviting-looking sites and eventually settling themselves on the second-story window sill of a building at 13 Patision Street. Within the hour, four people hurried to the scene, carrying hives to collect the runaway swarm. The first person to tackle the job, following a three-hour struggle, became the new owner of the swarm. It was subsequently revealed that the swarm had escaped from a bee colony temporarily established in the area of Votanikos.

———

From Patras, July 31, 1969

Itinerant Pretzel Sellers' Guild Patras expresses extreme repugnance criminal attitude actions "professor" Karagiorgas demands offender punished accordingly.

Dear Mrs. Mina—

I am in love with the surgeon who operated on my heart a few months ago. He is about 45, and I am 34. The operation was not a very serious one; it was simple, I was up in five days. I am now completely well. At any rate, the doctor showed me that he liked me from his very first visit. When I was in the hospital, he came to visit me twice a day. Each time he would hold my hand tightly and gaze tenderly into my eyes. I should also tell you that just a few months earlier I had broken off an eight-year-long relationship with my cardiologist. It was a miserable affair that helped land me even more quickly in the operating room. I mentioned this relationship to one of the surgeon's employees, who worked part time at the hospital and part time at the clinic. She and I quickly became friends and, completely beguiled by the affection she showed me, which I would later find out was false, I confided in her. One evening while he was making his rounds, he found her in my room. What are you doing here, he asked her? I came to see Miss Thea, says she. But it seemed to me he wasn't pleased by my knowing her. She was a shallow young woman about whom I had never heard a nice thing said in the hospital. Two days later she came to see me again. She said: I won't be able to keep you company at lunchtime because the surgeon's giving me a ride somewhere and we'll be leaving together. Two more days went by, the operation took place, and he was the same. Still gazing at me tenderly and squeezing my hand. Then suddenly his visits became more infrequent, and his attitude began to change. Even though other people in the room with me had already noticed his interest in me. A few days later I was discharged. I called from my home to thank him because he was out of town when I left the hospital. He was enthusiastic on the phone. He said: That little heart of yours is now brand new and ready for love. I told him that when I felt better I would go and see him. He was happy beyond words, at least that's how he sounded. Soon afterward I went to see him with a 3,000-drachma crystal vase my mother had bought as a thank-you gift for him. I think, Mrs. Mina, this was a mistake. His secretary, my friend, said that when she announced me to him, he was beside himself with excitement. She also asked me what I was giving him and how much it cost. Naturally, I told her the truth. When I went into his office, I found him sitting cool as a cucumber, not at all pleased, as she had told me, or as he had sounded on the phone. Please have a seat, he said. I sat down, all confused. We began discussing the operation. And just as he was telling me that I'm in great shape, he throws in something about finding a nice young man for me. And then, suddenly changing his tone of voice, he asks me: Or do you have someone already? I didn't answer, because I still had not recovered from the lukewarm reception. After a while I got up and started getting ready to leave: Sit down, he said, and let's talk. I opened the box with the present I had brought. I told him it was a small token of our love, meaning my mother's also: You're very kind, he said. He called his secretary and had her remove the vase he had on his desk: We will put this exquisite artifact that the young lady has brought in its place. Before I left, he recommended that in 15 days I visit a cardiologist he knew, who would speak with him on the phone about discontinuing some medication I was taking. I did as he told me. I went to see him a month later. The cold weather prevented me from going any sooner. He received me graciously, his eyes revealing nothing. In his office he said once again: You must find yourself a nice young man. I just smiled: No, he said, don't laugh, and don't let too much time go by like I did, and suddenly here I am, an old man. I tried to say something flattering, because he really is very young-looking, handsome and quite charming. But once again I didn't tell him all the things I wanted to about marriage. Mrs. Mina, I get hurt so easily, I'm scared of looking like a fool. At the slightest pretext I get angry, mostly at myself. So I got up to leave. He tried to keep me there. He talked about his work, and about a trip to the States for about 18 to 20 days, he said, and not more. I left without our discussing anything else. A few days later I phoned him on his Name Day. I asked him if he was leaving on the 1st of the month. He said yes: And you'll be back on the 20th? On the 21st, he said.

I wish you an enjoyable trip, I said. And I hope to see you. I need your advice, Mrs. Mina. Do you think I can visit him again? I'm afraid he didn't like that "I hope to see you again" I added. Please answer me under the pen name "Amaryllis," and don't mention the fact that he's a professor of surgery working at the clinic. Or anything about the operation.

Thanks a million,

Thea Zymvragaki

NEW YORK, AUGUST 9. *Reuters. After a number of attempts, American scientists succeeded yesterday in receiving the laser beam that struck the reflector placed on the moon on July 20 by Apollo 11 astronauts Armstrong and Aldrin. In their enthusiasm the scientists repeated the experiment five hundred times. In the meantime while (a) the astronauts' quarantine is still in effect, (b) the analysis and study of the rock samples is still underway, and (c) lab animals are being inoculated with moon dust, in anticipation of a new mission to be carr-*

The famous Parisian hair stylist Antonio arrived yesterday in Athens, by air, in the company of Mr. De Saint Leon, the general director of Garnier. The great hair stylist was welcomed at the airport by a delegation of Intercoiffure Hellas, headed by its president Mr. A. Kamer, and by Mr. N. George, the general director of Garnier/Greece, together with ten models who will take part in a special demonstration today, Sunday, August 11, at 7:30 P.M., at the Asteria Hotel facilities in Glyphada. Antonio, representing Intercoiffure of Paris, will be holding consultations with members of the Athens International Intercoiffure Conference which, as has been announced by the Prime Minister's office, will be convened here next March.

———

AUSTRALIA—THE FAR EAST
L U F T H A N S A
31 FLIGHTS WEEKLY

Omolion, August 13, 1969

Good-day, Sir,

I'm sending you my indigence paper. I'm a first-degree indigent and father of two children, all girls. Maybe I'm too late now, but we had a hard time with the mayor, he really gave us the run-around. Please could you see if maybe one of the girls could leave soon. Now about our invitation, for Ioannis Nousias, we haven't received one yet.

My greetings,

Ioannis Nousias

Omolion, Larisa

KALAMATA, AUGUST 18. *From our correspondent. Juvenile Court ordered that Sia, wife of P. Kontomanolopoulos, age 16, from Drys in Ileia, resident of Messini, be sent to reform school until such time as she comes of age because during the time period between May and November, 1968, she incited a fifteen-year-old woman to licentiousness, along with her husband, a musician, who kept her in their Messini home, cohabiting with them both for seven months. It should be noted that the young woman has already borne a child by the said musician.*

September 22, 1969

Dear Mrs. Mina—

Let me begin by reminding you which one of your listeners I am.
I wrote you twice two years ago. My pen name was "A Longtime
Sufferer." I was 15 years old then. I had written to you about our
family problem, about my mother living in Germany and being
divorced from my father. I raised my younger brothers and had to
endure all the hardships inflicted upon me by a tyrannical father.
That tragic chapter is over, but a new one has begun. In my desperation at that time, I used to think of marriage as a kind of salvation, and at the very first offer I said yes, God help me, and
rushed into it with my eyes closed. Unfortunately, I didn't choose
the right man. I have been married for a year now, and during this
time all sorts of things have happened. My husband is constantly
causing problems for me for no good reason. I don't know whether
he has sensed or suspected anything. The most serious thing is that
he beat me up. No matter what I say, he never listens. He's so
opinionated, only his word counts. Our characters are completely
incompatible, and this is the worst thing for a couple, as you know.
I have told my mother-in-law everything, and she does her best to
console me. She tells me he's still young, he'll straighten out.
They're all like that in the beginning. Mrs. Mina, he's 22 years old,
he may not be old, but he's not so young that he doesn't know how
to behave toward his wife. Perhaps it's because he doesn't have as
much experience as I do. Every day is just more of the same, or
worse. Give me some advice as to what I should do. I myself believe the best solution is a separation, because I don't believe that
he's going to change, as his mother says. I'm afraid of a separation,
however, because I have nowhere to go. Going back to my father's
is out of the question, because the abuse will begin all over again.
Mrs. Mina, he took me when I was 13 years old and kept me as his
woman for two years, but then, because he was afraid there'd be
talk, he had a doctor sew me up and married me off. Now, with
no reason to fear anything, he will want to have me again. As for
my mother, I doubt if she can have me come and stay with her in
Germany. I'm still only 17, and I'm afraid that I'll need signed

permission again. For this reason, I try my best to be patient and stay calm. I don't want to write my mother about the things I went through and am still going through because I will upset her. She no longer worries about me now that I'm out of my father's terrible clutches. How could she know that I have now jumped from the frying pan into the fire. I trust you, Mrs. Mina. I hope you will give me some good advice. I would so like to meet you in person and truly open my heart to you. I can hardly wait to hear your response. In closing, I send you all my admiration and appreciation and my heartfelt wishes for all the best.

My pen name is

Unhappy Newlywed

OCTOBER 25. *It has been announced by the Ministry of Public Order that, as of last night, the perpetrators of the bombing attacks that took place on the morning of Saturday the 18th of this month, as a result of which six Athenians were injured, are in the hands of the authorities and under investigation. Those arrested, who had in their possession explosive devices and other materials later confiscated, signed full confessions and are soon to be arraigned before a court of law. According to our sources, nine people have been arrested, two of whose names have not been released. The ministry announcement lists only seven, namely: D. Agiomerites, university student; Dimitrios Dodos, 21, university student; Ioannis Mylonas, 24, bank employee; Dimitrios Papaïoannou, 23, chemical engineer; Ekaterini Chouliara, 23, civil servant; Vasilios Rapanos, 22, university student; and Dimitrios Katsaros, 41, businessman. The age of university student D. Agiomerites was given as 14. This is obviously an error.*

To: The Emigration Department

I have written you repeatedly and you never answered. My name is Velisarios Dokos, I am from Larisa, and was born in 1952. I work at a body shop as a welder and painter. I want to emigrate to Australia. Tell me what I should do, so the Selective Service does not catch up with me. Answer me soon.

In Larisa, October 27, 1969

MILAN, OCTOBER 29. *By special correspondent. After many years of silence, the squeaky but imperious voice of the famous elderly industrialist Giovanni Meneghini was heard again. In a candid interview with an Italian journalist at his villa in Sirmione, he opened his heart, which he said never ceased to be full of Maria Callas, "the most lovely creature in the world." "For as long as I am alive," he said, "Onassis will never be able to make her his wife. Maria is going to be my widow. I am sure that someday she will return to me." The recluse of Sirmione repeated as though reciting a soliloquy: "My garden will be filled with her fragrance once more. I am waiting for her."*

PATRAS, OCTOBER 30. *From our correspondent. Following charges brought by the Patras Holy See, Security Police are searching for a monk, approximately 40 years old, who performed a belly dance as well as a "hasapiko" with a danseuse at the Spathakas Club, accompanied by a bouzouki band. He passed himself off to the patrons as hailing from Mt. Athos.*

Archanes, November 6, 1969

Dear Mr. Supervisor—

Will you please send me detailed information on everything I am writing you about. I have a married son in Australia, 27 years old, a sister, my sister's two daughters, one of them married, and they have all settled over there. I am 59 years old. I have two children here in Crete, a 20-year-old daughter, unmarried, and a son, 30 years old, married. I have no wife, she died. And now, Mr. Supervisor, my two children and my daughter-in-law want to move to Australia and live with the rest of my family over there. Can we emigrate? All of us over here, I mean, my three children and myself? Can we fly there, and how much, if you don't mind my asking, will our emigration cost? And if not by plane, then how about by boat, and how can we get our papers issued here? But I would prefer to go by plane, because boats make me seasick. And can my son who is over there with my sister send us an invitation, and exactly what else do we have to do to take care of this matter? And the most important question of all, Mr. Supervisor, is whether I, being 59 years old and single, will be able to live over there. What is your advice?

Love,

Iosif Kouskoubekakis

LARISA, DECEMBER 14. *From our correspondent. At about 8:00 P.M. a cherry bomb, placed by an unidentified person passing through our town, went off at the courthouse building under construction, making a terrible noise but without causing any injuries or damage. An investigation is underway.*

THANASSIS VALTINOS was born in an Arcadian village in the Peloponnesus in 1932. He studied political science, briefly, and film, served as an officer in the reserves, and held different jobs in the harbor of Piraeus and in Athens. He first achieved national recognition with the publication of work in the late fifties and early sixties, most notably his widely read novella *The Descent of the Nine*.

International recognition soon followed in 1970 with the award of a Ford Foundation grant for creative writing, accompanied by invitations abroad to the Deutscher Akademischer Austauschdienst (Berlin, 1974–75, 1987) and the International Writing Program (Iowa City, 1976) at the University of Iowa, where he is an honorary fellow. He is also a member of the European Academy of the Sciences and the Arts (Salzburg) and the International Theatre Institute.

His fiction has been translated into many European languages and his reputation in Europe continues to grow. He travels extensively and has received numerous awards for his work, both in Greece and abroad. His novel *Data from the Decade of the Sixties* won the Greek State Literature Prize in 1990 and was short-listed for the Aristeion European Literature Prize in 1991.

In Greece, Valtinos's work as a novelist earned him the position of president of the Society of Greek Writers, a post he held for many years. He is also a member of the Greek Society of Playwrights, and his translations of classical Greek drama—many of which were written for the Art Theater of the late Karolos Koun—are performed at annual festivals at Epidaurus and other ancient theaters throughout Greece. His novels, plays, and film scripts, including the award-winning script to the film *Voyage to Kythira* (Cannes Film Festival, 1984), in collaboration with the distinguished Greek film director Theodoros Angelopoulos, have established him as one of the most versatile and talented men of letters in Greece today.